Blood Never Sleeps

Blood Never Sleeps

Jane Morell

ROBERT HALE · LONDON

© Jane Morell 2011
First published in Great Britain 2011

ISBN 978-0-7090-9266-7

Robert Hale Limited
Clerkenwell House
Clerkenwell Green
London EC1R 0HT

www.halebooks.com

2 4 6 8 10 9 7 5 3 1

Typeset in 10.75/14.75pt Plantin
Printed in the UK by the MPG Books Group,
Bodmin and King's Lynn

Put not your trust in blood

for blood never sleeps

ANON

BACKLASH

The Flashpoint

BEIRUT November 2005 – 23.00 hours

The city lay quiet beneath a moonless starlit sky. Since the assassination of Prime Minister Hariri nine months earlier few of its
people place any trust in the safety of their streets – even in
daylight.

Travelling fast and using no lights, the sleek black Mercedes
drove from Muslim West Beirut into the largely Christian East.
They crossed over where the former Green Line used literally to
divide the city in two. Four men sat in the car, all of them Hizbollah
fighters. Clad in dark-blue combat fatigues, each wore a black-on-
white checkered scarf tied loosely around his neck ready to be
pulled up to cover his face before going into action. Three of them
were armed with Kalashnikovs; the fourth carried only a handgun.

The informant on the family they were about to hit is Muna
Ahmed. She is a forty-two year old Syrian woman employed by the
same family. Muna has provided this small execution squad – Unit
10, expressly chosen for this particular mission – with all the information required for a precisely timed, specifically targeted lethal
attack; one hour earlier, having served coffee to the family
convivially gathered around the dining table, she had unlocked and
unbolted the heavy, reinforced front door giving access from the
street into the villa. So that night the door will not protect the
family, and the next morning Muna will not be using her personal
key to let herself in to prepare the family's coffee and breakfast. She

will have to find herself another job fast since this betrayal-to-the-death of her employers will earn her no more than payment in kind – the 'traded' lives of *her* three sons will be her only 'reward'.

The driver of the Merc sat straight-backed and tense behind the wheel, his trimly-bearded face intent on the road ahead. He was the youngest of the four and would take no active part in the forth-coming assault. Nevertheless his duty at the target site would be of great importance to his comrades: while they are inside the villa he must keep vigilant watch on the street and, should he detect the slightest sign of a police patrol approaching, must punch out three short sharp blasts on the Merc's horn – *Get out of there at once!* This message to the assault team is an overriding order, on hearing it each Unit 10 man must stop what he is doing at once and make for the car outside at the double. *Whatever* he is doing he must obey that command immediately, because to delay for even a split second is to put the entire unit at risk of death or capture.

Beside the driver sat the captain of this 'Retributive Justice' team (a phrase favoured as having a more cutting edge to it than the simpler, but more honest 'Revenge Unit'). He was a gaunt man in his early fifties, experienced in most kinds of terrorist action. Nevertheless, the night's work will give him greater satisfaction than any one of the similar strikes he has taken part in before, because the man whose death it avenges had been his close friend and honoured fellow-combatant for over twenty-five years.

The man in the rear seat, behind the driver, was a cadet named Salim al Hami. This was the first execution operation he had taken part in and he was keyed up, elated and a little afraid – not of the death or injury he might suffer in the course of it if it went wrong, but of failing in proper performance of his duty, of not proving himself sufficiently fast, competent and ruthless in action.

But it was the young man sitting behind the captain, the one cradling the handgun in his lap, who was the feral heart of this mission.... And now suddenly, as the Merc passes beneath a tall streetlamp he glances out of his side window – and for a few seconds its brilliance flares across his eyes and they glint disturbingly ash-grey against his light brown skin.... They are the gift of his Irish mother—

'Nearing target,' he says. He is on a high of anticipation and his voice throbs with the bloodlust driving him.

'All three of the brothers are yours tonight, Hussain Rashid Shalhoub.' The words came hard and cold from the captain's thin-lipped mouth; he has a lined, raw-boned face and, as an active frontline terrorist for the last thirty-two years, he had neither mercy nor any warmth towards his fellow men.

'All three of them had both the opportunity and the motive to betray your father to his death. Therefore, since we have no way to determine which one of them actually carried out the fact of betrayal it is clear justice that, as his sole surviving son, you should avenge him: your hand alone shall kill all three. *Take their blood, Hussain!* It is both your duty and your right.'

'Also, an honour,' Hussain replied. Hussain Rashid Shalhoub had, so far in his twenty or so years of life, taken part in the implementation of four death sentences imposed by Hizbollah, two with the gun, two with a knife. Knives are his weapon of choice as at the climax of the act the body contact of the two combatants is much closer and the act of killing is, therefore, more ... satisfying to the victor.

As the Merc closed in on its target, the captain rapped out a swift resumé of the tactics Unit 10 would employ in the coming assault: tactics which, in this case, being tailored to achieve an unusual aim, did not conform to the customary pattern of such missions. 'My part in this,' he announced, 'and that of Salim beside you, is simply to hold at gunpoint all those present while you carry out the executions. Front gate and front door to the villa will by now be unlocked, I'll kick open the front door, we charge through the hall into the dining-room beyond where our target family is gathered. Once inside, myself and Salim will take firing stance one either side of the doorway and hold all present immobilized at gunpoint while you execute the three men. Our Kalashnikovs remain unused unless there is resistance to *your* actions, Hussain.... Nevertheless,' he ended harsly, 'our hearts and souls will be with you as you kill these betrayers. I repeat, *take their blood*, Hussain Rashid Shalhoub. And may God guide your hand in doing this.'

The Asleys had always been a close-knit family. Maronite Christians who had settled in East Beirut, their name was respected – had been honoured even – through three generations. Over years, its sons and daughters had built fine reputations in various fields of the medical and educational professions; the family had been careful to practise its religion in private while steadfastly maintaining a public – and therefore at times extremely perilous – refusal to use or condone violence in the pursuit of religious or political aims.

That evening Marcus Asley had been hosting a small family celebration in his villa to mark the birthday of his Palestinian wife, Katie. His guests were his only sister, his two younger brothers, and their grandparents (both his parents had been killed years ago when, as they walked along Hamra, West Beirut's busy 'shopping centre', a parked car they were passing by exploded, having been loaded with twenty kilos of explosives and one 'martyr').

The party had started at around 8.30, after the evening meal. Marcus's much-loved sister, Elianne, had arrived first. At twenty years old she was fifteen years younger than Marcus, and that evening arrived at his house eager, full of life and lovely; her long, glossy, dark hair was coiled into a chignon and her olive-skinned face was alight with excitement at the prospect of the evening ahead. She'll sweep all her male fellow-students off their feet when she gets to her London college next month for her course in criminal law, Marcus thought. Elianne's grandparents had come in five minutes later. Nadia, whose rather beautiful severe face had sharpened since the deaths of her son Francis and his wife Shams several years ago had, nevertheless, retained her gentle, courteous manner and interest in everyone she met. Because, as she said, whether they're Muslim or Christian, young or old, clever or stupid, anyone may be blown apart in the street any day, like Shams and Francis were, so surely it's only human to behave kindly towards every person you encounter as you go about your life? Philippe, Nadia's husband, tall and craggily good-looking, had become implacably bitter ever since 'that day' and his views had crystallised against a hostile world.

Last to turn up had been Tomas and James, Marcus's younger brothers. Both were engaged to be married, but were without their fiancées that night because the two girls both lived in Tripoli, far away in the north of Lebanon, along a road only travelled in daylight by those who valued their lives.

The evening began well. In the dining-room that opened out of the hall of the villa, the big rectangular table was graced with a special cloth of handmade lace. It stood brilliant with cutglass vases of flowers and set with small porcelain plates, wine glasses and elegant silver dishes, some offering chocolates, Turkish Delight, tiny sweet cakes or petit fours, others various savoury *bonnes mouches*. The sideboard was laden with a wide range of fine wines and liqueurs, and James and Tomas were in charge of serving drinks. Everyone was having a good time: personal news and good-humoured gossip and banter were being exchanged, family in-jokes had been retold and laughed over again, food and drink had been enjoyed. At just before midnight though, the party began to break up since all those present – with the exception of the grandparents, of course – had to be up early next morning for work.

From his seat at the centre of the long side of the table, his back to the door leading in from the entrance hall, Marcus Asley sighed. As host, in a minute or so he'd have to stand up and make a speech to bring the party to a close: he would thank them all for coming, wish Elianne good luck in London (making jokes about how useful it will be to have an expert in criminal law in the family). Then he'd say nice things about Katie (no hardship there) and round off nicely by saying a few words to the grandparents that they'll know mean they are an inspiration to all the family and that 'love for them runs in the blood of our hearts'—

But Marcus put off his speech-making for a moment; leant back in his chair and looked round at his guests, his love for each of them a source of strength to him. Elianne, seated next to him on his left and, beyond her, at the far end of the table, his wife Katie (her mother made the beautiful lace tablecloth as a wedding-gift for her daughter). On the far side of the table, facing him, were James and Tomas. Tomas's eyes looked tired behind his glasses, Marcus noticed and thought, doubtless he's dead-beat, he works too hard, always has done. Then at the right-hand end of the table sat grandfather Philippe, immaculately dark-suited, a glass of tonic to hand as usual at parties, he drank neither wine nor spirits. And finally, facing James across the table and on Marcus's right, his grandmother Nadia. She sat very upright, her long-sleeved, high-necked black silk evening gown was brightened at one shoulder by two small roses bound together: one white, the other red, they were from her garden. She had picked the blooms that morning for Memory's sake, to keep her dead son and daughter-in-law 'with' the family.... Looking round at their faces Marcus thought what a fine lot they were. I love each of you and I'm proud to be related to you....

At her end of the table Katie watched her sister-in-law, Elianne; the two have been friends since their schooldays even though Elianne is the younger by three years. Her sister-in-law's face strikes Katie as beautiful with its broad brow, serious cast and the firmly set but generous mouth. The nose is a little arrogant and the long amber-lucent eyes above the high cheekbones are very direct, warm and percipient. Katie had envied the girl her creamy petal-smooth skin ever since their schooldays – and she smiled a little, admitting the fact to herself, and recalled that, when they play tennis, sunbathe and swim together, Elianne's skin took on an attractive rosy tan. God, she's lucky, Katie thought, watching the girl turn to look up at Marcus—

'*Stay where you are or you're dead!*' a harsh male voice shouted as the door behind Marcus crashed open and three men with guns stormed in. 'Hands in the air – *now!*' Then all three stopped dead and took firing position between the table and the door.

But no one screams. There's a shattering of glass as Katie knocked hers over, but the men and women gathered round the table obeyed the orders knee-jerk fast; they knew about things like this, Beirut had lived with savage, factional strife for many years now, raids by gunmen have become a fact of life to its citizens and it is accepted that night-time often connives with the men of violence.

'One of you makes a move, they get a bullet!' The captain, who had stationed himself behind Nadia, snapped out the threat loud and clear and then for a second absolute silence locked these ten people together in a tableau depicting the absolute power of the gun: the seven men and women sat as still as stone around the festive table, weaponless hands held precisely as ordered by the gun. Between them and the door, in a line parallel with the table, the three Hizbollah fighters, their black-on-white checkered scarves pulled up to just below their eyes, their bodies tensed in firing stance, the two either end of the line armed with Kalashnikovs and the one in the centre with a revolver.

'Three executions will now claim blood for blood,' the captain went on, his gun trained on the back of the elderly lady in front of him wearing a long black dress (he had selected her because he's found that targeting a woman in such raids is likely to pay off, it usually kept the men present in order. '*How much* blood in addition to those three killings will depend on you yourselves! One move from any of you and this bitch in front of me gets a bullet in the back.'

As his captain fell silent the young man with the revolver took two steps towards the table, then halted.

'Marcus Asley, Tomas Asley, James Asley,' he said, spacing the names so that each stood alone, as he saw it, with its own guilt – an arrogant formality. He laid the names on the frozen quietness as one would a roll-call of the dead. All present have swiftly realized that this is exactly what it is about to become unless God somehow intervenes. In point of fact, only one of the brothers can even make a guess at the reason why this should be going on; then as the accuser-avenger continues speaking, he has his guess confirmed as almost certain truth.

'My father was betrayed to his death by one of you,' the man with the hand-gun went on. 'I will now take your lives in payment for his.'

In the tense silence that followed he killed Tomas first. Strode round the end of the table and shot him where he sat with his hands raised above his head: two bullets to the base of the skull.

As his grandson's body spasms in death then crashes forward on to the table, the dark head lying in its own flowing blood, Philippe Asley lets out a strangled cry then drops his head in his hands so as not to see. At that movement the captain's finger tightens fractionally on the trigger of his Kalashnikov, but then relaxes (the old man's clearly no danger to us so don't steal the avenger's thunder).

Standing over the dead man, 'Death to all our enemies!' Hussain Shalhoub declared, his voice not loud but powered by an exultant violence so strong in him that it gave the mantra immediate and terrifying power. Then he swung away, moved on towards the dead man's brother sitting next to him. As he does so, James lowers his arms and, with deliberation, lays the palms of his hands flat on the table.

'It takes a brave fighter to shoot dead an unarmed man sitting at table with his family, I suppose,' he remarks quietly as he hears his brother's murderer stop behind him. As he speaks he looks across the table into the eyes of his grandmother Nadia sitting opposite him. Just before Shalhoub pulls the trigger, she gives James a smile that says *I love you, James Asley.* Thank you, Madame, he thinks – then dies, his blood mingling with that of Tomas, running dark among smashed glass and the crumbs of cake and pastry.

'And it takes a fool to tell him so,' Shalhoub mocks, too elated to be marked by the insult. Then fixing his eyes on Marcus he went on round the end of the table, making for him. As he passed behind Katie a convulsive shudder shook her entire body. Is there nothing I can do to stop this? she screams inside her head. He's going to kill *Marcus* now – and I'm going to sit here and let him *do* that? But if

I make any move at all then Nadia will die and it still won't save Marcus....

Smoothly and slowly, keeping the rest of her body absolutely still, Nadia turns her head a fraction of an inch, watching the killer of two of her grandsons approach the third – Marcus, firstborn son to her own firstborn son Francis and his wife Shams—

Sensing the gunman closing in on him from the side, Marcus Asley gets to his feet and turns to face him, hands still raised. 'In the forehead, please,' he says to him. 'Man to man. That way there's some honour in it, even for you.'

Shalhoub stops dead little more than an armslength from Marcus, paying no attention to the girl close beside him. He has eyes only for Asley now, his last 'kill'. He raises his revolver (and at his side Elianne tenses ready to move because she *cannot* sit there and let this happen) – but at that moment the frozen silence in the room explodes into a chaos of noise and violent action as in one convulsive sideways lunge Nadia hurls herself bodily at Marcus to save him and the captain fires at her. She takes his bullet in her side and her body, out of control, drives heavily into Marcus's back. Shalhoub fires one shot at Marcus but the bullet only ploughs across his forehead since because of Nadia he's already falling. And from the street outside three blasts on a car horn blare a warning to the gunmen.

'*Unit ten out!*' yelled the captain, instantly turning on his heel and racing for the door into the hall, gesturing at cadet al Hami to do the same. '*Unit ten out now!*' There's mayhem behind those two, but neither turns back because both are sure Shalhoub will follow them on the instant – his orders command it, it's the Unit's bounden duty to act in concert and make a fast getaway *whatever the circumstances*, confrontation with the police must be avoided *at all costs*—

But Shalhoub's bloodlust has him by the throat. Looking down at Marcus Asley he sees him sprawled across the table with his body half covered by that of the woman, clearly both are unconscious, but Shalhoub fears that because Asley was already falling when the trigger was pulled the bullet didn't strike true so the son-of-a-dog might still be alive. Therefore, to give the bastard the *coup-de-grâce* he brings his revolver up again.

As he does so, a clenched fist on the end of a hard-swung arm smashes aside his forearm, then as the bullet flies wild a hand grabs his arm, hangs on, gripping tight. Glaring down he sees his assailant is the girl who'd been sitting beside Asley. Seizing her free arm he forces it backwards cruelly – then as her clutch on him weakens he jerks his right arm free and smacks his gun barrel across the side of her face. But it's not enough. Driven by fury and despair, feral with grief and loss, she reaches for him with her right hand, hooks her nails into his masking scarf and claws it down. For a fraction of a second the girl and the man stare into each other's eyes, dead still. His eyes are close to hers, grey and brilliant: searching their depths Elianne Asley knows that the visceral hatred she finds flaring in them is mirrored in her own—

'Hussain! Hussain, *get the hell out! Get out now!*'

Grey eyes blink once as the furious command from the hall gets through to him – then Shalhoub shoves her violently aside, whirls round, makes for the door and races on through the hall and out into the street where he is picked up by the already moving Merc which, as soon as he's aboard, gathers speed and roars away into the night.

At his going a heavy, blood-soaked silence holds the room in thrall. Fallen to the floor, Elianne is lying on her back, dazed, blood running hot across the left side of her face.... Suddenly pushing herself up to lean on one elbow she looks fearfully towards the door into the hall – but there's no one there now. He has gone....

'Elianne!' From behind her, Katie's voice reaches for her, thin and questing, trembling.

Inside her head Elianne is with the man who has just sped out through that door; the man who, before her eyes, has just shot dead, in cold blood, her three brothers. She is seeing that man's face, the olive-skinned face with those pale grey eyes, disturbing eyes in a face never to be forgotten....

'By your face I shall know you.' She whispers the words near silently, speaking them to the image of his face that's burnt into her memory, the image of him staring down at her with the gun still in his hand and Marcus lying in his blood across the table. 'One day I'll find you. When I see you again, I shall know you and I'll kill you then.... It won't be easy to find you, I know that. But I've got a life-time. God willing, I've got a lifetime. Your face will give you to me and I'll *kill* you then—'

'Elianne, Elianne!' Katie's voice suddenly stronger and a strand of hope in it. 'Look at Marcus! I think ... I think he's still breathing!'

CHAPTER 1

THORNTON HEATH, London
28 October 2007
The garden of Charles Gray's house in Carlton Road

Elianne Asley's attention wandered away from the textbook she was studying. Interesting and absorbing as criminal law undoubtedly was, on a warm autumn afternoon a lovely English garden was a beguiling place to be. Quietly so as not to disturb Charles, she slipped a marker between the pages, let the book slide down on to her lap and, leaning back in her cushioned garden chair at one side of the big lawn at the back of Gray's house, lifted her face to the sun and, with closed eyes, breathed in the scent of roses and newly mown grass.

Charles Gray was at work some ten yards away from her across the lawn, sitting at a beechwood table set at one end of the paved terrace which ran the length of the back of his house. It was an attractive greystone building of medium size and, like his informal but still blooming garden, the house had a welcoming atmosphere. A dark-haired, wiry man in his late forties, Gray was an ophthalmic surgeon of considerable international reputation, and to him his work was the most important thing in his life. The most important *thing*, that is. Late in 2005 Elianne Asley had become the most important *person* in it – because her need had been so great and so very immediate. That afternoon he was engrossed in reviewing case-notes relevant to a lecture he was scheduled to give the following day: hunched forward in his upright chair he was evaluating the information in the file open between his hands.

Whee-eee-eee-eee! The peace was shattered by the piercing howl of a police car's siren as it raced by in the street – and Elianne started in her chair, staring wide-eyed, her face taut in shock. But quickly the ensuing calm flooded over horrific memories and drowned them; relaxing, she looked across the lawn at Charles Gray. The whooping of the siren had apparently bounced off the force-field of his concentration, she observed. Smiling wryly, she studied his familiar face, in profile to her now. His straight black hair fell across his forehead, the nose was rather long and the thrust of his bony jaw betrayed a certain arrogance, she knew – but knew also that his arrogance was confined to his work, to fighting his corner in order to serve his patients. She had come to know about him from what her brother Marcus had told her, way back before she'd come to England and had since taken him to her heart as a father.

'Hey Charles! You asleep there?' Light and joking, a male voice came from over by the corner of the house beside Charles's table. Looking that way Elianne saw a tall, rangy man with untidy fair hair whom she had never seen before coming around the grey stone wall and heading towards Charles. Clad in a black sweatshirt and khaki chinos, the man was somewhere in his late thirties, he held his head high and at once gave the impression of possessing a forceful personality kept on a tight rein. He had not noticed her, she realized, and watched him with interest as he reached out a hand in greeting as Charles, hearing his call, turned his head then got to his feet and faced him, smiling.

'Locksley! Good to see you back!' And from Charles's voice Elianne knew he meant it, meant it in spades. 'How was Amsterdam this time? You got what you went for?'

'No dice – again.' A shake of the head as he pulled out a chair and sat down across the table from Gray. 'One vital witness was recently found in an alley with her throat cut, consequently wherever one looked for information one met a solid wall of silence, people too afraid—' But Gray was turning away from him so he broke off.

'Elianne!' Charles called across the lawn. Looking that way, Locksley noticed the girl for the first time and saw her get to her feet. 'Come and meet a friend of mine,' Charles said.

Standing up again, Locksley watched her walk towards them. As he did so he found himself experiencing feelings he had never known before. He stood very still. *Watch yourself here*, he thought. 'Never again,' he reminded himself, recalling three years ago when his wife had walked out on him for her 'much more fun to live with than you are, Matt darling' millionaire lover.

'Elianne, meet Matthew Locksley, who for my sins recently became my neighbour. He's with the Met but presently on second-ment to MI6. He's been my friend for many years.' Gray was smiling as he took her arm and introduced them, pleased that these two should meet. 'Matt, this is Elianne Asley. Her home is in Beirut, but she's over here studying criminal law.'

The two shook hands, smiled and made conventional greetings. But knowing them both, Gray intuited a mutual – though slightly wary – interest sparking between them. Elianne turned to him uncertainly and he suggested they all had tea together out there on the terrace.

'Great idea. I'll go and make it and bring it out,' she said grate-fully, then as she passed Locksley on her way to the French doors standing open halfway along the terrace she gave the MI6 man a conspiratorial grin. 'Charles can do the washing-up afterwards,' she whispered to him. 'That is a chore I do not like.'

As she walked away across the stone paving towards the house, Gray sat down again, but Locksley's eyes did not leave her until she went inside: a girl with a lithe and lovely figure stepping blithely along through the sunshine in slim-fitting jeans and a daffodil-yellow kaftan top. She's young in years, he thought, but inside, she isn't young. Her eyes give her away; inside, she seems somehow old. Old, I guess, with grief and anger, if she's from Beirut she'll doubtless have her reasons.

'She's too young for you, Matthew.' Gray spoke dryly, noting the intensity of the younger man's regard of the girl.

'Sad but true.' Swinging round to him and quickly smiling, Locksley sat down and folded his arms on the table. 'Added to which I'd bet there's a long line of handsome young students only too eager—'

'And you'd be wrong there. Not Elianne; she works extremely hard, doesn't play much.... There is one young fella she likes being with, though, I recall. Bloke called Brad Ellis, I've met him a couple of times. Like her he's studying criminal law. Actually, though, he's dead keen on photography and journalism. She tells me his doing law is due to parental pressure.... I think she's a bit lost, Matt.' Gray looked down at the table, frowning, and when he went on his voice was thin and hard. 'Deep down she's lonely and lost in grief.'

Locksley knew him well. 'She's from Beirut, you said. What happened to her there?' he asked. Then, suddenly, having asked the question, he felt annoyed at his own forgetfulness, and recalled how, five or six years ago, a Lebanese consultant had come over to London on a two-year Exchange Programme and stayed with Gray while he did it. He was an eye surgeon, like Gray, and Matt remembered meeting him several times. 'Is she tied in with your Lebanese friend?' he asked. 'I don't recall his surname—'

'Asley, Marcus Asley,' Gray interrupted harshly. 'He was her brother.' He had become close to Marcus during those two Exchange years, both personally and through their work. As a medical man from a country engulfed in civil war, he had had first-hand experience of wounds seldom encountered in peacetime Britain. 'Marcus Asley learned a lot while he was over here,' he went on sombrely, 'but my God, we gained even more from him. He'd used techniques that won *time* for accident and emergency casualties, you see, Matt. It's sad for him and his patients, but greatly to the advantage of eye-surgery in general, that he'd had the opportunity to practice—'

'Tell me about this sister of his, then.' The suggestion was made partly to bring Gray back to the present, but mostly because Locksley wanted to know more about her; he felt strongly drawn to the girl.

'Yes, I'd like to do that.' Pushing himself to his feet Gray turned and, thrusting his hands into the pockets of his black trousers, stared out across the lawn at the four tall silver firs bordering his property. Ever since Elianne had come to London he had wanted to tell the Asley story to someone. It had seemed to him one which deserved to be heard – with the proviso that the person to whom it was divulged was one who would respect the knowledge. Knowing Matt Locksley was such a man, he told him all that had taken place in the Asleys' dining-room on the night in 2005 on which Elianne and six other members of the Asley family had gathered in the villa of its eldest son, Marcus, to celebrate his wife's birthday. All that was known to him, that is. Gradually, he had slotted together into one coherent whole the pieces of it which – on one occasion with uncontrollable tears – Elianne had entrusted to him. He now relayed to Matt how the Asley family had paid the price for the arrest – which led to his death – of one of the men who had played a lead part in the assassination of Lebanon's Prime Minister Hariri. The pared-to-the-bone facts of the case struck Matt as having the dry precision of an official resumé of a witness statement.

Locksley heard him through in concentrated silence, missing nothing. In the course of his working life he had dealt with worse situations than those Gray had described, with more savage killings, but those only served to make the horrific events of that night in Beirut more graphically real to him.

Coming to the end of it, Gray stood silent.

'So why were all three sons targeted like that?' The MI6 man broke the sombre quietness of Gray's garden. 'D'you know?'

Gray shook his head, tight lipped as he turned to him. 'I do not.... I have a feeling Elianne may know, or at least suspect, but when I ask her, she won't tell me,' he said. Then dismissing the question, he went back to the main thread of his narrative. 'Her grandfather got in touch with me a few months afterwards. Told me the university at which Elianne had been accepted for 2005 had agreed to postpone her studies for a year and that, consequently, she would be arriving here in 2006.... Then he asked me – for Marcus's sake – to be kind enough to, as he put it, "watch over" his grand-daughter when she came to London to finish her courses.' Looking up, he searched Locksley's eyes. 'So I did that,' he told him quietly. 'I'm still doing it, Matt, because – you know something? – I feel she's my daughter. Which is something I never dreamed could ever happen for me. But it has.'

The daughter, or son, of course, that you never had, Locksley guessed in the privacy of his mind, recalling that some eighteen years or so ago Charles' wife of fifteen years had died in childbirth, the baby with her—

'There's one thing in all this I haven't told you yet,' Gray said suddenly, sitting down again.

'Which is?'

'Marcus Asley, Elianne's favourite brother of the three—' His mouth twisted and he broke off, looking away.

'Go on. Say it, Charles,' Matt said quietly.

Gray looked up at him. 'You see, Marcus didn't die that night. I should have mentioned that when I was telling you about it just now but.... What Elianne did at the time shifted the gunman's aim so the coup de grâce he intended didn't come off and Marcus ... he wasn't killed like the other two brothers. Shot in the head, he's been in a deep coma ever since. Medical diagnosis is irreversible brain damage.'

'*Christ!* ... Poor Elianne.' It came from the heart.

'The grandfather refuses to accept the diagnosis. Won't allow life-support to be withdrawn.'

'And the grandmother?'

'Was dead within a few months. She didn't want to live, Elianne said. Just slipped away.'

'So Marcus Asley ... lingers on?'

Gray nodded.

'And Elianne still hopes. After she told me, I think she wished she hadn't and since then she won't talk about it.' Suddenly, frustrated at his own uselessness to the girl boiled up inside him and, slamming both hands palm-down on the table, he pushed himself to his feet. 'It's keeping her shut up in her dreadful past, Matt! I can't seem to get through to her. Can't persuade her to get on with her life – she's in her early twenties, for God's sake, she should have fun sometimes, do something other than work.'

'She seems....' But Matt Locksley's voice trailed away into silence as he realized he had been about to say 'happy enough' – which, remembering the expression behind her eyes, he knew to be far from the truth. So he tried again. 'Her face … she looks to be a very serious-minded girl—'

But Gray interrupted, an impatience in him to get to the plan that had been forming in his mind since he had seen that tentative empathy between the girl and Locksley as they met for the first time a short while ago. 'I was thinking, just now, maybe you could help her with that? I'm a dull old stick on the social side nowadays – but you get out and about more than I'm interested in doing. You go to the theatre and the cinema and so on, and you've got friends in the country.' Sitting down again, he sought to advance his newfound cause. 'Elianne's quite an "outdoor" sort of person, like you,' he went on. 'When she does take a break from studying she likes to go off into the country or spend a couple of nights at some coastal place. Somewhere that's got some history to it—'

'Yes, just like the villages and towns along Lebanon's north-south seaboard on the Med, most of them had been fought over, sacked and torched since long before Vikings raided our shores.' Linking his hands behind his head, Locksley fell silent for a moment or two and sat staring out across the garden, his imagination roaming wide. Then he shrugged and, smiling wryly, turned again to Gray. 'D'you know,' he remarked, 'if you ask some people in Lebanon their nationality they still answer "Phoenician"?'

'Sounds a bit over the top to me, did you read it somewhere?'

'I've had it said to me, face to face.'

'You've been in the Lebanon, then?' Surpised and interested, Gray forgot for a moment his rapidly developing scheme for drawing Elianne into mainstream life. 'You've never mentioned it before. How come you were there?'

'It was back in the mid-nineties, warning bells regarding activities in Syria, Lebanon and Iran were ringing in Western Intelligence circles. Low level, exploratory work was all I got, I was small fry then. It wasn't a long-term assignment; six months only, all in Lebanon: Beirut, Tripoli, Byblos.'

'What was your cover?'

'Trade Representative: educational supplies including IT equipment.'

'This is great, Matt!' Seizing on this surely heaven-sent opportunity, Gray pressed on more confidently with his plan. 'Elianne will be thrilled, and it'll be so much easier for her to relate to someone like you who's been to her country.' Then, frowning suddenly, he half turned away, recalling the horror of the waking nightmare haunting the girl. 'Three brothers she had, Matt, all surgeons of high repute – and she's lost all three to terrorism, two dead and the third, my friend Marcus, condemned to lie in a hospital bed like some bloody zombie. And, *she saw it happen....* Such a thing *marks* you. That's why I regard her as being *in my care.*'

'I'm glad to know you do,' said Locksley, thinking back to the grief he had seen in Elianne Asley's eyes and, recalling that other emotion he had sensed lurking there, underlying the grief: a passion fraught with vengeful intensity.... Maybe the girl needed more than simply 'caring', he thought. There's a deep-rooted anger in her that's looking for—

'So will you help me with Elianne, Matt? Help by getting her out and about doing ordinary things, meeting people.... Marcus Asley was a good man and a fine surgeon in his field.'

'Why do you speak of him in the past tense? He's still alive, isn't he?' Locksley's eyes met his; and for a second both men were very quiet.

Then Gray asked, 'Do *you* call that "being alive"?'

'Only in the sense that it may keep *hope* alive in those who love him, I guess, and yes, Charles, I'd like to do what you ask—'

'Hey, can someone give me a hand, please?' Elianne called, coming out on to the terrace carrying a large, obviously well loaded tray. 'It's heavier than I thought, I'll drop the whole thing if someone doesn't – oh thanks! Saved!'

Locksley took the tray from her, and within a few minutes the three of them had settled down and relaxed into the happy state that afternoon tea in an English garden generally induces.

In the event, Elianne Asley and Matt Locksley did the washing-up together, deciding against using the dishwasher in favour of the sink positioned in the big airy kitchen overlooking the vegetable garden at the side of the house. They were already finding pleasure in talking together and discovering more about each other – Gray such a socially experienced, perceptive man that strangers invariably found themselves quickly at ease in his company. Both Matt and Elianne intuited that beneath the easy chatter, any barriers either might wish to erect would be respected by the other.

'This chap Brad Ellis you mentioned earlier, is it … well, serious between you?' Locksley asked, carefully placing washed-and-dried china on the table behind them then turning back to her.

'God, no! I haven't got a boyfriend, there isn't time, I'm too busy studying. Brad's a friend, a good friend to me. We discuss lectures together, go for a coffee, maybe a film sometimes. We *like* each other.'

'He's in the same year as you in college.'

'Yes he is, but his heart's not in criminal law, what he really wants to do is photography, that's his passion: action photography – catching people's emotions on film. He dreams of a career as a press photographer specializing in crime and warfare.' She placed the cup she had been washing on the draining board, and gave Locksley a sudden gamine grin, her eyes alight with laughter. 'You have to be careful when you're with Brad, you know? Sometimes he's quite embarrassing to be with. You see, he carries his camera with him all the time, wherever he goes. He likes to photograph people's *faces* – their expressions as they go about their ordinary lives. You have to watch out when you're with him or he'll catch your face looking some way you'd rather other people didn't see it … he calls what he does "recording life in progress", and he's very good at it. He sold four pictures to a newspaper a while back, faces in a football crowd.'

As she fell silent, Matt said, 'Your English is near perfect. How come?'

'Oh, we speak it a lot at home. Besides, ever since I was eleven I studied it four days a week at the British Council in West Beirut, one hour, from five to six o'clock.'

Laughing, he went back to drying up. 'Well, they did a good job.… Go on about Ellis. Charles told me his parents don't want that sort of career for him.'

'They don't, but he's winning them round, I think. He's a very persuasive sort of guy. Clever, too, and very knowledgeous … if there is such a word?' Placing a well-washed silver milk jug on the draining board, she quirked an eyebrow at him.

With a quick grin, 'Not sure, you'd better ask Brad,' he said, then got on with the drying up. And after a few moments asked her – because the silence between them felt so companionable – whether all her brothers had been married.

To her surprise, since usually she would regard such matters as private, she found herself quite happy to answer him.

'Only Marcus is married,' she said quietly. Then smiled to herself, enjoying good memories. 'We are a very *proper* family, you see,' she went on. 'Very traditional, I suppose. What some of my fellow students would probably call "stuffy", I guess. Neither Tomas nor James would think it right to marry until they were well established in their professions. They were both engaged, though. Being older than them, Marcus had been married for quite a while.'

'Does he have children?' Matt asked, careful to use the present tense.

'One son aged three. His wife's name is Katie.... Katie nearly died in childbirth because at the time the hospital she was in was under attack from a local Hamas group, street battles were going on all around it and ... well, at least she survived and so did the baby. Unlike two doctors, four patients and a baby girl born that night to a woman who....' But her voice trailed away into silence. Her hand reached out automatically for the next thing waiting to be washed – but there was nothing there, the washing-up was finished. Straightening up she turned away from him and stood silent, her head down, lost in remembering.

'At that hospital, a woman who *what*, Elianne?' he asked, watching her.

'A woman whose husband was one of the gunman outside attacking them,' she said, the words running out of her in a flat stream without expression. 'She died, but her baby lived. Sad, wasn't it.'

After a moment, 'Let those things go,' he said, wanting to touch her hand but – not doing it.

It was as though she had not heard him. 'How does that man live with it, though? The husband, how does he live with having done that? That's what I can't understand.' She faced him, her eyes searching his, haunted. 'Can *you*, Mr Locksley? Because if you can I'd very much like you to explain it to me.'

He thought, I suspect that gunman in all likelihood doesn't brood upon it much, especially since the baby was a girl. He said, sombrely,

'If I could explain things like that maybe I'd be able to save the world.'

And strangely, almost at once, her memories slipped out of synch with present time and she 'came back' to him he intuited, glad of that yet also, in some unfathomable way, humbled by it. She smiled, but he knew the smile was not for him, her eyes kept it secret to herself; then she turned and made for the side door opening on to the kitchen garden.

'I promised Charles I'd dig over the herb bed,' she said over her shoulder, 'but I'm not that keen on digging, so would you help me? That's if you've got time, of course—'

'Yes, I have time.' He was by her side as she reached the door, and he opened it for her. 'As a matter of fact I often make myself useful in Charles's garden – I've always enjoyed gardening, but living in a flat I have to settle for growing tomatoes on the balcony.'

As she passed by him and stepped out into the sunlight she looked up at him. 'Thanks,' she said, her eyes direct to his. Then she went on her way, leaving him unsure whether the grace-word was for the offer of digging or for something else.

'Yes, she's had her own bed-sit room here in my house for the last eight months, to use whenever she likes and wants a change from her digs and sharing with her flatmate. She doesn't use it all that often, but the point is, she knows it's always here for her whenever she wants to escape from the pressures of college life in what, to her, is a foreign country.'

'It must have been difficult for her, at first,' Matt said. Sitting one either end of the sofa in the sitting-room and enjoying a brandy together after supper – once Elianne had gone up to her room – the two men were both interested in talking about the girl, each for his own reasons.

'When her grandfather first contacted me and asked me to keep an eye on her when she came over here, I agreed for Marcus's sake, he was a good friend of mine and a man I'd known as a fine surgeon with a great future ahead of him,' Gray went on thoughtfully. 'But then later, once she was here and I got to know her and she began to trust me enough to talk to me about what had happened to her family....' Breaking off, Gray sipped his brandy, then put the glass down and looked at Locksley again. 'As I said, I care about her; she has become dear to me,' he said. 'That may seem trite, maybe even weird, but that's how I see it.'

Then you're a lucky man, Charles, that there's someone in your life for you to love, Locksley thought. Then he got to his feet and, taking his brandy with him, strolled across to the window, stood gazing abstractedly out over Gray's garden, and after a silence asked him about a crucial point relating to the appalling events of that night in Beirut.

'*How* did it come to happen, Charles?' he asked. 'How did the gunmen know it was the Asley brothers? Do *you* know? Does *she* know?'

'*I* know. The grandfather told me. I needed to know, because if Elianne had been involved in the reason for the killings she might well be in great danger over here. When I first asked, the grandfather clammed up at once, saying he didn't know, that none of the family did. But then a few days later I had a letter from him. In it he apologized for lying to me earlier: then he told me all he had been able to find out about the whole thing.'

'And *had* she been involved in whatever it was that provided a motive for the killings? Was it only the brothers, or did she come into it somehow?'

'Come and sit down again, Matt. You've said you'd be willing to try to open her life out and be a friend to her, so please, come over here and sit down again, because if you're going to try to help her you need to know *why* her brothers were shot that night since it's because of that she shuts herself away as she does. It's not a story I want to shout across the spaces of my sitting-room. It's ugly.'

So Locksley returned to his place on the sofa, put down his brandy and listened, and didn't touch his drink again until Gray had recounted what lay behind the Asley killings.

'It was tied up with Hariri's assassination in Beirut in 2005,' Gray said, chin sunk on chest, eyes down. 'After the assassination the police moved in hard and quick, and many of the Hizbollah fighters engaged in the actual murder were arrested or shot. However, the 2i/c of one of the assassination/support units escaped the scene of the assassination *and* the ferocious police and military action immediately following it. He was wounded in the running battle that went on as he fled though, and was pursued; a police bullet ploughed across his forehead, but he got away. His wound healed, but it left a faint scar.' Gray paused, sipped his brandy. And then as he replaced his glass a narrow smile flickered for a moment on his face and he glanced across at Locksley. 'Treacherous, tricky bastard luck can be, can't it?' he observed wryly.

'I've know it hand one goodies one minute then kick you hard in the teeth the next,' Locksley said. But he knew Gray was hardly aware of him as he told the 'story' – he was in a sad, lost Lebanon with his friend Marcus Asley.

'Luck let this terrorist Hizbollah fighter – he was operating under the assumed name Ahmed bin Hamid at the time – run free for fourteen days in Beirut,' Gray went on, leaving his friend's remark to die its death unnoticed, 'then it turned on him. Late one night he drove his car into a tree – almost certainly he was forced to do it, but nothing was ever proved. The fire service cut him free and he was taken to A and E at the nearest hospital. This happened to be in the Christian sector. There, examination showed that bin Hamid had got glass in his eyes and required urgent surgery. And by chance, the eye surgeon on call at that time was Marcus Asley. He operated, bin Hamid's sight was saved, and in a matter of days he was discharged, subject to out-patient treatment.

'*However*, in the course of making the necessary close examination of his patient's head and face prior to surgery, Marcus Asley had seen and taken careful note of the scar of a recent wound running across the man's forehead, above his eyes. Therefore, being a man who regularly followed news programmes with deep interest, he put two and two together and came to the conclusion that his patient's true ID was almost certainly not "Ahmed bin Hamid". He reported this conclusion to a Fatah activist whom he knew from his work. And it happened that, a few days after his discharge from hospital, Ahmed bin Hamid was shot dead outside the front door of the house he was staying in at the time. It was a drive-by killing, he was just putting his key in the lock. The death was neither reported in the media nor recorded in any official report. Later, Marcus was informed of the killing by the activist to whom he had passed the information on "bin Hamid"....

'So, clearly, somehow Hizbollah Intelligence must have discovered that an eye surgeon by the name of "Asley" had fingered their man to Fatah.' The story told, Gray fell silent and sat back with an open-handed gesture of resignation.

'So in one way, justice was done.' Locksley remarked quietly.

'A kind of justice for Hariri, yes. But at what a price for the Asley family. And I doubt the thing will end there; given Lebanon the way it is, I doubt that. Each revenge killing sows the seeds for the next, so there's no end to it. Follow it through, Matt. If Hariri was assassinated for his perceived anti-Syrian bias – then, any of his killers who escaped death or arrest in the aftermath of the event, of whom "bin Hamid" was one, could be murdered by their Fatah enemies as soon as opportunity offered. That leads straight on to Hizbollah having the Asley brothers killed in revenge for "bin Hamid's" death.'

'But Marcus is still alive. So are you saying he'll be next? They'll go for him again?'

'No. What I'm saying is that sooner or later some close relative or friend of the Asley's may find out who it was that pulled the trigger on the Asleys that night, and go gunning for him.'

But Locksley's mind had swung back to a point which had puzzled him earlier. 'But Charles, what I don't understand is why the gunman shot all three of them. It was Marcus, Marcus only, who ID'd "bin Hamid", so why kill all three brothers?'

'I asked the grandfather that. He put it down to straight blood lust.'

'If you don't know which one it was, kill them all…. *Christ.* What a way to live your life.'

'I'll never forget something the grandfather said when I asked him about it. Just before he ended the call, he said, "Mr Gray, that murderer needed no *reason* to kill all three: *he had the gun,* and if you are the one holding the gun on unarmed fellow-men you can do to them whatever you choose." … But all that's incidental,' Gray said, suddenly impatient. 'The deed is done, two men are dead and nothing can bring them back to life. But here and now there's another side to this question, one that's infinitely more pressing—'

'My God, you're scared for Elianne, aren't you!' Abruptly, Locksley had intuited Gray's underlying concern. 'Forgive me, I should have realized it before.'

'I am indeed, Matt. The way it seems to be, she is vulnerable even over here.'

'That could be true.' Locksley was frowning and troubled on the girl's behalf, he probed deeper. 'Tell me, did she see the killer's face? Or hear any *names* used by the three-man group?'

'I asked. She said not, but … that could have been simply to escape my questioning, now I think back to it.' With an effort, he shook off his sombre mood, got to his feet and picked up the bottle of Corvoisier from the table. 'Now, let's you and I get down to a bit of forward planning,' he went on, topping up both drinks. 'You'll help, about Elianne?'

'I'll be happy to give it a go. Hopefully, with you to vouch for me as a man of honour she'll not reject me and my companionship out of hand.… And I'll watch out for her, Charles, I promise you that.' Then, smiling, Matt Locksley raised his glass as in a toast. 'Here's to Elianne Asley,' he said. 'To her continuing safety, success in her studies – and her increasing enjoyment of life.' But even as he and Charles Gray drank to the girl, Matt knew in his heart that the story behind her presence in London, while awakening his deeply felt sympathy for her loss, had also aroused his professional interest. The gunman who shot the Asley brothers had, obviously, been a member of a terrorist group – probably Hizbollah – and experienced gunmen from national groups frequently progressed to involvement in international terrorism, not only as frontline combatants, but also as instructors in training camps and, more insidiously, as agents provocateurs within domestic communities – and, therefore, such individuals were best identified and kept track of whenever possible.

★

12A Lime Tree Road
Hammersmith, London
Elianne Asley's bedroom at 01.30

A brilliantly lit dining-room in a chaos of violence. She knew her brothers were dead. The pain of a pistol-whipping is sharp across her cheek and he has her arm in an iron grip, he's forcing it back further, further, the pain's beyond enduring. She hooks her nails into his masking scarf, wrenches it down – his eyes glare down into hers and they are grey and brilliant with the urge to violence driving him. He'll kill me now, she thinks. 'Hussain! *Out now!*' a man's voice shouts across the flaring shadows, his eyes blink once – then he hurls her away from him and she's falling, falling—

Breaking free of the nightmare, Elianne pushed herself upright, turned on her bedside light then threw herself back against the pillows. She remembered her dead family then – and *how* they had died.... Remembered those who were still alive – and the way they lived now: how Grandfather Philippe had become a remote man, hard with bitterness and grief, but determined to keep what was left of the family together. She remembered Marcus. Marcus's devotedly cared-for body lying in its immaculate bed – the core of him gone.

Lastly, she recalled the words she had whispered to herself earlier that night – and now whispered them again. 'One day I'll find you and when I do, I'll pay you back in your own coin.'

Then, getting out of bed she slipped on her dressing-gown and, going out into the kitchen of the small ground-floor flat she shared with Roz Hunt, a fellow student fifteen years older than her, made herself a mug of hot chocolate and sat down at the table to drink it. Later, she went back to bed and, after a while, found refuge in sleep.

CHAPTER 2

MI6 HQ
Central London

Entering his own office Superintendent Locksley went straight across to the computer standing on a desk of its own against the far wall, sat down facing it and switched it on. It contained all the data known to MI5 and MI6 on already-suspect individuals from the Middle East countries rated 'hostile to British interests' who were currently resident in the UK and, therefore, subject to Medium-level surveillance by its Intelligence services. Accessing the names he presently required, he read the following:

A. ROSE DALEY (Married name: Roisin SHALHOUB (See note 4 below)

  1 Irish-born (1960 Dublin) to Republican family
     Parents IRA activists (Both deceased see att notes for details)
  2 Belfast University 1978 to 1981: English Lt plus Lang
  3 1981. BEIRUT Teaching Eng at The Lebanese University
  4 1982. Married Mohammed Hussain SHALHOUB (Palestinian
        by birth – family resident Beirut 1950 onwards)
        N.B. Suspected arranged marriage, politically motivated
           (IRA/Hizbollah. Shalhoub, 51 at time of marriage
           Daley, 22)
  5 1984–2001. Very little info available. Verified info as follows:
      a Daley gave birth to 3 sons Ramadan, Soheil & Hussain
      b Ramadan and Soheil died 2001. Cause of death
        unknown suspected but unproven to be in combat
        during raid into Israeli territory
      c July 2005 Mohammad Shalhoub died. His personal
        MO certified death by natural causes, but that diag-
        nosis is suspect

6 2007. 14 March Rose Daley returned to live in UK bringing with her the third son Hussain – his name changed by deed poll at the same time as his mother when she resumed her maiden name.

7 Rose Daley currently resident Flat I, Brookside House, 10 Park Road, EALING, LONDON.

A PERSONAL
1 ROSE DALEY
48 years of age
Average height, light brown hair (artif col maintained) grey eyes
Sophisticated dress sense, good quality clothes unostentious and stylish
Languages: English and Arabic (fluent verbal and written) Spanish (verbal: good, written: average)

B SOCIAL LIFE
    a   comfortable lifestyle
    b   fellow occupants at given address report her good neighbour, considerate, friendly without herself offering or accepting offers of close social contact
    c   works part time on casual basis at local library mornings only regular voluntary stint 2pm to 5 at local RNIB chairty shop
    d   member of local Bridge Club
    e   apart from her son has few visitors (see later note)

A. ROBERT DALEY (né Hussain Rashid SHALHOUB)
  1 Born 1986
  2 Presently resident 12 Nelson Road, EALING, LONDON shares accomm. with two other male students both res term time only
  3 Occupation: student EATON TOWERS COLLEGE, RICHMOND, LONDON subjects cybernetics plus business studies

2 ROBERT DALEY
College reports him hard working student of above average scholastic ability – keen sportsmen. He is fit and athletic with fast reflexes and

good hand-eye co-ordination – untutored in all sports, bar football, at which he's said to possess natural talent but given to 'selfish' play. Well liked by both tutors and fellow students – appears to be well adjusted to student life in the UK – has several good friends no girl-friend in particular, but some contact with several female friends

CONCLUSION He's a handsome attractive young man. Nothing suspicious has been observed about him and his activities. However, there are inevitably periods (particular evenings) when his where-abouts, activities and social contacts are unaccounted for.

3 MOTHER-SON RELATIONSHIP and SOCIAL
Relationship appears amicable, but not particularly close. Robert visits frequently but has not been observed to stay overnight.
Mother very hands-on re. son's educational progress and attends most college-related social-study meetings and events.
Mother attends local Cath. church regularly, but does not appear to have any particular closeness to religious personnel there.

VISITORS Rose Daley (apart from her son)
1 Fairly regularly ladies visit for morning coffee (acquaintances from Bridge Club, staff from Library and RNIB and local antiques shop)
2 One Arab male, mid-fifties, shortish but well-built – expensive business clothes.
Visits minimum once a week, no routine to the timing of visits, earliest recorded 11.00, latest 20.30
Agents have been unable to discover either a) the name and personal details of this visitor or b) what links him to Rose Daley
Please note that a) above would be possible given more manpower for surveillance. The man presumably arrives and leaves by car which he parks several streets away then walks to Daley's. We have no designated vehicle, and tailing him is too slow to be effective.
3 Mr and Mrs Steven Gilkes, resident owners 11 Park Road Ealing (nextdoor neighbours to Daley). Retired couple, he previously sea captain and wife has common interests with Daley, i.e. theatre and bridge. They and Daley on good terms, but never visit each other's houses.

The report ended there. Leaning back, Locksley stared at the wall in front of him, lost in thought. He was intrigued by the strange, or at the very least unusual story of Rose Daley's life to date. It had been the '1981 to Beirut' entry which had jumped out at him and claimed his special attention – partly because of that city's connection with Elianne Asley, he admitted to himself in passing, but mostly for professional reasons. Then, as he had continued reading, other facts in Rose Daley's CV had made him suspicious and at points stretched his credulity to breaking point.

Action should be taken, he decided: Rose Daley, and a male Arab visitor, a regular visitor whom surveillance had been unable to name or track down.... Checking the identities of the two officers responsible for the report on Rose Daley and her son, he found one name he knew: William Carson, a man Locksley had worked with many times before, a man dedicated to his job beyond the norm and prodigiously knowledgeable in the highways and – even more importantly – the byways of surveillance procedure. Hoping that Carson at fifty-four was nearing retirement and wished he weren't, often wondered despairingly how he would fill in all the hours of the days when the job wasn't there for him to give his clever policeman's mind to, Locksley called through to his office. After a moment—

'Carson.' The voice was as he rememered it, curt; he resented interruption when he was engrossed in work.

'Locksley here. I've just been studying your latest report on Rose Daley, Bill – a good job you made of it, too. Off the record, though, how do you feel about her surveillance rating? I'm having a re-think on that. I was wondering ... well, it gave me cause for thought.' He must not *lead* him, he reminded himself, mustn't plant the word 'suspicion' in his mind.

He had no need to. 'I'm glad you've brought it up, sir,' Carson said. 'I've been debating with myself whether to come and talk that one over with you, ever since I made that last summary.'

'Along what lines, your debate?'

After a brief pause, 'She seems too good to be true, sir,' Bill Carson said. 'Both she and her son, they don't ring true when you see them in the round, as it were. Her life in Beirut and all that, and her life here, now – the two don't *fit*, if you see what I mean. They look to be so ordinary, she and her son, that any suspicion about them seems almost insulting, it'd be like suspecting your own mum of being a terrorist. But to professionals like us, Mr Locksley, it could be that Rose Daley and her son are too damn' carefully ordinary to be exactly and no more than what they seem to the casual eye. Charity work, the library, bridge, the theatre – it seems altogether too quiet a life for Rose Daley – bloody boring, you'd think she'd find it…. Plays well with the neighbours, of course—'

'And with the professionals unless and until something prompts them to look at the whole thing from a different perspective.' To himself, Matt Locksley smiled wryly, then he moved on. 'I think you and I are in agreement on this one,' he said. 'You got time to come up to the office and talk about it with a view to upgrading surveillance on the woman?'

'Be with you right away, sir.' Bill Carson had got what he had begun to hope for as the conversation developed.

Saturday, 7 June 2008
The garden of The Foresters' Arms, a country pub an hour's drive southeast of London.

'I'm so very glad you brought me here.' Elianne was sitting comfortably in a beechwood chair, her eyes roaming over the rolling countryside finally settling on one particular knoll in the middle-distance known locally as Hermit's Hill. The woodland surrounding it crawled a little way up its gentle lower slopes, but its highest point stood treeless and, poking up through the rough grass growing there rose a circle of large, time-worn slabs of grey stone marking out the perimeter walls of some long-dead anchorite's primitive dwelling.

She and Matt Locksley had been rambling through those hills since they'd had lunch at the pub, and, now back there, were sitting over cool glasses of cider. Situated on the fringe of a hamlet a mile off the main road, The Foresters' Arms was a large, friendly place. It had stood for over two hundred years, but had changed very little during that time.

'Charles and Marcus were true friends,' she went on softly, 'and I love Marcus, so although Marcus isn't properly with us yet, Charles is my guardian angel.' For a moment she sat very quiet, then in a quick change of mood, she threw him a gamine grin of self-mockery. 'That's a bit over the top, isn't it,' she said. 'Forgive me!'

'Nothing to forgive.' He smiled across at her, thinking how much more self-confient she had become, how much more at ease she was socially; and it seemed to him that, now, she trusted him completely and felt no need to hide her thoughts from him.

However her gamine grin was quickly gone. 'It's interesting, isn't it, Matt, how one thing in your life leads on to another, often in a way you'd never dreamed,' she said, her face returning to its customary serious cast, her eyes on the hermit's ruined cell atop its serene and separate hill.

'Do you mean how the friendship between Charles and your brother Marcus resulted in you being here, now? With me?' He watched her as he spoke; and as she turned to face him directly he caught in her eyes the last thing he had expected – a flash of anger, of hatred even. The perception shook him – but her expression changed almost at once, by the time her eyes met his fully, they reflected only her usual thoughtfulness.

'You are a clever man, Matt – no, that is not the right word, I mean you are very *intuitive*. Would that be the correct word?'

So her gamine grin hadn't been quite such a giveaway as he had thought, he realized. She *was* hiding from him in some way, hiding something that she felt strongly about. But then of course she had every right to do that if she wanted to. He must move at *her* pace, then maybe in time she would really open up to him.

'It was work that brought Marcus and Charles together in the first place, wasn't it?' he said at last.

She nodded, flicking her long dark hair back behind her ears. 'Yes. Like Charles does, Marcus lived for the work he did,' she said.

'Ophthalmic surgery ... many people have suffered because of what was done to Marcus that night, people whose sight he might have saved had he been whole.' She smiled to herself, then went on, pensively. 'There was a day I saw that very clearly, back in 2004. Marcus and I were strolling along Hamra together, and there was this man coming along the pavement towards us, he was in his late '20s, tall and well built, fair untidy hair, not particularly handsome but sort of good-to-look-at, a lively intelligence in him, you know. Then as he came nearer I saw him recognize Marcus – and as he drew level with us he stepped in front of him, very politely but very firmly, so we stopped. Now he was close to me I could see that the skin of his face was pitted all over – *all over* – with little red scars and that there was a lot of deeper scarring around both his eyes, too. "You probably don't remember me, Mr Asley," he said to Marcus, "but I will remember you with profound gratitude every day of my life until I die. My name is Pierre Hammond, you operated on me and saved my sight eighteen months ago after I was in a car crash, I went headfirst through the windscreen.... You are a gift of God to me and to many others in this country, Mr Asley, I wanted to tell you that: a gift of God." Then he smiled at Marcus and went on by.' Through the passing of a few seconds she sat silent then she blinked, gave a small shake of her head and looked away. 'We are an emotional people, we Lebanese,' she said quietly. '"A gift of God": it sounds corny, I guess, but it didn't at the time. Sorry, though.'

'Not corny. Humbling, perhaps. To me, anyway.... And, don't be sorry.'

'Why shouldn't I?'

Her abruptness took him unawares. Quickly, he changed the subject, asking her whether she planned to go back and work in Lebanon when her studies in London came to an end.

'The legal system in Lebanon is seriously ... contaminated. I hope to stay here,' she told him, seemingly relieved to be speaking of other things.

'But it's the country of your birth,' he protested, 'and your whole family's still there—'

'*You fool!*' The words came low and vicious out of a face suddenly convulsed with fury and despair. 'My *family?*' She leaned towards him, narrowed eyes stabbing into his. 'I had three brothers and now all three are lost to me, two dead and buried, the body of the third in a hospital bed. I saw them killed, Mr Locksley: Tomas first, then James – and James being James he stood up and faced the gun, didn't he, but of course the result was the same. Then the killer came round the table—' Abruptly and with some effort she obliterated the memory and broke off. Closing her eyes she sat back, her whole body slack, vitality drained from it.

Locksley went to her side, hitched one hip on to the edge of the table close beside her and gently took her hand in his from where it lay loosely on the arm of the chair. 'There's nothing I can say to ease that, Elianne,' he said to her, 'nothing anyone can usefully say, I think. Words can't really do that, at least I don't know any that can. So I'll leave it lie, and kiss your hand.' Which he did, uncurling the passive fingers one by one and pressing his lips lightly to the palm of her hand. Then he put her hand back on the arm of her chair, returned to his own place and sat down to wait for her.

But she recovered her poise quite quickly (self-defence mechanisms had taught her how to do that, he thought). 'Lebanon was doomed, Marcus used to say,' she said, looking up at him again, clear eyed. '"It's doomed to be fought over, and through, again and again,"' he'd say, '"and that'll go on until everything in it that *makes* it "Lebanon" has been leached out of it and it's governed by either a Syrian satrap or some Hizbollah terrorist supremo".' But then suddenly the hatred in her burst out through self-control and her voice came low but raw with the anguish of lost hope. 'I love Marcus but – what use am I to him now? There's nothing left but to....' But she did not finish her sentence; she left it hanging in the air, keeping its ending secret to herself.

He could not bring himself to give her an answer to her question. So, turning away from her, he stared unseeingly at the surrounding countryside and sat in the sunshine waiting for her to come back to him. But she stayed silent, and after a couple of minutes he fell to wondering again – as he did from time to time since he'd first met her at Charles Gray's house – about the hatred he sensed in her.... Hatred of what? And at whom was it now directed? Was it the common generalized hatred of 'terrorism'? Or was it of a more personal nature?—

'Do you know anything about sailing, Matt?'

Her voice was light and clear again and he turned back to her at once. She was embowered in sunshine, with cascades of dark hair falling in disarray around her shoulders and a careful smile curving her lips: yes, the girl was reaching out for new things now, and he was with her in that.

'Sure, a bit. I grew up near Dover, we had a small boat, my dad taught me.' Then realising that therein might lie opportunity he gave her smile for smile. 'I inherited it when my parents died,' he went on. 'Me and another guy share it now, he lives nearby so looks after it, keeps it in good nick. Would you like to go out on the water with me? I can promise you you'd be in safe hands, I may be a bit out of practice, but I haven't forgotten the things that matter.'

'I'm sure of it – and yes, I'd like to go sailing with you. I'd like it very much.'

Her smile was no longer careful, he saw; it came from the heart and lit her face in a way he had not seen before, there was a glow to it. Nevertheless a second later he warned himself that his feeling of sensual gratification had no place in the relationship he was seeking to establish with the girl.

12A Lime Tree Road
Hammersmith LONDON

—stifling air foul with the stink of blood.
The killer's head is close to mine
grey eyes glare into mine but black/white scarf masks his face
he's killed Marcus now so
I must see his face.

Oh God, his grip hurts, I
can't get my hand free he's got it tight. I
try to knee him, but he's too strong and he blocks it.
I've got my right arm free so I reach up clawing at the scarf, but
can't get there. I
try again, I must see his face— My hand is
a swift sly claw, I hook in my nails and drag the scarf down.
Oh God, his eyes are wild he'll kill me—
'Hussain! Out now!'

'Elianne! Elianne! Wake up…. Quiet now. It's me, *Roz*. You're safe here, you're here in London in our flat, you're in your own bed, there's no danger here…. It's me, *Roz*. I'm with you and there's no one else here. It's only you and me. You're *safe*, no one can hurt you here.' Roz Hunt's voice. Roz Hunt helping her out of bed, into a dressing-gown….

Roz talked her along to the kitchen, sat her down at the table, then made tea for them both. And she was right, of course: there was no danger to Elianne Asley lurking in that house.

They drank hot sweet tea together in the friendly, untidy little kitchen in their flat in the quiet, leafy street in Hammersmith.

Back to bed. All is well now, the memories won't come again tonight. She turned out the light on her bedside table, lay on her back with her body stretched out straight and rigid. She concentrated on hatred – then stared up into the dark and said the words:

'I saw your face that night. Some day I will see it again, track you down then – *pay you back in your own coin*.'

CHAPTER 3

Brookside House
10 Park Road
Ealing.

10.30 Thursday morning

Sitting behind the wheel of his black Toyota, parked opposite the paved entrance to Brookside House, Bill Mason looked to the casual eye like someone simply awaiting the arrival of a mate, girl-friend or business partner. He decided to give the job another hour and then, if nothing interesting had occurred in the Daley flat, to turn his attention elsewhere; he had two other surveillance jobs in progress, one of them rating a higher level of vigilance than this one on Rose Daley....

The Daley woman had been visible to him fairly clearly for the last ten minutes or so, over in her ground floor flat she sat at a table facing across Park Road to the small park beyond. She had walked into his view in the flat carrying some files in one hand, come straight across the room to the deep bay window at the front of it, sat down at one end of the long table there and put the files down in front of her. Since Park Road allowed only one-way traffic, and offered parking space only on its far side from her, Mason (aided by the high-definition, slightly magnifying spectacles he used on such occasions) was able to see with reasonable clarity the upper half of Daley's body and – should she turn her head to look out of the window – her face. He knew that face well by now: first from the photographs in her file at MI6, then in the flesh from his surveillance of her. Framed by short, stylishly coiffured, nut-brown hair, it showed her to be both a handsome woman and one of character and determination: her features were strongly defined, a certain stubbornness evident in the line of her mouth and jaw, a suggestion of arrogance in the slight curve of her nose.

Mason was hoping she would have visitors that morning; she often stayed home on Thursday mornings and usually someone came to see her on that day.

Rose was indeed expecting a visitor; written in her diary as a caller due at 11.30 was the name of the man described in MI6 records as being 'Arab male, mid 50s, short but well built' – the man for whom, due to lack of manpower, the surveillance team had been unable to establish an ID or place of residence.

The two files Rose had brought with her into her sitting-room contained notes she would need to refer to during the 'business matter' she and her visitor intended to discuss; his plans would doubtless have developed further since his last visit three days ago and she had some sharp questions regarding them to put to him.... The bastard thought he ran the entire show, she thought resentfully as she realigned the files in front of her but then, grudgingly, she admitted to herself that as a matter of fact, he did: she herself was only one of his 'second in command' officers, the other being the Afghan, Khaled Ras. But then, letting her mind roam a little, Rose allowed herself a measure of self-congratulation: boss of the major operation they were working on together here in England her expected visitor might be – nevertheless, he didn't know *everything* that was going on in the line of subversion here in Britain, did he? He didn't know that in addition to working with him on 'Wayfarer', the big op he was heading here, she herself was running a small one of her own *and* using some of Wayfarer's personnel on it. That sideline op of hers was a small one, granted; it was simply a matter of private revenge due on an incident long ago in her life – but it was her own, and he had no idea it existed. Operation Cold Call was hers alone, right from its inception – with the ready co-operation of her son Robert, of course (he was always eager to get stuck into the hard action, up front violence). That eagerness for violence – how did it get into a man? she wondered. Likely it was part hereditary. That would certainly fit for Robert: it would have come into his blood from both sides, gifted to him by both his father and herself, born to IRA activist parents.

Through his car window Mason saw her lean back and rest her head against the high back of her chair. Maybe she's dead-beat, he thought. Christ, I wish she'd just go to sleep, then. Nothing much ever seems to happen here with her that's of any fucking interest to us.

Rose Daley began to reminisce about Caitlin, her mother, the only person to whom she had ever given unquestioning, selfless love. Only when she was in her early teens had Rose realized her mother belonged heart and soul to the Cause and that, being a clever, manipulative and ruthless woman, she had deliberately set out right from her daughter's early years to make the girl her own in order to put her to service in that same Cause. But this realisation had made no difference to Rose's unconditional devotion to her mother: when Rose came to appreciate fully that her mother saw her purely for her potential use, she had given sincere thanks to God and The Virgin Mary that Caitlin had not been able to conceive again – thereby ensuring that she, Rose, was Caitlin's only hope. Since she had had no other children, Caitlin had treasured her daughter, despite near-hating her for not being a boy.... I still belong to Caitlin, Rose Daley thought, and I always will. Then with her eyes half closed and her beautifully manicured hands resting lightly on the arms of her chair, she traced the pattern of her life which had brought her to this flat where she had continued the way of life her parents – her mother in particular – had inculcated into her during her malleable years. She had accepted marriage in Beirut to Mohammed Hussain Shalhoub. 'Use the gifts God gave you for The Cause,' Caitlin had said to her (which translated, Rose well knew, as use your sexual attractions for The Cause). Caitlin had set up the mixed marriage to facilitate co-operation between the IRA and certain Islamist terrorist organizations active in

Britain and the Middle East, arranging for her to take a job in Beirut as an English teacher under the auspices of the British Council.... Rose recalled how she and her mother had laughed together at the savage irony of that, laughed at how they had conned the Brits....

Watching her, Mason saw her suddenly put her head back again and – yes, the woman was laughing. So what the hell was she thinking about? he wondered and, taking off his glasses, he looked away, passed a hand across his eyes.

Mohammed Hussain Shalhoub: how lucky I was there! she thought. Before I met him he was only a name to me, he was merely 'an Arab whom you must marry to advance The Cause', as my mother said. But then I met him in person and – he was tall and well built and severely handsome so I … well, Mohammed gave me a good life. And Caitlin was pleased with me because he and I were able to facilitate communications – also several 'robust' operations. And by God, Mohammed was glorious in bed! she mused. I'd only had local boy Brendan Brady before, I hadn't realized what sex could be like. Three sons we had, Mohammed and I, with less than a year between the first two.... I remember the first time we met, how I was instantly sexually aware of him: although he did not so much as touch my hand he excited me.... But then later, soon after my third son, Robert, was born Mohammed—

Settling his glasses back into place, Mason looked across the road into her front room again and saw her suddenly jerk upright, slam her forearms flat down on the table and throw up her head, fury evident in every line of her profiled face and body....

Then the Arab bastard wanted a woman younger than me, didn't he! And his 'law' allowed it so he took one, put me aside and 'married' her.... But she didn't give him any children, did she! Barren bitch!

Mason saw the door by which she had entered the room open again then saw the tall young man he knew to be her son Robert come in and go straight to her, kiss her hand, turn away and go to sit down facing her at the far end of the table. All the info on

Robert Daley currently held by the Intelligence services proclaimed him to be a law-abiding citizen and a young man who was hard working, sports-loving and popular with both staff and fellow students at the college he was attending. Mason knew it all, but he still doubted that the 'presentation' of Robert Daley as a perfectly 'ordinary' young chap told the whole story. There was more than met the eye to Robert Daley: acknowledging his own intuition of that belief, Mason was always on the lookout for the opportunity to prove himself right. And now as he watched Rose and her son talking together, his frustration mounted. Christ, if only he could hear what they were saying to each other....

'Robert! You should have phoned me to ask if it was convenient—'

'Sorry, sorry.' Smiling, he released her hand then sat down at the far end of the table, going on as he went, 'I hadn't realized my mobile wasn't topped up. Besides, I haven't come to stay, I just wanted to collect that report your mole in Beirut got on Faris Adjani. Is it ready?'

'No, it is not. I wish to study it further. I will inform you when it is available to you.' Her mouth was tight. Since they had come to live in London she had observed in Robert a tendency almost to question her authority over him as both Operation Wayfarer's second in command *and* as Cold Call's initiator and commander. 'And you will remember, please, that Cold Call is *my personal* affair—'

'Also, however,' he interrupted, smoothly mocking her, 'that if Wayfarer's chief Abu Yusuf discovers you are running it concurrently with Wayfarer *and* without his knowledge, he will cut you down to size without a qualm. And that size would be very small indeed.'

'Should that happen you would certainly be punished as hard as I.' She challenged her son, disregarding the smirk on his face.

'So, we're both safe.' He gave her a quick smile, gesturing apology with his hands. 'Don't be angry with me, Rose, I know my place,' he said, to placate her (but adding mentally, However that doesn't mean I accept *your control over me* as set in stone, Mother mine).

'Cold Call is indeed a small operation, certainly in comparison with Wayfarer; but it is of immeasurably greater importance to me because it is … its success will be a high point in my life.' She knew very well though that she must prosecute it in absolute secrecy: Abu Yusuf, a seasoned terrorist, had been appointed Commander of the two al-Qaeda-supported cadres involved in Wayfarer, the 'spectacular' designed to rock to its core the Brits' confidence in the ability of their own security services to safeguard their lives and property from terrorist attack. He was indeed a man she could not afford to offend – and, therefore it was imperative he remain unaware of Cold Call.

Watching her, Robert saw her sitting very still and very tense, her chin up, the long, sensual lips slightly parted in a smile of triumph. He intuited that she was gloating over the prospect of Cold Call – also, that the actual deaths it would cause did not matter to her; it was Martindale's coming emotional suffering because of them that she was now relishing. In that moment Robert Daley (aka Hussain Rashid Shalhoub) learned a truth about himself that he had not perceived before. He realized that, in himself, he was not a self-appointed 'avenger of past wrongs' such as she was (and as her mother and father had been, she'd told him, reciting a litany of revenge killings); rather, he recognized that he was simply a terrorist – and a good one – because he enjoyed killing.

The mobile on the table to Rose's right hand rang and, expecting the call, she picked it up and answered with one word, 'Rose'. She listened to a three-second reply then replaced the mobile without further response and looked across at her son.

'That was Minder,' she said sharply. 'Abu Yusuf will be here in four minutes' time. Leave by the back door of the house, it is better he does not find you here.'

Robert was already on his feet and on his way out. At the door he paused, looked round at her.

'I owe you everything that is good in my life,' he said to her with great simplicity. 'Take care, with Abu Yusuf. The man is jealous of you, of your position and standing in the organization; he will always be on the look-out for a way to bring you down.... And Rose, I would never betray you. Please believe that.' Then he turned on his heel and went out.

But the words of his little 'speech' meant nothing to her: she did not believe them.... It was strange, not to trust your own son, she mused, sliding the 'Wayfarer' file in front of her in preparation for Abu Yusuf's arrival.

Mason saw Robert Daley leave his mother's front room and saw Rose sitting on alone there. Looking along the street he caught sight of her Arab visitor striding purposefully towards Number 10, briefcase in hand. As on all his previous visits that Mason had witnessed, he was wearing the same dark-grey business suit and a black homberg. Turning in at Number 10, he crossed its narrow courtyard, reached out a hand to press a button on the panel beside the door and, a few seconds later, he went inside.

Shifting his attention back to the front room, Mason saw the Arab enter it, greet Rose Daley then sit down at the far end of the table in the chair her son had recently vacated. Placing his briefcase in front of him, he took from it a sheaf of papers, riffled through them, then extracted two and slid them across to her....

The greetings between Rose Daley and Abu Yusuf were formal – patronizingly polite on his side, coolly so on hers. There was no personal empathy whatsoever between them. She envied and resented his position as commander of Operation Wayfarer, having hoped for that honour herself as the widow of Mohammed Hussain Shalhoub, having been his aide-de-camp in many terrorist operations in Lebanon. Whereas Abu Yusuf had always lived by the basic tenet that all men are, irreversibly and as of right, superior to all women. Nevertheless, each trusted the other on the current job, having total confidence in his or her respective commitment to aggressive terrorism as a political tool.

'Khaled Ras reports that Robert has been co-operating

extremely well,' Abu Yusuf remarked, still using Arabic. 'The young man is an asset to us, I am pleased with him.'

Self-satisfied bastard, she thought. 'I have no doubt of either fact: we brought him up to it, Mohammed and I,' she said, aware that her words would remind him that her husband had died a martyr to his Cause and was a man whose standing in their organization had been far higher than his. 'And, if you please, we will speak English in my home,' she added, then went on reading the papers he had passed to her.

Smoothly smiling, he switched to English, which he spoke fluently. 'Perhaps your Arabic has become slightly rusty owing to lack of use,' he remarked, 'and doubtless you find it pleasanter to use your native tongue—'

'Good God! What action should we take about this?' Tensing suddenly she looked up, shot the question at him.

'I have already initiated the necessary dispositions.' No smoothness in his voice now. 'As you see there, our IT expert in the Paddington area has been involved in an accident.'

'It says here that he's close to death!'

'In point of fact he died half an hour ago. I was informed of his demise on my mobile during my journey here. Obviously his death is very regrettable, but our main concern now is of course to appoint his successor with all possible speed. I have ordered that Sahil Shakir will replace him—'

'I should have been consulted about such a matter!'

Coldly, Abu Yusuf smiled upon her. 'It is true that in normal circumstances as my 2i/c you would be involved in such things. However, in affairs of such immediacy the need for rapid action demands rapid decisions.' His tone hardening, he went on curtly, giving orders now to a subordinate. 'The young man is fully qualified, as Wayfarer's administration co-ordinator you will immediately take all steps required to establish his promotion. Is that clear?'

Her mouth tight, Rose Daley took it – because she had to, Abu Yusuf was well within his rights as commander of the operation. Holding his eyes, she made a smile.

'Why should it not be?' she answered coolly. 'The required admin. will be done at once. May I offer you coffee before you leave?'

Refusing the offered refreshment, Abu Yusuf took his leave with all due politeness but without delay. As was customary on his visits to her, Rose did not see him out of her home; they both preferred it that way, he waiving the courtesy for security reasons, she citing those also but, in her heart, fiercely glad of even such a small opportunity to demonstrate that she held herself equal to him, not merely 'a senior member of his staff'.

Getting to her feet she went to the window and watched him walk away down the street: the dapper businessman, briefcase in hand as he went about his legal or financial affairs. Who could have guessed at his true identity as a high-powered terrorist master engaged in an operation intended to bring carnage to his chosen targets in the country he was presently residing in as a harmless citizen?

Sitting down on the cushioned window seat built into the curve of the bay, Rose Daley gazed unseeing across the road to the small park beyond it and dreamed on Operation Wayfarer. She had been attracted to its working hypothesis from when, just before she left Lebanon, the Hizbollah group, of whom she and her now dead husband had been high-ranking members, had offered her an active part in its prosecution; she would be Abu Yusuf's on-site 2i/c. The op's key action was relatively simple and although its ancillary aspects called for extremely complicated logistics, Wayfarer had appealed to her immediately.

Wayfarer:

1. Four suicide bombers
2. Their targets: four trains travelling on separate mainline routes either to or from summer holiday destinations or industrial towns
3. On-train bombs to be detonated simultaneously as the trains close in on the target towns.

4. Zero-hour for the martyrs – and God knows how many others, fellow-travellers in the widest possible sense of the word – to be 11.30 on Friday 15th August 2008

5. DESTINATIONS of Target trains:

Rugby

Exeter

Southend

Brighton

As she thought about those named cities Rose smiled, the prospect of the operation's success gave her great pleasure. But, suddenly, her mind arrowed off in a different direction and the smile died swiftly. Her mouth compressed to a rat-trap gash of red and the blue-grey eyes narrowed as she thought of what she had in mind for the man who was Cold Call's target. Unlike Wayfarer, Cold Call was hers, and its motivation and objective were highly personal. It was also infinitely simpler: it would only bring about four deaths, as against the unknown but surely far, far greater number Wayfarer would cause, Abu Yusuf's minimum imagined 'harvest' was 200 dead.... But to Rose Daley, Cold Call's four deaths would be beyond price; they would be *wergild*, blood money to give honour to a woman long dead.

As Bill Mason watched Daley's Arab visitor walk away along Park Road he smiled to himself, then swung round to his mate sitting well back in the rear seat.

'He's all yours now, Mike,' he said. 'Get going and *don't lose him*.'

And as Mike Jones slipped out of the kerbside rear door and set off after his 'mark', Mason murmured to the quietness of his car, 'Good on you, Mr Locksley, sir! You got us a man to tail Rose's Arab and now we've got one we should be able to track him 'home' today: with the help of police prowl cars and foot patrols we should be all right – Good hunting, boys and girls. Have at it!'

Charles Gray's house
A Saturday evening mid-December

'Always I feel at home here, quite literally.' Curling herself into the corner of the big sofa in the sitting-room, Elianne settled herself comfortably back against its large, soft cushions. 'It's partly because I know Marcus spent a lot of time here, happy time; but mostly it's because of Charles himself. He's made me feel I'm truly welcome here, not just some "outsider" asked in for a social event.'

That evening Gray had gone up to central London for a business dinner. She was staying at his house and, by arrangement with him, had asked Matt Locksley to come over and spend the evening with her. 'You've taken me out, given me so many good days,' she had said to him, 'so please, let me cook you an evening meal, Lebanese style.' So that evening he had walked along to Gray's place from his own flat further up the road.

The dinner she had prepared for them had been simple but delicious: and after it they cleared the table and loaded the dishwasher then made coffee and took it into the sitting-room, where Locksley found brandy set ready for them on the low table in front of the sofa. As he poured the two drinks he noticed that the brandy was a very good one indeed, and complimented her on it as he handed her the glass and sat down at the far end of the sofa with his own.

She grinned at him. 'Oh, that belongs to Charles,' she explained. 'He said you were his friend, and for me to present you with anything less than really good French brandy in his house would be an insult to you.... And neither he nor I wish to insult you, Matt Locksley,' she added softly. 'Apart from Charles, you are the best thing that has happened to me for a long time.'

She was wearing a rose-red dress of some silky material, her dark hair was swept back from her face and tied high at the back of her head with broad, leaf-green ribbon. Locksley found her very beautiful; but now, as previously, he sensed in her two emotions: grief, and embedded within it a violent hatred that never relaxed its pressure on her. She was being driven on, but to what? he wondered. And suddenly, he felt sure that he should ask her about it: the time was right, the place was right and she would not run away from his questions.

'Tell me about that night, Elianne,' he said to her. He had meant to say more, but stopped himself and waited for her, realizing that too many words might destroy the rapport he felt was developing between them.

Putting her brandy down on the table in front of her, she clasped her hands in her lap, fixed her eyes on them and laid the facts before him. At first her voice was a cold monotone. She described the family party being violently interrupted by three gunmen, two of them staying, Kalashnikovs at-the-ready, just inside the door – the third, the killer, advancing on the gathered family – the 'execution' of Tomas and James: she laid out the terrible acts for Locksley's inspection, truth by dreadful truth.

'... Then the man with the gun came towards me and Marcus,' she said – Locksley saw her knuckles turn white as her clasped hands held each other in a vice-like grip. Her voice rose as she recalled the horror of that evening. 'He was coming for Marcus, I realized he was coming for Marcus to kill him so, as he fired at Marcus, I bashed his arm up and the bullet didn't strike true. He was hit in the head, though, and as he fell forward on the table there was blood on the food and spilt wine.' Suddenly her head came up and she stared straight into Locksley's eyes, he saw hers wide and haunted. '*I saw the killer's face then*,' she said, a steely ferocity in her voice, her whole body tense and rigid. 'I fought him then. The only thought in my head was that I had to *see the face* of the man who'd shot my brothers so as we fought I clawed at the scarf hiding his face and I pulled it right down—' Breaking off she sat for a moment silent and very still, concentrating on that moment in which every feature of the face of her brothers' murderer was seared deep into the fabric of her mind. Locksley perceived the calm in her for what it was: a quietness loaded with hatred. When she went on her voice became thin and hard, fey.

'Then almost as the same moment as I saw his face a car-horn blared out in the street,' she said, 'and it must have been their warning because one of the other two gunmen shouted that "Unit 10" must get out of there – but me and the killer went on staring into each eyes, it seemed as though we were frozen together in time, eye-contact binding us together. I shall never forget that face. *Never.*'

Locksley let the ensuing silence remain between them. Then he said – only half believing it – 'Time will soften the memory.'

Looking away from him, Elianne leaned back into the corner of the sofa. 'You think?' she mocked. 'In my book, it is plain justice that those who are killed in cold blood have a right to be avenged.'

CHAPTER 4

2008 - A Saturday in early March
The two-acre property of Judge Anthony Martindale (retired)

That cool, sunny afternoon was only the second time Robert Daley had surveillanced Oakdene, the house and extensive garden of Anthony Martindale. This time he was standing in for his college friend (and Cold Call collaborator) Johnny Blake who had crashed his motor bike in the small hours of the previous night and, consequently, would be out of action for a couple of days.

The layout of Oakdene House made surveillance fairly straight-forward. The six-bedroomed greystone residence stood four-square at the centre of the property; the only access to it was from the minor road, known as Pilgrims' Way, that passed outside its front gate. From that gate a broad asphalt drive led past lawns and a thirty-yard deep shrubbery straight up to the front door. Like the rest of the house, the solid oak door dated from Victorian times, and in summertime, like the casement windows either side of it, it was garlanded with yellow roses.

Robert had no eye for the roses. From his cover in the shrubbery bordering the right-hand side of the drive, he was observing Martindale, the target of operation Cold Call. The op was Rose's own, and although Martindale himself would suffer no physical injury on the night of Cold Call's climax, he would undoubtedly suffer emotionally for the rest of his life because of the hit. You had to hand it to Rose, her son thought as he spied on the man against whom, years ago, his mother had sworn vengeance: while anyone who hurt her in any way was alive he would never be safe from Rose, she'd pay him back for the hurt, however long it took – and in Martindale's case that payback would be fourfold....

Martindale was mowing the big lawn at the front of the house. Now seventy years old, he had retired four years ago, and since then had taken a seriously hands-on interest in the property, keeping house and land 'ship-shape and Bristol fashion' as he liked to phrase it having been a proficient yachtsmen in his time. In achieving this he was assisted by his wife (mostly in summertime) and by Rod Smith, a three-times-a-week local gardener and handyman some twenty years younger than him.

That afternoon, seated on his motor-mower, he had started cutting the grass on the far side of the lawn from his hidden watcher. Now he was within a few yards of the drive and the shrubbery beyond it, and thinking of taking a break soon to give the motor a rest and stretch his legs a bit. He thought he'd stroll up to the terrace running the length of the front of the house and have a chat with Tiger, his golden retriever, at present stretched out on the paving, half asleep in the sun as befits a dog of fourteen summers.

Concealed within the shadowy darknesses of the shrubbery, no more than a yard back from where it met with lawn, Robert had nothing to 'surveillance' other than the house and Martindale himself trundling up and down his fucking lawn on his fucking motor mower and his dog muzzle-on-paws snoozing over on the terrace. Robert eased the strap of his small but powerful binoculars at the back of his neck and considered Cold Call. 'A small op but – mine own', as Rose had termed it when she had first broached the subject with him – and, he recalled, there had been a tight, bitter smile as she said it.... Well, her op was certainly small, just the four of them involved: himself and Rose, of course, Blakey and Jenner, both of them mates of his from his college. There was also the bomb-maker, naturally, but he would be excluded from the action; he was doing it for Rose, she explained, and didn't know anything about the op itself.... Its smallness was one of its strengths, she'd told him; and he, Robert, had agreed with her on that as soon as she outlined its details to him.

He and his two college mates made a good team for Rose, Robert mused in his shaded hideout: he her on-site commander to Vince Jenner and Jonathan Blake. Vince – good-looking, but painfully shy with the girls – had dreams of 'making a difference' in the world by becoming a member of some terrorist organisation and hoped Rose and Robert would give him an 'in' to that world if he performed well in Cold Call. Jonathan Blake, Blakey, who, although he would never publicly admit it, Robert knew to be the op's greatest asset. Blakey was already an experienced house-breaker, having learned the necessary skills from his father. Ten days earlier, while Martindale and his wife were enjoying a four-day break with one of their two sons, Blakey had forced a kitchen window at the back of the house, slipped in and sketched a rough plan of the layout of both the ground floor and the approach to the two bedrooms Cold Call would target. Using this, Rose had drawn up the plan of action for the afternoon when Robert and Blakey would gain access to the house and place the incendiary bombs.

Briefly, Robert's thoughts went back to Jenner, handsome Vincent Jenner, only child to a wealthy widowed mother who indulged him with a huge allowance on the condition that he complete his 3-year college course in family law. He was too good-looking for his own good, thought Robert with a smirk, envying him the lolly; he was also too fucking serious, too given to discussing the political philosophies of the world – so that after the initial attraction of his good looks, his generosity, and solici-tous attention, girls grew bored with him because he was no *fun*, dates with him were no fun at all, he was in fact dead boring.... I wouldn't trust Vince in hard action, Robert decided as he watched Martindale on his mower heading towards the house. Likely Vince'd throw up at the sight of blood, there was in him no lust for the high that came from driving a knife into enemy flesh and feeling enemy blood spurt warm against your skin. And as he thought this, Robert's right hand slid down to his waist and his fingers traced the lines of the hunting knife below the belt of his jeans, secreted in the thin suede sheath stitched into place at the hip.

Stopping the mower a yard or two short of the terrace, Martindale switched off the engine. Silence descended sweetly over his garden once more as, his mind firmly fixed on a long, cold drink, he climbed down on to the grass and stood flexing the muscles of his arms and back, breathing in the green smell of newly cut grass and admiring the result of his work so far – the long straight lines of his mowing patterned the lawn. Then he mopped his brow with his handkerchief and, well pleased with life (and himself, he had to admit), walked up on to the terrace. Tiger roused himself from open-eyed dreaming, set all four legs firmly on the paving then gave himself a vigorous shake, his eyes on his master saying so-glad-to-see-you, I'm your devoted retainer but, please, don't ask too much of me just yet as I've only just woken up. Martindale paused to stroke him then went in to the house through the open door. After brief consideration of the situation, Tiger followed him.

Robert watched man and dog disappear into the house then stood irresolute, running his eyes over the house and garden, wondering whether to call it a day and go home—

Striking out fast from the leafy shadows hard by Daley's back, a man clapped one arm tightly round his throat, grabbed his left wrist with the other hand, and yanked it behind him. The man thrust Daley's hand against his spine, then spoke, his mouth close to his prisoner's head.

'Seen yer here before, ain't I, you bastard,' he snarled in Daley's ear. 'So I gotta teach yer that this place is *our* mark, see—'

But Robert Daley had learned close-quarters combat on a level of brutality far beyond the experience of an English country-house burglar. Hair-trigger fast he'd reached for his knife with his free hand and, twisting round on his assailant, drove his left shoulder into the man's chest. He tore his wrist free, ignoring the enemy nails digging in to his skin and drawing blood there – then straightened up, whipped out his blade and slashed it hard and lethal across the man's bare throat.

Blood spurted from the gaping wound across Tom Richards's neck, gushed viscously over his chin and shoulders as he collapsed and lay sprawled on his back, head pillowed on leaf-mould already sodden with his blood. He choked briefly, spasmed and then died.

The man who had sneaked into Martindale's property that afternoon – Tom Richards – was the 'muscle' for a gang of house-breakers based in south London. He had been sent there by them to frighten off the stranger whom he and his mates, casing Oakdene as a possible subject for plunder, suspected of watching Martindale's house with that same purpose.

Robert Daley did not give him a second glance. High on the adrenalin surge of the successful kill, he roughly cleaned his blade on a patch of moss, re-sheathed it, then left fast, wrapping his handkerchief around his still bleeding wrist as he went.

A quarter to eleven, and an almost full moon was high in a cloud-less sky. In the front garden at Oakdene, Anthony Martindale was taking Tiger for his last walk before bed. It was a gentle night, serene. With an unused torch held loosely in one hand and brown suede windcheater on against the night chill, Martindale strolled along the drive towards the road, a certain smugness in him as he surveyed the moonlit well-ordered reaches of his property. Tiger, canine senses alert to the nuanced scents adrift in the still air, was rooting about in the whispery leaf-mould beneath the trees at the edge of the shrubbery where it met the lawn.... 'Surprisingly pleasant out here, think I'll go on right to the gate, give Tiger time to enjoy himself,' Martindale murmured to the uncaring night. Then as he strolled on he fell to remembering when he and his wife Olivia had moved into the long-empty and neglected house that Oakdene had then been. Olivia had been pregnant with their first child, they had set about making a home of it. It had been a good time with lots of laughter, tears too, of course, just as it is now when the grandchildren come to stay—

He stopped dead as from within the gloom of the shrubbery on his left, Tiger gave tongue in a long mournful keening that quickly rose to a sustained howl, a blood-chilling threnody running the night air, feral and infinitely sad. The hairs rising at the nape of his neck, Martindale stood stock still – then as abruptly as it had begun the eerie lament broke off. Switching on his torch Martindale pushed his way into the shrubbery, wondering what the hell was up – Tiger not one to cry over a dead rabbit! – homing in on the whining, whimpering sounds—

His torchlight froze on a patch of ground ahead of him. Tense with shock, Martindale stared at the body of a man sprawled on its back on the dark earth there, arms outflung, head and shoulders drenched in blood. At the man's feet the big, pale-gold dog stood with his beautiful head cast down as he mourned the dead.

'Tiger! Tiger, *quiet!*' Snapping out of shock, Martindale ran forward to the body and stood gazing down at it, one hand resting lightly on Tiger's head. That the man was dead was blindingly obvious.

'Poor sod,' he murmured. 'What a rotten way to die.' Then turning on his heel, he started back to the house to report the fatality to the police. '*Come*, Tiger,' he called quietly. 'Come on old fellow. Home now.'

The dog did not obey immediately though. For a full minute he stayed where he was, whining, his head lowered. Then he padded home after his master, leaving Robert Daley's latest victim – his first in England – to the night and the living trees.

'I still don't understand why you don't tell your parents now, straightaway,' Elianne said, walking along High Holborn towards Kingsway at Brad Ellis's side, a grass-green linen overblouse loose over her jeans, her hair caught at the back of her head with black ribbon. 'I know I've said it all before, but I really do think that keeping it hidden from them is, well—'

'Immoral?' Lean and lanky, Ellis slanted a grin at her, lightly mocking her for what seemed to him her anachronistic attitude to his present situation. 'I'll only tell them when I'm sure they're both ready for it—' He broke off, leaping out of the way as a brightly clad young woman, arguing furiously on her mobile and oblivious to all else, clove passage between them then forged ahead still locked in her own closed world.

'I have to say that after those wonderful photographs we've just seen I can understand why you feel as you do about camera studies. Those were works of art, weren't they, Brad: they captured moments of great beauty, and things so terrible as to break the heart – all of them pictured *on film*—'

'We have to go left just ahead,' he interrupted, taking her elbow and steering her towards the turn. Earlier that day he had taken her to a lavish international exhibition of photography – presented in creative, journalistic and commercial sections – and to his delight had found her so enthralled that they had stayed on there for hours, taking a short break for lunch at a snack-bar nearby. And now his face lit up at the prospect of an interesting discussion with her on what they had seen, once they had settled at Antonio's, the coffee house he was taking her to.

As they turned the corner, however, they saw and heard mayhem ahead of them. Outside the entrance to a bar thirty yards or so along the street, a fist fight had spilled out on to the pavement. In a small space at the centre of a circle of onlookers two young men were slugging away at each other in no uncertain fashion. It was no holds barred, obviously, and some of the onlookers were goading them on, jeering a feeble blow, cheering when one of the combatants drew blood.... As Elianne and Ellis drew closer, they sensed the mood of the crowd turning nasty, voices baying for more blood—

'Christ, I've got to get pics of this!' said Ellis suddenly, and in a few seconds he had the high-tech camera he always carried with him out of his tote bag and was heading at speed for the fracas – all else gone out of his head at this heaven-sent chance to get street-scene photos of 'life in London'.

'I'll wait for you in Antonio's, then!' Elianne called after him, and saw his left hand swing up in acknowledgement as he ran. Crossing the road she passed by the fight as fast as possible without actually running, her head down and eyes fixed on the pavement as she tried to shut out the violence. When she was well beyond it she slowed down and lifted her head: Antonio's pink awning was just ahead and, reaching the café, she went inside.

Its serene, well mannered atmosphere closed comfortingly round her at once. Slipping into a chair at a table for two alongside one of its big street-side windows she relaxed. Then smiling up at the pretty young waitress who arrived to serve her, she explained that she was waiting for a friend and would order a little later. After a moment, grateful to be at one with the world again, she fell to recalling the most arresting photographs she had seen earlier on—

'Hi. Sorry to be a pain, Elianne; the chance was there in front of me, I couldn't walk away. I've got some beaut pics, by God it was worth it!' Ellis was grinning at her across the table, his boyish face alight with excitement, half a dozen photographs in one hand as he pulled out a chair for himself with the other. 'I ordered as I came in, coffee and cakes,' he went on, dropping his tote bag to the floor and sitting down. 'I did them straightaway, couldn't wait to see what I'd got, and guess what? They're *good*, they're really good stuff! I've got a couple here I reckon are on a level with my best ever to date—' Breaking off he put the prints he was holding down on the table beside him. 'Hey there, Ellis, stop bragging,' he chided himself still grinning, and started checking through them for the ones he wanted her to see.

'*No*, Brad.' She sat right back in her chair, frowning. 'Not now. My mind's still full of what we saw at the exhibition.' Then seizing on the first thing she thought of to take the edge off her rebuff, she went on, 'There's questions I'd like to ask you about some of those—'

'Okay, okay,' Ellis countered, but he was not a man to give in easily – especially about his photography. 'But Elianne, dear Elianne, please spare me just a couple of minutes now,' he entreated. 'Because there're a couple of faces I got back there you have to see, you just have to, I won't let you off. Because, actually, the interesting ones are not those of the two men fighting. The two I want you to see are a couple of *onlookers* – and Christ! Elianne, I've got something there. I've caught that disgusting vicarious excitement, the enjoyment of watching violence-in-action, revelling in it, always greedy for more even when—'

'You can stop there. I know exactly what you mean,' she said quietly. 'And I'd like to see your photographs, please.' Brad is *my friend*, she thought, it's the least I can do for a friend. God knows he gives me enough of his time.

Ellis smiled at her. 'Thank you,' he said, meaning it. 'I'll just show you those special two now, the ones where I've really caught ... raw stuff. Then we'll settle down to coffee and cakes and talk about the exhibition.' And, picking up the two prints he wanted her to see, he passed them across to her.

He watched her as she looked at them, holding them close in front of her, one after the other. He knew what she was seeing: the top one showed a woman in her mid-twenties, showily dressed in bright pink and black; she was half smiling as she watched the two men fighting, a salacious excitement obvious on her heavily made-up face.

Ellis perceived no change in Elianne's expression as she looked at this photo. A little disappointed, he said, 'The other one's the better.' And watched her as she slipped the first behind the second of the two in her hand. 'It's the full-face, head-and-shoulders of a young man. 'You can see the bastard's just *loving* it, he's right in there with the violence—' Abruptly he broke off, seeing Elianne staring transfixed at the second image. Her face was frozen in a mask of total disbelief at what her eyes were telling her.

'Can I keep this?' she asked after a few moments, her voice expressionless and her eyes never leaving the face of the young man in the photograph. It was the face of the man who had murdered two of her brothers and left the third in a coma. Without a shadow of doubt it was *him*. And that murderer was here in London! He was there in the picture, mobile to mouth but the pale eyes not missing a moment of the fight—

'I'll have it copied for you,' Ellis said quietly.

'No. I want it now.'

But so did Ellis, it was the best of the lot and he thought he knew a market for it, 'Elianne, have mercy! Copying'll only take an hour or so, I know a bloke—'

'Brad. Please. I ... need it.' The words came out desperate and anguished.

Hearing this he said, 'It's yours, take it.'

She was on her feet at once, slipping the photograph of the young man into the back pocket of her jeans. 'Thank you,' she said to him, then turned and walked out into the street.

She might have been saying thank you to some perfect stranger who'd just opened a fucking door for her, Brad Ellis thought, momentarily resentful, but then, picking up the photograph she had left behind on the table, he forgot all about her and proceeded to enjoy both his coffee and hers, poring over his treasure of 'pics' and debating each one's merits or faults with his usual unforgiving honesty.

Elianne had been in Holborn before. She remembered that the Inns of Court lay just off the High Road and to one side of them was a small public square with shrubs and trees and seats for people to sit on and feed the pigeons if they wished.

Sitting on the end of an empty bench in this small green place, late afternoon sunshine around her, Elianne dropped her head and closed her eyes. The horrors that she had managed to hold in check until she was alone came back to her. It was all further away these days. Mercifully, she had learned to put distance between them and herself; nowadays she could usually isolate them from her present life.

Except for one: the memory of Marcus in his special-unit hospital bed, his devotedly cared-for body lying log-like beneath its covers, his beloved face bereft of 'life' in the full sense of the word. If she laid her hand on his brow his skin felt warm against hers and it *was* Marcus she was touching, whatever his doctors might say, some day he would 'wake up'—

She reached into the pocket of her jeans and slid out the photograph Brad Ellis had taken less than an hour ago. Holding it on her lap she stared down at the face of the young man pictured there and for a second it seemed to her that his eyes stared straight into hers, and that she and the killer were locked together again in mortal combat.

'Murderer,' she whispered to him, holding his eyes. Then closing her hand round the image she stood up, slipped the photograph back into her pocket and walked quickly back to the spot where the street-fight had taken place. She found combatants and onlookers long gone; outside the bar, the road and pavement were quiet, cars were passing and several people were going about their business. Opposite the entrance to the bar she stopped and fixed her eyes on the spot where 'he' had stood watching the fight, mobile-to-mouth as, according to Brad, he saw one of the fighting men pull out a knife and called the police.

I will kill him. Silently, she re-stated her vow.

Sitting opposite Abu Yusuf at a table in the office-like room in the Balham safe house, Rose Daley looked up from the file she was holding and addressed him directly.

'So I will confirm to Base Commander in Damascus that Operation Wayfarer is of this date on course to climax at 11.30 on Friday the 15th of August,' she said, confronting his veiled eyes coolly, aware of his concept of the female of the human species as immutably inferior to the male *and* his bitter hostility towards her, personally.

Meeting her eyes with practised passivity, he answered, 'That will indeed be in order,' then watched in silence while she gathered together her papers. As Abu Yusuf's 2i/c she seldom stayed for the discussion period of these regular meetings of Wayfarer's senior officers. She stowed the documents inside her briefcase, took her leave of the four men gathered round the table with an all-embracing Arabic farewell and left the room.

As the door closed behind her, Abu Yusuf looked in turn at each of the other three men. He chaired these twice monthly meetings at which each of Wayfarer's section captains presented a progress report and had the opportunity to ask questions and voice relevant opinions. That day the meeting was going well: all section commanders' reports had been straightforward, so now all that remained was the 'questions and opinions' session (which he would not have permitted had the choice been his, but 'orders' laid down that it should be so, and he was a stickler for rigid adherence to regulations).

'Finally, then, to "open discussion",' he said, in Arabic now and using his own favourite phrase for this democratic procedure. 'You may put forward any matter you wish to see talked over or clarified.'

As they sat silent, each busying himself with the papers in front of him, Abu Yusuf studied his section captains one by one.... Khaled Ras, sitting opposite him, the Afghan in charge of security and the training of Wayfarer's four martyrs: at fifty years of age a tall, thin, gaunt-faced man of wiry strength and fitness.... To his left, Faris Mansoor, Palestinian by birth whose family had been resident in Beirut since 1949. Younger than Ras by a good ten years, Mansoor looked the perfect businessman in his well tailored charcoal grey suit, his thick auburn hair close cut, dark brown eyes lively and intelligent. He was blessed with a pleasing personality, was at ease in any company and was counted chief among the operation's antennae to the outside world. He worked closely with Rose Daley (who found him sexually attractive and was unaware that he preferred women no older than eighteen).... And lastly, on Abu Yusuf's right, sitting with his arms folded across his chest, Mahmoud Afsanjani. Middle-aged and stockily built, the Irani terrorist's facial expression and body language were well-controlled in his public life and presented a quiet, ordinary persona well-suited to his job as personnel officer with an IT company. But now, being as it were among 'friends', he showed his true self, that of the religious fanatic, aggressive and self-righteous. His dark eyes were alight with fervour, and throughout the meeting he burned with grim anticipation of the now not-so-far-distant day when his present 'dream' would become a reality; for he was the operation's bomb-maker, and it was work to which he gave his soul....

As Abu Yusuf had expected, no questions were put forward, no matter for discussion was raised. Within minutes, therefore, he announced the date and venue for their next meeting and then ended the present one. He sat back while the three men rose to their feet, made their salaams to him and went their various ways. Khaled Ras was the last to leave, covering his delay (Yusuf noticed) by a show of annoyance at being unable to find some paper he had apparently misplaced. By the time he had found this both Afasanjani and Mansoor were gone.

'You have something private you wish to discuss with me?' Abu Yusuf asked as, finally, Ras got to his feet. He knew the Afghan was always alert for the slightest hint of anything with the potential to damage their mission – and, also, a man with many high-placed contacts within the various al Qaeda-inspired groups. He was in touch with both the nascent and the well-established ones in Britain and other European cities.

Ras invariably spoke bluntly and to the point. 'The woman now known as Rose Daley is betraying your trust in her,' he said, staring Abu Yusuf in the eye, thrusting the accusation forward without preamble.

At once, Yusuf sat very still. Being aware that the woman aspired to rise above him in the hierarchy of their organization he had personal reason to mistrust her, but – outright treachery? Treachery in the course of an operation they were working on *together*? Surely such a perfidious act was inconceivable in a woman with her CV; her marriage to a Hizbollah terrorist of repute and the sons she had borne him – and lost to the enemy in combat.

'Be careful what you say, Khaled Ras.' Playing for time, Yusuf met the hard dark stare. He knew the Afghan was famed for ruth-less commitment to the Islamist cause, but he realized that in this particular case he should also bear in mind the man's proven misogyny. In Ras's mind the presence of any female among the executive élite of an Islamist terrorist mission – barring only her possible use as either suicide bomber or as bait to entrap a male enemy – was anathema in the eyes of Allah. 'Remember that Daley gave two of her sons to the fight against the Israelis, both died in battle; also, that working with her husband Mohammed Hussain Shalhoub she herself facilitated at least four major missions in the Lebanon—'

'She had no choice in the matter, Shalhoub would have cast her out had she refused.... I tell you to your face, Abu Yusuf, *she is disloyal to you*, Wayfarer's commander. Such conduct *in the course of a mission* constitutes treasonable action, and within our organization there is only one punishment for such a criminal. That punishment is death.' He drew himself up, stood erect, stood tall, arrogantly challenging his commander. 'Sir,' he said with formality, 'I would be honoured to carry out the punishment.'

Abu Yusuf's first thought was that as far as he was concerned Ras was welcome to go ahead and do that, but then he reminded himself that Ras was not only a woman-hating zealot, but also invariably a remarkably well informed one in regard to the security of Wayfarer, so calling his mind to order he set about getting to the root of this extraordinary accusation against Rose Daley.

'As her accuser you must first make a case against her,' he observed dryly. 'In what way is she "betraying my trust" in her?'

Khaled Ras's eyes burned bright in his lined, grim face. 'She has planned and is presently carrying out an operation of her own, it is an act of personal revenge—'

'*You have proof of this?*' Abu Yusuf demanded, his face a mask of barely controlled fury. In his heart he already half-believed Ras's allegation against Daley simply because, hating her, he wanted to; but his mind required words giving form and substance to that charge before allowing total acceptance of it as the truth.

'Sir, I will name my sources for that information only when you agree to act upon it.' Then Ras stood silent, waiting, his eyes challenging his commanding officer.

'Are you suggesting that, having been informed of proven

treason, I might *fail to act* against those practising it?' The question cut through the air like a striking whip, Abu Yusuf's head jutting forward as he spoke.

Ras moved not a muscle. 'Sir. In order to operate successfully as Wayfarer's security officer I depend on the reports of many informers. Such men lead double lives and they will give me nothing unless they have faith that I will *protect their identity....* You know this,' he added, concealing his anger.

Accepting that he was in error Abu Yusuf forced himself to relax; then he sought to regain the Afghan's trusting co-operation. 'I will not press you,' he said with a conciliatory hand gesture. 'Sit down. Tell me all you know.'

Khaled Ras sat. 'Daley is running an operation against an English judge, now retired, who many years ago sentenced her mother to life imprisonment—'

'For what crime?' Yusuf interrupted, all eagerness now: the prospect of having a weapon to use against Rose Daley renewed his long-held hopes of weakening her position within the organization.

'Sectarian murder. It occurred in Ireland. As you know, she was born to a committed IRA family.'

'Her mother – is she still alive?'

'She died in prison.'

'Ah. So there you have it. Daley now seeks to avenge her mother's death.' Sitting back, Abu Yusuf folded his arms, frowning. 'Yes, she is a woman who would not be afraid to do that.... Does she plan the murder of this judge?'

'Her mind is more subtle, also more vicious than that. The judge concerned has four grandchildren he cherishes. She will strike at him *through them.*'

'In what way?'

Ras's thin mouth stretched into the mockery of a smile. 'During their summer holidays, the grandchildren usually spend a lot of time with the judge and his wife, at their home. Through her agents – a small group of young men, her son among them – Daley has discovered that on such visits the children, two boys and two girls, sleep in two bedrooms, the boys in one, the girls in the other next door to them.... Daley will have all four of them blown to pieces in their beds.' Ras's smile had died on his face. 'A fine revenge, to my mind,' he added, a touch of admiration in his voice.

Slightly repelled by it, in spite of having authorized equally vile killings in the past, Yusuf frowned. 'You will keep the entire situation closely monitored, Ras. Report to me—'

'You do not intend to discipline the woman immediately?' Aflame once again with sudden anger the Afghan thrust out his hands towards Abu Yusuf, reaching for him as if to grab hold of him.

'*Enough! Control yourself!*' Stiffening where he sat, Abu Yusuf stared him out eye to furious eye. 'As yet you have presented no *factual proof* to substantiate your accusations; they stand on your word alone, therefore I *cannot* act against her yet!' But then he leaned towards Ras and went on, quietly, intently. 'From now on you not only have my authority to pursue this matter further, you have also my support in doing so. *Covert* support; I must not be seen to be, shall we say "investigating" the actions of my 2i/c in Wayfarer.... You understand me?'

Through a tense ten seconds the Afghan held his eyes, searching them for the truths buried in the mind behind them. Finding there the requisite intent and hatred, he murmured, 'I understand, sir.' Then he drew back and stood as he had before, but aware now that he might consider himself his commander's accomplice in their hoped-for removal of Rose Daley from her honoured position in their organization.

'Smoke her out, Khaled Ras,' Abu Yusuf said softly. 'You and I are of one mind in this, and such an opportunity may not come our way again.'

'With Wayfarer approaching its climax, surely it would be better to take action against her at once? We—'

'Not so, Ras.' Rising to his feet, Yusuf cut him short impatiently, fearing he might have been unwise to give away to him the depth and strength of his hatred of the woman. 'Daley must remain untouched until after Wayfarer had been carried out. It would not be good to have to replace her at this stage of the operation.'

'But if I discover this private hit of hers is scheduled to come to fruition *before* Wayfarer?'

'Think, man! She holds all Wayfarer's administrative plans in her hands. Her continued wellbeing and competence in ensuring our operation's success *must* be our first concern. We do not touch her until it is completed, or very nearly so.'

'You will allow her this … this satisfaction?'

Yusuf gave him a narrow smile. 'She will not have long to enjoy it,' he promised him. 'Rest assured, Khaled Ras: you shall have her blood.'

Carlton Road, Thornton Heath

As he let himself into his flat at around six o'clock that evening, Locksley heard his telephone in the sitting-room begin to ring. He went straight through to answer it.

'Hi, Matt,' a voice said.

'Elianne! What gives—'

'Yes, I know, you're coming round here to Charles's after dinner, but I'm calling you now because I need your help in something that's just come up.... Need it very badly,' she added, her voice suddenly low and shaky.

'It's yours. Yours any time, as you know.' Christ, I wish I was with her now, she sounds as if she's dying inside.... Then into her silence, he asked if Charles was there with her.

'No-no. Sorry. Just for a moment I … lost it.... You see, Matt, you're the only person I know here in England who might be able to help me, it's a special sort of help I need.'

'Is it a police matter? Christ, Elianne, *what's wrong?*'

'No, don't worry, I'm not in trouble with the police or anything of that sort.'

'What, then? Tell me!'

'I can't, over the phone like this. I have to be *with* you so that I can make you understand, properly understand.'

It seemed to him that her voice had taken on a different quality on the last few words, and he intuited in her a baleful excitement that shocked him and made him fear for her.

'Hell, Elianne, you sound.... I don't like this.'

'Leave it now, *please*. When we're at Charles's, after we've all had coffee, he'll retire to his study as he usually does, to work. You and I can talk then. See you soon. 'Bye.'

An hour later he walked along the road to Charles Gray's house.... Since their first meeting, the relationship between himself and Elianne had blossomed, become close. Only Locksley had realized that on his side it might become love.

On his arrival he found Elianne and Charles just settling down to coffee in the sitting-room.

'Timed it well, haven't you, Matt,' Gray remarked with a grin, looking across at him from the sofa facing out through the French doors. 'Washing-up's done, brandy's ready and there's a fresh pot of coffee waiting. Come and sit over here where you'll get the last of the evening light.... Let's all have a drink together, then I'll take myself off to the study and get a bit of work done.'

For ten minutes or so the three of them sat chatting over their drinks. Then Charles put down his empty coffee cup and got to his feet. 'Well, all this is very nice, but I've work to do – that GBH case I told you about, Matt, it's taken an unexpected turn, one of the prosecution witnesses got smashed up in a road accident, he's in a coma. There's a lot of rescheduling to be done.' Pouring himself another small shot of brandy, he picked up the glass and made for his study. 'See you later.'

'I'll look in on you before I leave,' Locksley called after him, then turned quickly back to Elianne. 'Sorry he brought that up,' he said, having seen her stiffen as Gray spoke of the man in a coma.

'Don't be.' But she was tight-lipped and tense, and her voice was as hard as her eyes.

Getting up from his armchair he went across and sat down on

the sofa, a little closer to her than Gray had been but not touching. He had only seen her as uptight as she was now once before; she had been wild with grief then, drowning in misery just after she had read a letter she had received from her sister-in-law telling her – again – that there was no change in Marcus's condition, he still lay in his hospital bed, cared for but himself seemingly impassive. But this time was quite different, she was seething with … not grief, nor fear … not exactly anger even. It was something crueller than that, it was hatred. It was pure, unadulterated hatred. The grief in her had somehow found a focal point and homed in on it. Intuiting a feral urge in her, Locksley feared for her.

'What's happened, Elianne?' he asked. 'If it's secret, it will be safe with me, you know that. So tell me. That's what I'm here for.'

'I want to tell you because being MI6 you must know about such things … or have ways of finding out about them.' But there she stopped and sat looking past him into the darkening garden.

Standing up he went to the French windows and stood gazing out, hoping she would go on. But the silence grew too long, so he turned to her again: he saw her sitting still and very controlled. Controlled and … unbearably lonely.

'Please go on,' he said to her across the huge distance which seemed to separate them.

'I saw a photograph,' she said levelly, speaking in his direction, but not to him. 'It showed his head and shoulders and, even though he was using his mobile at the time, it showed his face quite well, showed it *enough*. So I saw the face of the man who killed James and Tomas and hospitalized Marcus.'

'Christ!' Then, 'Are you sure? How *can* you be sure, everything must've happened so fast that night—'

'You bastard Brit!' Off the sofa and close up to him in a flash, she was on fire with fury. 'I was as close to him as I am to you now,' she said to him, her voice small and tight. 'He shot Marcus once and he fell across the table then the killer raised his gun to fire again so I smashed that arm aside and I grabbed the scarf over his face and I pulled it right down to his chin.' Reaching out she seized Locksley's upper arms, dug her nails in and held him tight, their faces inches apart. 'I was this close to him,' she whispered. 'We stared into each other's eyes from this close, and I shall never forget his face until the day I die.' Then her hands fell away from his arms and she stepped back. 'Do you *understand* now, Mr Locksley?' she asked him quietly.

He did not give her a direct answer. 'I should not have doubted you,' he said. 'I have no right to question that the man you have seen in the photo you have is the gunman who assaulted your family. I apologise for doing so,' he said, then walked past her and sat down again on the sofa. 'I'll help you in this in any way I can. I'll need the photograph, or a copy.'

'I brought one with me.' Swiftly resuming her seat she picked her handbag up from the table, took out of it a slim transparent plastic envelope containing a photograph and passed it to him.

Without removing it from the envelope he studied the pictured face. Mixed blood was evident in its features and skin-tone: the photo showed a good-looking young man holding a mobile to his mouth, the lower part of his jaw partially obscured by it.

'How did you come by this?' he asked after a few moments, still intent on the features of the young man, noting with interest the long, heavy-lidded grey eyes which, quite clearly, were riveted on some object or event that was fascinating and exhilarating him. 'Tell me the circumstances in which it was taken.'

'There were two men fighting in the street, and a small crowd watching them. Brad Ellis and me – he took the picture – we saw the fight going on ahead of us. I passed by as fast as I could because I hate to see that sort of thing, but Brad.... Well, it's people living their lives that he wants to get on film, wants to ... he wants to capture their emotions, he says—'

'But why did Ellis pick out this particular face?' He looked up at her. 'I'd have thought the faces of the combatants were more interesting.'

'I said the same to him, later.' As their eyes met she felt that, suddenly, in a way she could not define, the relationship between herself and Matt Locksley had subtly altered: they had come to a deeper understanding of each other and somewhat to her surprise the realization made her feel safer, more secure and therefore stronger in herself. 'He said it was because of the expression on the face, it was so revealing. And when you look at it you can see what he meant, can't you? That man in the picture, he is enjoying every minute of the fight, he's *revelling in it*, isn't he?'

'Yes.'

'Brad's always trying to get people's expressions on film, to capture their mood in unguarded moments - in this case a man getting a kick out of watching a knife-fight.' She paused a moment, searching for the right words to use; she found them and went on. 'For Brad it's entirely objective, so he ... he has a record of it. But for me, Matt, it's not like that. The sight of violence makes me feel physically sick so I walk on and don't look.' But then her voice hardened. 'It's not that I'm *afraid of* seeing it, though, I don't want you to think that. It's that I'm afraid of what it can make people do, of how it can change people.'

'Go on,' Locksley said after a moment.

Pushing herself to her feet she swung a little aside from him. 'The man in that photograph is a terrorist!' she cried. And Locksley realized she had 'left' him again and was back in that world where terrorism ruled and the people lived and frequently died under the heel of that rule. 'I saw him shoot dead members of my family. He is a killer and he enjoys what he does, and Marcus is locked away in his private hell, God knows what that hell is like, what's going on inside his head—'

'Nothing, perhaps.' He spoke harshly and deliberately, to stop her.

It did. 'Nothing.' Quietly, she repeated the one appalling word to herself. 'Yes. The most dreadful possibility of all.'

But then she turned back to him. 'So what are you going to do about this terrorist who is alive and well and presently living a free man in your country?' she asked, her voice flat.

'That remains to be seen. May I borrow this photograph?' He answered her crisply.

'How long for?' An instant suspicion in her eyes.

'No more than a few hours if that's what you want. Why? Does it matter?'

Giving him a narrow smile, she shook her head and sat down on the sofa again. 'No, of course it doesn't.... What will you do with it?'

'Run it through the ID checking database covering foreign nationals resident here, see if there's a match.'

'And if you find a match? What then?' Her eyes bored into his. 'You will act against him at once—'

'Elianne, Elianne!' He reached out and touched her hand. 'We have nothing to arrest him for. Should I find a match we shall go by the book. We'll search out his background over here, where he lives, what he's doing—'

'But things like that take a long time, surely? And God knows what he might be doing, against Britain, I mean – he's a terrorist, I tell you.'

'If he's involved in anything of that nature over here he's likely to be under surveillance already, and now with your identification of him we'll tighten up immediately. Don't worry, I'll have it in hand straightaway.'

But she looked away; stayed silent. So Locksley too sat quiet, thinking things over, recalling what she had said earlier and considering her reaction to the presence in London of the man who had assaulted her family so devastatingly. Then for the first time he considered the emotions and attitudes he had sensed in her previously and thought how they fitted in with what he was intuiting in her now. He came to the conclusion that it was surely only natural that her desire to see her brothers' killer brought to justice should be so fierce and implacable.... Looking at her he saw her head bent a little, the glossy black hair falling forward. He could not see her face – but he did not need to, for suddenly the desolation and yearning consuming her invaded him and he got up and stood close in front of her.

'Elianne.' His voice carefully controlled. 'Elianne, you have to—'

'"Search", you said.' She echoed his word with bitter derision then turned on him, accusing. 'Even if you find this "match" for him so you know it really is him, what will you actually *do*?'

'Blanket surveillance, wide-ranging investigation of everything he does and everyone he has close contact with.' Stepping back, he was keenly aware that manpower would dictate how stringently the actions he had listed would actually be implemented. 'But don't build your hopes too high. Think it through now. Even if I find a match for this man, he may prove innocent of any discernible criminal intent over here, in which case no action can be taken against him. Remember, too, that there are mirror-image look-alikes—'

'So why bother? Is that what you're saying, that I must "stay cool"? But I'm not English, I can't do that! I won't—'

'You'll have to!' he snapped. 'If you want my help in this you'll bloody well have to be patient! This man in the picture may be perfectly innocent—' He broke off as, shrill and insistent in the hall behind them, Gray's front door bell rang. A couple of seconds later Charles came in from the study and headed straight for the door into the hall.

'I'll get it,' he said to them in passing. 'I've just remembered, I asked Richard round for an after-dinner drink and a talk.'

Elianne had quickly moved further away from Locksley as Charles came in, but now as he went on past them into the hall she went to the MI6 man, her hand reaching out for him.

'Sorry, so very sorry,' she whispered to him, her eyes assuring him of the truth of her words. 'I lost it just then. Please don't give up on me, Matt. Please don't do that, I don't have anyone else to talk to about … things.'

He took her hand in his, but he was still unsure of her, the change of mood had been so fast. 'You have Charles,' he reminded her. 'He's been there for you much longer than I have. And, he knew Marcus.'

She let his hand go, was silent for a moment, at a loss for the words to use to say what she wanted to say. Then, 'It's different, with Charles,' she said. 'I don't know how to say what I mean in English, to explain this. I've told Charles a lot about what happened, but with him I would never let him see that what was done that night made me so angry. With him I've always been very … selective, there are things I haven't told him, things about myself, I mean, my 'hang-ups' I think Brad would call them.' Her last words came out with a fleeting grin of self-mockery and a quick glance up into Locksley's eyes. 'But with you I can let it all come out. I feel *free* with you, I could tell you anything about my feelings, really anything. Because I'm not afraid of your knowing me, really knowing me. I trust you.'

'Come on through into the study, Richard.' Charles's urbane voice came to them from the hall, and she broke off as he ushered in his next-door neighbour. 'Elianne's here for a couple of nights. Locksley you already know – he's here for the booze, of course, knows I stock the best brandy on the block....'

CHAPTER 5

Oakdene House
Pilgrims' Way

29 April 2008

In the course of his career Anthony Martindale had acquired a well-earned reputation as a man of probity with an unsparing dedication to the pursuit of justice and the rule of law. Now retired, his conscience was clear that no criminal he had sent down could rightly dispute either his conviction or the length of his sentence. Despite this his five-bedroomed house was comprehensively fitted with burglar alarms connected to the local police station thirty minutes' drive away. He loved Oakdene: he and his wife Olivia had brought up their two sons there and, now in his retirement, he found great happiness in two things. Firstly, in a loving family life with Olivia and his four grandchildren: Melinda, Jack, Elise and Nicholas; and secondly, in maintaining and continually beautifying Oakdene, both the house and its extensive grounds.

That afternoon he was weeding his young courgette plants in the kitchen garden at the back of the house. It was a fine day: quite sunny with puffy white clouds sailing along on a light breeze from the south. Beginning work after lunch, he had kept hard at it for a good hour and a half, stripping off his shirt after twenty minutes, loving the feel of the earth in his strong sunburned hands. The smell of the earth and the vitality of the plants around him satisfied a need in him; he acknowledged the need, aware that over thirty-five years of living and working with serious crime and those who planned and perpetrated it had left its mark on him. His work had bred in him a longing to get hands-on close to the good, useful and enduring things to be had in life.

'Time for a break, darling!' Olivia's voice floated out from behind him and, glancing over his shoulder, he saw her standing by the long wooden table outside the back door, a tray of what he knew to be lemon tea in her hands. 'You look as if you need one,' she went on, putting the tray down on the table as he straightened up and went to join her. 'And remember the Meesons are coming for drinks so you must come in in plenty of time for a long, long shower.'

'I know, I know.' Gratefully, he sat down on the bench alongside the table, rubbing his hands relatively clean on the damp towel she had brought out with her. 'You rang Sergeant Thomson?' he asked as she poured him a mug of tea and passed it to him. He sensed she had done so even as he spoke, for he could read what the policeman's answer had been in her beloved face. She was three years older than him. Her thick, straight, light blonde hair was cut into a bob. Her calm, regular-featured face was blessed with very direct, very perceptive seagreen eyes.

Seating herself opposite him, Olivia gave him the answer anyway. 'They've called off protective surveillance at Oakdene,' she said.

'And doubtless are no closer to finding out who knifed Tom Richards that night. You know, I'm sorry for him,' Martindale said. 'Housebreaker or not, Tom Richards was simply a man in the wrong place at the wrong time.... Bloody hard luck for him, it was a foul way to die, knifed to death by a rival thief. He was no slouch himself in a scrap it seems, but according to the police he never carried a weapon so he didn't stand a chance.'

'Leave it, Anthony.' Olivia frowned; she and her husband had talked over the grim murder of Tom Richards – a housebreaker with form who lived in a nearby town – over and through again and again, finding the horror of it not easily put behind them. 'The strawberries look as if they're coming on well,' she went on, quickly

83

changing the subject. 'Will there be plenty when the grandchildren are here? It isn't that long now.'

'What're their dates again? I've forgotten.'

'I could hate you for forgetting a thing like that, but I won't.' Her eyes and tone forgiving him all, as usual. 'They arrive on Saturday, 9th August and will be with us for ten days.'

'Which has them leaving on the nineteenth—'

'Well done! Brilliant deduction!' They were smiling at each other. 'So back to the strawberries— Will there be plenty for the young?'

'Should be, depends on how many we and our friends consume....' Then leaning back he closed his eyes and thought about his grandchildren.... He'd taken the boys, Jack and Nicholas, sons of his own younger son, out in the sailing dinghy down on the coast last year: God, they'd had fun on the water that day, aged eleven and twelve the boys were already pretty good at handling the boat.... Melinda, their sister, had already turned thirteen, and then there was little Elise, the 'baby' of the family who was hopelessly spoilt but adorable anyway. They'd be celebrating her ninth birthday while she was at Oakdene this August, big kids' party, glorious mayhem, hide-and-seek in the garden, strawberries and ice-cream for tea—

'Lottie just called to say she won't be able to come in this evening, her sister's not well.' His wife's voice brought Martindale back to the present and unavoidable realities. Whenever Lottie – Charlotte Grover, their housekeeper, a twenty-four-year-old girl from the nearby village of Oakchurch – rang in to say her sister was ill (or whatever) it usually resulted in extra chores for him.

'I'm coming to think her sister being ill coincides remarkably often with the times that new chap she's going out with visits the village, suspiciously often.'

Olivia laughed. 'Vince Jenner, yes. He's very handsome, you know. Comes down from London in his splendid sports car. Village gossip has him rolling in money and spending it on Lottie like one truly besotted.... Don't grudge a young girl the goodies her face and figure bring her, darling! And give Lottie her due, she always repays us by working really unsocial hours when we entertain.'

'I suppose so, and she's marvellous with the children, they all like her.'

Martindale dreamed a little longer, then roused himself, got to his feet. 'You wanted lettuce for tonight, you said. I'll get some now and bring them round to the kitchen for you.'

Rose Daley was well pleased with the progress so far of her planned revenge on Anthony Martindale. Cold Call, she had code-named her mission, calling it so because, she reasoned, Martindale could have no expectation of any such act of revenge, it was many years since he had handed down sentence on Caitlin Daley....

On her return to England following the death of her husband in Beirut, she had at once set about planning appropriate revenge for what she saw as the 'unlawful imprisonment' of her mother. Within weeks she had discovered Martindale's present status and place of residence. Having done so, she had devised an action plan for Cold Call. Drawing her son Robert into the mission she had used him to recruit for its use two of his fellow students at Eaton Towers College in Richmond. First of these had been Vincent Jenner who would be her 'spy' via his 'dating' of Charlotte Grover, the Martindales' housekeeper who, obviously, was fully informed on the routines of the household. The second had been John Blake, a fellow 'star' of her son's college football team who, well taught by his father, was already an accomplished burglar and conman. Her team recruited, only one further accomplice was required, and that, for Rose, had presented no problem: she had contacts from her glory-days in Beirut who had found refuge in London and 'owed' her. Abdul Rahman was an experienced bomb-maker; Iraqi by birth, he had agreed to work with her in honour of her late husband Mohammed Hussain Shalhoub.

Rose convened a meeting of Cold Call personnel for 10.00 in an ex-IRA safe house which still served 'old friends' providing they knew the right people to arrange the matter. Tucked away at the rear of the house, the room put at her disposal was small and windowless, lit by two white-domed ceiling lights, and furnished with the bare necessities for her meeting – a centrally placed table surrounded by six upright wooden chairs.

She made her entrance at 10.15 to find her team members already seated. Smoothly dressed in a stylish linen two-piece in a flattering shade of crushed raspberries, her blonde hair elegantly coiffured, she greeted them with cool authority, then sat down in the chair left empy for her at the head of the table. Taking three slim files from her briefcase, she put them down in front of her, leaned back and took swift stock of the men who would be at the sharp end of Cold Call. Three of them were young, in their twenties, the fourth was in his late fifties. She had met them all before, naturally, but considered it wise to maintain regular contact with all the members of Cold Call's action unit.

Her son Robert was sitting immediately on her right; next to him was John Blake, whom they all called Blakey. Rose could see that as usual the red-headed young man was brimming with energy yet was his very controlled self.... Opposite him across the table sat Vincent Jenner, Cold Call's spy on the Martindales. Lastly, on her left sat Abdul Rahman. Resident in London for many years, Rahman had to her certain knowledge been clean of terrorist activity for the last seven of them; he had agreed to work with her on Cold Call because in 1978 her husband had saved his life at risk to his own so he felt honour-bound to come to her aid when asked. As she looked at him with his eyes downcast, his brown, veined hands clasped loosely in his lap, he seemed a man apart from the others, and she acknowledged herself still a little ... not exactly afraid of him – Rose would never admit to that – but warily respectful of him. She had had no choice in co-opting him since he was the only bomb-maker she knew in Britain apart of course from the man serving operation Wayfarer in that capacity who, obviously, was sworn to exclusive loyalty to Abu Yusuf.... Straightening up, Rose started on the agenda for the meeting.

'At last we have an exact date for Cold Call's climax,' she announced. 'Martindale's grandchildren's planned holiday at Oakdene will be from Saturday the 9th August to the following Wednesday. Therefore our action will, provisionally, take place on the Thursday after their arrival at Oakdene, i.e. the 14th August.'

'So we will work towards that as the definite date?' Jenner leaned forward as he spoke, smoothing a hand over his thick black hair, grey eyes meeting hers briefly then dropping nervously away.

Thank God you are, basically, unsure of yourself, Jenner, Rose thought, smiling at him. 'To a large extent that will depend on you, obviously,' she observed. 'As our spy on the Martindale household it is your responsibility to find out *in advance* if there's any alteration in the plans for the children's visit, and to make sure – closer to the chosen day, naturally – that the housekeeper will be alone in the house then long enough for Robert and Blake to do what is required.'

'From what I have learned from Charlotte Grover so far, that last requirement will present no problem for us since when the grandchildren visit them Mr and Mrs Martindale take them out somewhere every afternoon—'

'Thank God you're so brilliant with the girls, Vince.' Robert grinned across at him, knowing that Jenner's problem with the female sex lay not in his ability to attract them in the first place but in being able to retain their interest in him despite his earnest desire to discuss with them only literature and politics. 'How is the lovely Charlotte, anyway? Still your girl, I hope?'

Jenner greatly admired Robert Daley. He envied him his easy excellence at sport, and, more importantly, his 'in' with the (in Vince's present opinion) wondrous world in which men and women committed themselves to undertake terrorist missions that would change things for the better, would right wrongs that had been done. Robert had spun him stories of his 'missions' in Lebanon and it had all sounded so soul-stirring, so meaningful that Jenner longed to be part of it all.... Looking at Robert now, Jenner hoped that, later, Daley would keep his promise and bring Jenner to the notice of Abu Yusuf who would then enrol him in his terrorist cadre in Britain.

'Is she playing ball with you, your Charlotte?' Robert pressed him.

'Oh. Yes. Sorry, I was just.... Yes, it's going fine, Charlotte and me.' Jenner leaned towards him, eager to report progress. 'When I ask her about her job she's just so pleased I'm interested. I show her a good time, I guess, so she wants to keep me happy.... Besides, I call her "Carlotta" and she likes that—'

'See to it that you keep her interest in you productive for us until Cold Call is done,' Rose interrupted. She considered Jenner a very dull young man. Conceding that he was free with his money and very good looking she had gone along with her son when he suggested Jenner would be useful to Cold Call, would be able to get information on the Martindale household by sweet-talking their housekeeper. If the price for Jenner was to put in a word for him with Abu Yusuf – well, why not? Handsome young recruits with a ready flow of cash were usually welcomed by terrorists as well as by private citizens.

'Blakey and me, we shan't need a lot of time on the day.' Robert was frowning, irritated by his mother's wasting time on Jenner. 'You, Rose, will already have provided us with the fake IDs we'll need, so all we'll have to do is collect the bombs from Rahman here' – he made a quick hand-gesture towards the Iraqi – 'then call on Charlotte at Oakdene.'

'That is correct.' Abdul Rahman's voice was calm, almost uninterested: to him, Cold Call was a small affair, it was only for Shalhoub's memory that he had agreed to become part of it. 'I shall have the four incendiary devices assembled, armed and ready for collection.'

'Thank you, Abdul Rahman,' Rose said. 'Blake, outline your and Roberts' action again for me.' She turned to the redhead sitting beside her son. She had a lot of time for John Blake, respecting his solid grasp of the basic principles of criminality, his way with words, his quick wit and articulate commonsense – also, his skill at defeating locks which sought to deny him entry. 'Keep it brief, but Abdul Rahman should be informed of the entire course of it, so far he has only heard it piecemeal.'

'Ma'am.' Blake got to his feet. 'The chosen afternoon will be one on which Mr and Mrs Martindale take their four grandchildren out for the day. The only person left in Oakdene will be Charlotte Grover, the housekeeper, a local girl enslaved to the charms of Jenner here.' He shot a grin at Jenner, who looked down in embarrassment. 'Around 2.30 Robert and I ring the bell at Martindale's front door. Charlotte opens it, sees before her two personable, very correctly dressed and businesslike young men, both carrying zipped-up holdalls. She asks their reason for being there. They say they are from the local council tax department, produce papers to prove it, then explain that their department is carrying out a survey of properties prior to the issue of revised council tax charges. They have come to establish the number and approximate size of the rooms in the house. To back this up I open my holdall for her inspection; it will contain a small high-tech camera, a glossy booklet detailing the rights and regulations covering all aspects of the inspection, and four small plastic "Lunch Boxes" containing, as we explain to her, our sandwiches for a tea-break at 3.30—'

'In fact, of course, they contain the four explosive packages,' Robert interrupted impatiently.

'Allow Blake to finish, Robert!' Rose, imperiously.

'Sure.' Robert grinned at her, then turned to Blake. 'Sorry, Blakey. Your story.'

'Yours too, mate, when it comes to the action, which is where it really counts.' Blake was a very observant and perceptive young man; having early on intuited Robert's inner resentment of his mother's 'control' over him he was always careful of his friend's resultant prickly pride and of that innate arrogance he tried to keep hidden from his mother. 'So, Robert and I spin the story to the lovely Charlotte – lovely of face and body but usefully gullible in mind, according to Vince here – who then lets us in to Oakdene to carry out the local council's diktat. Once in the hall we explain that our modus operandi is for one of us to "do" the ground floor while the other "does" the upstairs rooms—'

'Your ID from the council, it covers house inspection according to English law?' The Iraqi's dark eyes were levelled piercingly at Blake.

'I have it on good authority that it does, sir,' Blake answered, aware that the Iraqi usually softened – a little! – when afforded the courtesies he considered his due from the younger members of Cold Call. He went on quickly then, wanting to get to the end of the thing. 'Charlotte lets us in, then Robert leaves me with her while I do the ground floor and himself goes upstairs, taking his bag with him – he'll explain if need be that he may require the camera to snap the views from the bedroom windows which, apparently, can count when tax is being set. I'll have explained to Charlotte that it would be helpful if she stayed with me to help me with the layout of the ground floor.' Pausing, he turned to Robert. 'Best you tell the next bit,' he said to him with his quick, disarming grin. 'You'll be the one doing it.'

'Sure. OK.' Robert got to his feet and, glancing from face to face as he spoke, told his gathered comrades how he would finalize the operation his mother had planned. 'As we all know,' he said, 'the lunch boxes contain the timed limpet bombs fashioned by Abdul Rahman here; each contains not only high explosive, but also incendiary and accelerant materiél. We know from Jenner's under-cover work that the Martindales' grandchildren, two boys and two girls, sleep in two bedrooms when visiting Oakdene.' He fixed his eyes on his mother then and, as he went on, he was really speaking to her alone: he gave her what he knew she had hungered for through the years, her horrific revenge. 'That Thursday afternoon I shall attach a limpet bomb to the underside of each of the four beds, below where the children's heads will lie. Then at one a.m. the following morning, all four bombs will detonate.' He stopped there and stood silent. His mother could – and would, he was sure of that – imagine what would happen at the Martindales' house when the four bombs exploded.

'Thank you, Robert.' There was a smooth satisfaction in her voice and a kind of gloating serenity in her face as she broke the silence which, for a moment, had possessed the room; then she picked up a second file, opened it on the table and proceeded with the next matter on her agenda for the meeting. This was Blake's latest report on the progress of the police investigation into the knifing of Tom Richards at Oakdene. She already knew that it concluded that the only suspects presently in the frame for the crime were all known housebreakers, and that little progress had been made in building a case against any of them, but she wished to question Blake on certain details given in his report....

Locksley had wasted no time in trying to establish the identity of the man in the photograph Elianne had given him. He passed the computer search to Sergeant Simon Matola first thing next morning; nevertheless it took time. At 16.00 hours Matola had reported on all sources available to him checked, but no match had been found.

'Sir,' he said then, 'there's only one other place to look, far as I can see. If this guy hasn't been in the country long, isn't it a possibility that his photograph is in the Foreign Entrants section which'll be—'

'Hell, I should've thought of that!' Locksley interrupted, and at once got to work on his own database.

'*Jesus!*' Locksley whispered as, half an hour later, his eyes made a match between the face pictured on the screen in front of him and the one shown in Elianne's photograph which he had placed close beside him on the work-surface his computers stood on. 'Robert Daley, ne Hussain Rashid Shalhoub, is Rose Daley's son, and now Elianne has ID'd him to me as the terrorist who carried out the assault on the Asleys that night!.... Hussain Rashid Shalhoub.' Leaning back in his chair he breathed the Arabic name aloud again as if giving it audible form might afford him control over the name's owner. Up to a point, it did so: he found he could recall, from Elianne's account of it, certain items of information regarding the assault on the Asley villa which supported her present identification of Robert Daley/Hussain Shalhoub as the killer in that attack. And since the Foreign Entrants section would have his address on record he, Locksley, could use that as a firm base from which to run close surveillance on the man, and check on his activities here in London.

Getting to his feet Locksley crossed to the south-facing window in his office and gazed out over the city.... Elianne's identification of Robert Daley as the gunman at the heart of the assault on her family in Beirut opened up an entirely new aspect of the case – quite possibly one of extremely threatening potential. Strangely, perhaps, there were no details on record regarding Robert Daley's lifestyle, activities and so on in Lebanon.

Within minutes Locksley decided to pursue the matter further himself and, sitting down at his desk again, he considered when he would reveal to Elianne the true identity of the man her friend Ellis had so fortuitously captured on film. Then he wondered whether it would be wise to give her that name at all? He had sensed her hatred for the killer and it made him afraid of what she might do if she came to know his name and address here in London.... Yet, surely, he had no right to keep those facts from her? He had to tell her, he decided – but before doing so he would exact from her a promise that she would make no attempt to contact Robert Daley unless he, Matt Locksley, told her it was OK for her to do so. Elianne would never break a promise to him, would she?.... And even as he thought that, he recalled the last time they had gone to The Foresters' Arms together. They had spent the whole day there. Climbing up Hermit's Hill he had got to the top first and sat down on the rough grass, linked his hands round drawn-up knees, then turned to her, starting to josh her for being so slow. But the words had died on his lips as he saw her: she had climbed a little off to one side of him and had almost reached the top already: in profile to him she was standing straight and still in the sunshine, gazing out across the countryside below them, her long black hair lifting and falling in the breeze – and to Locksley at that moment she had seemed fey, living in a world of her own.... If I ever made a promise to her, he had thought then, I'd never break it – never, whatever the cost to me might be. And as he thought it she had turned and come straight to him, sat down beside him and smiled at him – yet behind her smile he had for a moment sensed in her a coldness, a sort of deadly malevolence.

That latent malevolence had vanished even as he perceived it, but now it returned to haunt him. He loved the girl (privately, he acknowledged that) but now he realized that there was a dark side to her which she guarded from outside eyes, his own included. And for a moment he wondered about the nature of that 'world' she sometimes seemed to inhabit. That dark side of her surely brooded in anger and hatred on the events of that terrible evening. He must, therefore, be extremely careful as to how much he told her about Robert Daley.

Elianne was in when he called her at home in Hammersmith, the house she shared with her flatmate Roz Hunt.

'Things are beginning to look promising about that ID you wanted,' he said to her. 'It's likely I'll have a positive ID on him by the weekend, so why don't I pick you up around ten o'clock on Saturday morning and drive us out to The Foresters for lunch, followed by a walk in the country? That'll give us time to talk the whole thing over.'

'I'd love to do that. And Matt, you'll really have an ID by then? You'll know who he is and stuff about him and be on the point of arresting him?'

Locksley could hear it then, as she spoke: at first there had been in her voice the natural enthusiasm for a problem solved, but then as she went on the tone of her voice changed subtly and as she spoke the last couple of sentences her words were corroded with hatred.

'I'll be at your door around ten, then,' he said quietly, asking himself why he should be surprised by the change?

'Promise?' she asked.

'Promise. See you then.'

As he put down his mobile, Locksley brought to mind the age-old justification for the fact that he did not intend to tell her everything he knew about Robert Daley: 'It's for your own good, Elianne,' he said to himself.

Then he set about acquiring as much information as he could regarding the life of 'Hussain Rashid Shalhoub' before his arrival in Britain. First he requested from MI6 all the facts they had on him that were not available via 'the usual channels'; namely top secret info going right back to his childhood in Beirut as the third (and last) son born to Rose Daley and her husband, a known terrorist activist. He called in to his office Sergeant Todd of Special Service Communications (Middle East).

'Fast track, top secret to Beirut wanted, Jaz,' he said, waving the burly, grey-haired IT expert to a chair across the desk. 'Routes all clear, I trust?'

'No problem, sir.' Jasper Todd's round, benevolent face gave an impression of a kindly man of, perhaps, slightly lazy disposition. His pale deeply set eyes belied the latter, they possessed a peculiarly invasive and perceptive quality, as if he could, if he so wished, read your inner thoughts. 'It'll be coded?' he asked.

Locksley nodded. 'Agent Ramadan Shasri.'

'Working name "Pearl Diver".... I've always liked that; it *belongs*, like.'

'His father was one, over in Qatar. The story goes he got lucky one day, seriously lucky; he had a big find on the seabed, sold it for a packet and stayed out of the water from then on. Moved the family to Beirut, opened a general store – and gave his four sons and two daughters the good education available there.'

'Interesting. I didn't know that.'

'He's a good bloke, and very valuable to us. He teaches maths at the local secondary. Married, one son now aged around five or six.'

Sergeant Todd nodded, smiling. 'Long may he prosper,' he murmured.

'Agreed. We could do with more sleepers like him.... So, his instructions: he is to conduct deep level research into the possible political activities of Beirut citizen Hussain Rashid Shalhoub during period 2002 to 2007—'

'That's Rose Daley's son, isn't it?'

'It is. Now, take this on board, Jaz. As you surely know, following their applications for a) residency permits and b) a name change by deed poll, both Rose Daley and her son were closely investigated on account of her deceased husband's terrorist activities in the Middle East. Nothing to taint either of them emerged from that, and their applications were granted.'

'Yeah. Both were opposed by you early on, though, if I remember right?'

'You do. But cold fact prevailed: no evidence of criminal or terrorist activity came to light—'

'Doesn't mean there wasn't any, though, does it?'

'The investigations followed standard practice: there's no going against what they produce – unless, of course, new evidence emerges. And – hear this – recently I've learned things that suggest Robert Daley engaged in terrorist activity in 2005 – which is why I'm putting Shasri on a job as of now.'

Todd's face was grim. 'What "terrorist activity", sir? If I may ask.'

'You'll be dealing with Shasri from now on so you need to be in the loop. It's the Asley killings: Beirut suburbs, 2005, consequent on the Hariri assassination. I have reason, good reason, to believe Robert Daley – Hussain Shalhoub as he was then – was at that time acting with Hizbollah and took a lead part in those killings.' Locksley stood up, put both hands palm down on his desk and leaned across it towards the sergeant. 'I want proof against Robert Daley, proof that he shot all three brothers,' he said harshly, 'so get Shasri digging. Fast as you can.'

As the sergeant went out Locksley's mind had already moved on. Obviously further and more penetrative surveillance on Robert Daley should be initiated; but first, he decided, he would visit Rose

Daley and, hopefully, get the 'feel' of the Irish woman who had
been wife to a known Islamist terrorist.

'Mrs Rose Daley? Good morning, ma'am. I'm Alistair Elliot; we
spoke earlier, on the phone.'

Locksley stood at the door of her ground floor flat in Brookside
House in Ealing. Opening the door, Rose liked the look of him at
once; tall and well built, grey suit well cut, his blond hair capped
neatly to his head. He had a pleasing voice and a manner that
spoke – always very important this, to Rose Daley – of good social
standing. Smiling graciously upon him she invited him in, led the
way into her sitting-room at the front of the flat and suggested they
sit in the big bay window overlooking the road and conduct their
business there.

Seating himself in the chair she indicated at one end of the table
alongside the window – (I guess Mason watched her from out
there, Locksley thought) – he extracted a file from his briefcase,
put it down in front of him and waited for her to sit down opposite
him at the far end of the table. She had an air of comfortable
means and effortless self-assurance.

'It's good of you to see me, Mrs Daley,' he began. 'You've
quickly made yourself a respected member of the community here,
but my department has a policy of keeping in contact with recent
arrivals in our country.'

'My son and I are hardly new arrivals, Mr Elliott.' Half smiling,
she met his eyes quizzically. 'We have been here quite a while now.'

'True. But some people in positions similar to yours take many
years to integrate as successfully as you—'

'And doubtless some never manage it at all.' Pleasant but firm,
she interrupted him. 'Please, ask me the questions you have doubtless come to ask. Is there a problem of some sort about Robert and
me?'

'Not at all, ma'am. Just a few questions to bring us up to date.
If you wish, you may of course refuse to give answers.'

Rose Daley had always prided herself on having the perceptiveness necessary to determine whether a man just met for the first time was indeed what he presented himself as. In her case this skill had been acquired rapidly in circumstances in which doing so correctly could dictate whether you got cooperation or a couple of bullets in the back of the head. Now, her grey-blue eyes examined 'Alistair Elliott', searching him out; nevertheless, that morning she jumped the wrong way in her assessment of him.

'I don't think I'll need to do that,' she answered coolly, leaning back in her chair, entirely at ease with him. She smiled, adding, 'If I refused to answer even one question I would probably acquire a large black mark against my name in that file of yours, no?'

He laughed, smiling into her eyes. 'I'm sure you would never merit one, ma'am, so if I may I'll just run through these jobs you have. The one at the library earns you a salary, but the one at the RNIB in the High Street, being charity work, is of course unpaid....'

It seemed they enjoyed each other's company that day, Rose Daley and 'Alistair Elliott'. After half an hour of increasingly pleasurable conversation – about Rose's work, her neighbours, and friends made at bridge parties and various social events – she remarked that they had reached her coffee-break time and suggested he join her in that. It was an invitation he gladly accepted: it would give him more time to assess all he had learned about her so far, about the real person behind the carefully maintained 'front' she presented to the world. He sensed a break would give him an opportunity to turn their talk to Robert, the main reason for his visit.

As soon as she had left to prepare the coffee he sat relaxed, head down and eyes half closed, letting the ambience of the room assert itself now she was no longer there to dominate it.... The place had a false, synthetic feel to it, it seemed to Locksley: it was surely a 'made' room, one fabricated by Rose Daley, *widow of Hizbollah terrorist Mohammed Hussain Shalhoub*, to suit the personality and lifestyle behind which she might lie low and integrate herself into contemporary English life—

To what purpose? he wondered and then suddenly a likely format slipped into his mind: mother and son working together, Hizbollah connections, a mission being planned in Britain and both of them part of it—

Christ, *stop*! Pushing back his chair, Locksley stood up, cursed himself short and sharp then blocked 'the room' from his mind and concentrated on his present intentions: he had come hoping to obtain some impression of Rose and her son because Elianne was convinced that Robert was the Hizbollah terrorist who had gunned down her brothers.... Roaming thoughtfully around the room he stopped by the bureau against the far wall, picked up one of the framed photographs among the half-dozen standing on top of it and studied it carefully. Apparently an enlargement of a happy family snap, it pictured a beach scene: sand, sea and sun and, in the foreground, facing the camera, a young man clasping a beach ball and obviously engaged in a game with the other long-limbed, bronzed and smiling young men and girls around and behind him. The young man shown was well built and clad in very brief shorts; he was looking straight at the camera, his face alight with a huge grin, but his eyes obscured by sunglasses—

'That's Robert you're looking at, I think.' Her voice light and clear. She has just come back into the room.

'I thought it must be.' Turning as he spoke, Locksley replaced the photograph and went to her, took the loaded tray from her and set it down on the table in front of the chair she had been sitting in. 'He's a fine young man, Mrs Daley. He seems to be enjoying himself there. Looks good.'

'He *is* good, Mr Elliott.' Seating herself, she smiled up at him: a sophisticated woman nearing her fifties, happily – and innocently? – living a comfortable and locally useful life in the capital of the country she had no cause to love. 'And I mean "good" in both its senses, the socially-and-politically orientated one as well as the general one you intended, I think.... We are good citizens, Robert and I,' she added quietly, then looking down poured coffee from a sweetly shaped porcelain jug into each of the two bone china cups standing in their saucers on the tray, going on in her cool, softly cadenced voice as she did so. 'I learned my lesson when, having already lost two sons to the cause of militant Islam, I lost my husband to that same relentless ... chimera. So, taking the one son left to me, I left a doomed country and came to live in one which, unlike Lebanon, owns itself.'

Nice little speech, Locksley thought; and as he took the proffered cup of coffee from her manicured hand said, with a sincerity equal to hers, 'I sympathize with your losses, Mrs Daley.' Then carrying the cup to the far end of the table, he sat down again. The aroma of the coffee drifted up to him, fragrant, delicious – faintly erotic, he had always thought, and now leaned down to inhale its scent. 'From the Yemen, isn't it?' he offered, smiling.

Compared with most of the people from British Intelligence who had come to 'assess' her, she found this one both physically attractive *and* gifted socially. 'It is always pleasant to receive a compliment, even if it is only on the quality of the coffee one serves,' she remarked, then slid the conversation back to her son. 'Robert is progressing well at his college; as you know he is studying at Eaton College over in Richmond. His academic reports are excellent, and here in England his brilliant sporting abilities serve him well.'

'The fact that he is of the Muslim faith – any problems with that?'

Her quick ready smile gave her face a certain beauty, he thought, then added to himself the natural corollary born of long experience that women well practised in the tricks of visual deception meant trouble.

'Neither of us has encountered any difficulty of that kind in your country, Mr Elliott,' she said, her eyes frank and alight with disarming honesty. 'We have always felt welcomed here.'

'Robert's friends—'

'He has many. Most are Christian, two or three are Islamic, and most – but not all – are fellow students.' She had interrupted with a touch of impatience and her face now showed a half-mocking expression implying, perhaps, she felt he was a staid 'oldie' in such matters of the young. 'Robert is a clever, athletically gifted, hard-working young man, and he revels in being the way he is; he enjoys his talents to the full. His attitude is that as he's young and life's great he should go ahead and *live* it!' Relaxing, she reached for her cup. 'Don't you remember what it was like, being really young?' she asked him softly, elbows on the table, coffee cup held between her hands and she looking down at it.

Wondering why she should feel it necessary to shift the thrust of the conversation, he let a silence lie for a few seconds; but then as he was about to restart communication with her, she did it for him.

'Robert's friends – you wanted to know about Robert's friends.' Putting down her cup, Rose spoke in a measured tone, then sat quiet for a full minute. When she went on her voice had changed; she spoke, he thought, with a cold detachment he found slightly unnerving. 'I don't really know much about his friends,' she said, 'and what I do know comes from him, he doesn't bring them here.... Well, nothing strange in that, I suppose; in a small flat like this there's nothing whatsoever for sports-mad young men to do, is there?'

'What's his favourite sport?' Locksley asked, aware that sometimes one can learn a lot from general 'chat'. 'Football?'

She laughed – spontaneously this time, he thought. 'How *did* you guess? He plays for the college.'

'I used to enjoy football myself. What position does he play?'

'It's somewhere in the middle, I don't remember what you call it.... Now I come to consider it, I don't think Robert is temperamentally suited to any *team* game, he's too ... self-interested. In football, I think, he always wants to score all the goals himself – either that, or be in the goal and make dramatic "saves" from brilliant ... "shots", does one say?'

'One does.... Tell me, is your son a good loser?' When you strike a potentially rich seam of information, he thought, it usually pays to go on working it as long as you can!

'*Robert*, a good loser? Never!' She laughed again at the thought, but then realized she was perhaps relaxing her guard too much with this man who was, after all, from a British government department; he was a 'checker-up' on foreigners, no more than that – in any case, he was attached to the enemy.... Straightening in her chair, she eyed him coolly. 'And you, Mr Elliott? Are *you* a good loser?'

Locksley took it, smiling. 'I do all right at it, Mrs Daley. I set out to learn how to be one because it seemed to me to be worth doing so. People respect you for being a good loser so in a way you have won.' And getting to his feet, he apologized for taking up so much of her time, thanked her for the delicious coffee and took his leave.

The Foresters' Arms
Saturday, midday.

'Julie said she and Tom were very busy so I was to help myself and bring it out, so I did.' Putting the tray he was carrying down on the picnic table in front of the inn, Locksley passed one of the two glasses of cider to Elianne. He took the other for himself and sat down facing her.

'What were they so busy about?' she asked.

'Julie was in charge of the bar serving a crowd in there, and she said Tom was out the back taking a delivery.' He raised his glass to her. 'Cheers,' he said; drank deeply then put down his pint and looked her straight in the eye. 'But you don't want to talk about them, do you?'

'Hussain – Rashid – Shalhoub.' Leaving her drink untouched, Elianne spun the name out slowly, giving each part of it great emphasis. Locksley had given her that name within minutes of picking her up at her house earlier that morning: 'That's all I'll tell you for the moment,' Locksley had said as she settled back into the passenger seat of his dark blue Renault. 'Right now I need to concentrate on driving. We'll talk about it as soon as we're there.' And she had nodded, then stayed silent as they drove out of the city. But a little later, as they were speeding through sunlit countryside, she had whispered the name to herself, low and hard.

Now, looking across at her, Locksley found himself deeply moved by the intensity of her grief. 'In time, we'll find out all about him,' he said, prevaricating, and slightly ashamed to be doing so.

'Where does he live?' she asked, her eyes on the table in front of her.

'This is not the time to tell you that.'

Frowning – as though he was rejecting her – she looked up, let her eyes rest on the surrounding hills and said after a moment,

'Marcus has been moved to a nursing home in the hills behind Beirut. Katie told me in her last letter.'

'Is that a good thing?'

'Oh yes. I know the place and it's lovely up there, and Katie says the nursing care he receives is faultless.'

'Does she write to you often?'

'At least twice a week. And to me, always proper letters, with time given to them. To her, e-mail is great for business, but for friends, it's different.' Elianne looked at him again then, smoothing back her hair. 'Katie and me, we both love Marcus, she as his wife and lover, me as his sister. We all grew up as kids together, our families were friends, we all *knew* each other.... Now I'm away, she keeps me close to him.'

And, probably, keeps alive your hatred of the man who ripped the heart out of your family, Locksley thought – and fuels your craving for revenge.

'Let's take our drinks inside, finish them over some lunch as usual then go for a walk and feel grass beneath our feet!' Suddenly Elianne pushed back her chair and stood up, keeping the memories at bay with present, everyday concerns.

'Julie said she'd make up our usual Ploughman's Lunch and leave it in the kitchen for us, it'll be ready by now.' He was quickly at her side and, glasses in hand, they headed for the big, airy kitchen at the rear of the mellow redbrick inn.

★

They walked through the peaceful hills that afternoon, and felt blessed. They didn't talk much at first, each aware that in the immediate present there lay between them only the one matter to discuss – and that it would be best left until they had reached Hermit's Hill and sat down to rest. They trod narrow tracks through cool woodland, their feet soundless over moss and leaf-mould; crossed farmland (carefully opening and closing farm gates as they went) rich with grass and lazy with cud-chewing cattle; they heard birdsong in hedgerow and treetop and, once or twice, they laughed together over some inconsequential thing said between them. And in time, reaching the summit of Hermit's Hill, they sat down side by side on the grass with their backs against a sun-warmed, greystone wall poking up through rank grass....

'In this country, he has committed no crime, Elianne,' Locksley said, breaking the silence that had grown between them as they sat in the sunlight.

'*To your knowledge* he has committed no crime here.' Drawing up her knees she linked her arms around them. She was wearing brief shorts and her legs were bare.

'True. I stand corrected.'

'He is under your department's surveillance?'

'He is. Nothing ... invasive, though. We have no right in law.'

'So there could easily be parts of his life here in London that you know nothing about—'

'We receive reports on him from various people who know him well.... Fairly well.'

'People he ... spends time with, at work, or something, you mean?'

'Yes.' There was a disquiet growing in him because he guessed what she was leading up to, but knew he ought to refuse her the knowledge she craved.

'But surely, now you know what he *has been* you will—'

'Surveillance will be pitched higher.' Scrambling to his feet he moved a few steps away from her alongside the ruined wall then turned to look back at her. Saw her in profile, the loose fitting daffodil-yellow overblouse, the way her hair was caught up at the back of her head then fell free.

'Does he go by his own name, here?' Her voice clear and sharp, her eyes still on the distant hills.

'No. He changed it by deed poll.'

'Changed it to what?'

'Why should you wish to know that?'

After a slight pause, and her voice lower, 'Because I would like to … personalize my hatred…. And because I have a *right* to know.'

'Perhaps.' Then he let the conversation lapse again, waiting for her next move. When it came, it took him by surprise.

Quite quietly she said, 'He didn't come to England alone, I think?'

'No. And Elianne, I can't tell you who came with him any more than I can tell you his name. Please, leave it be. I've given you the name he went by in Beirut and it's best you stand aside from it all now; you must leave us to deal with the situation. If we find he is engaged in subversive activity of any kind here, he'll be arrested immediately,' he added harshly. 'I can promise you that. Then you'll have the satisfaction of knowing that, in effect, it was you who caused it to happen.'

But that was not enough. She got up and came to him. 'Matt,' she said, 'all I ask is the name he lives under now.'

'Why? Why do you want it?'

Her mouth twisted. 'Not "want". *Need*: need to identify him so I have something definite to hate.'

It seemed to Locksley an appalling thing to hear anyone say, but most appalling to hear it said by this young woman who had so many other things to live for. But after a moment he understood why she felt the way she did – and there came to life in him an irresistible desire to give her at least something, not leave her with only what she had now – which was indeed, he realized, practically nothing, nothing she found of any value to her.

'Matt,' she said. '*Tell me.*' She said it very quietly and, looking into her eyes, he saw she knew she had 'reached' him. 'Give me the name he lives under, here in England. Give me that.'

I can do so, provided she gives me her word not to *act* on the knowledge – I can, because I trust her, I have faith in her given word *to me*. 'Promise me two things, and I'll do it,' he said.

Suddenly, hope burned in her eyes. 'Tell me what they are.'

'It's two things in one, really,' he said and, slowly, giving weight to each word, laid on the line what he required of her. 'First, that in the matter of this man you ID'd to me as Hussain Shalhoub, you will from now on make *no attempt whatsoever* to contact him, either in person or through any one else.'

She frowned a little, but all she said was, 'And – the second thing?'

'It's no more than a confirmation of the first: you must give me your word as a solemn oath that you will keep your promise.'

She looked down, and for a moment stood before him silent and self-absorbed. Then, 'I promise I will make no attempt to contact this man in any way,' she said, looking up at him. Then reaching up she put one arm around his neck, moved in close and kissed him on the cheek. 'A kiss means a lot to me, Matt,' she said. 'I'll keep my word to you – that kiss seals my promise to you, makes it binding on me.'

12A, Lime Tree Road, Hammersmith. London
Late the same night.

'Robert Daley,' Elianne whispered to herself. She was alone in her bedroom. Sitting on her bed, showered and cool in cotton pyjamas, she thought about the name she had won for herself that day – with a promise she had no intention of keeping. Then, bowing her head, she concentrated on working out a way to find out where 'Robert Daley' lived. Once she knew that – and given time, she realized it was not a thing to be achieved either easily or rapidly – she would give to him what he had given to two of her brothers.

Quite soon she rose to her feet and slipped into bed, the thin, crooked smile of schadenfraude ugly on her face; she had decided on the new move she would make and was impatient for the next day so that she might go out and set about making it. Sleep did not come to her easily that night. When she closed her eyes, her mouth remembered the feel of his skin – and he was with her then: Matt Locksley. The kiss that at the time had been for her simply a pledge to keep her given word to him had, she was aware, been more than that to him. And now, as she lay quiet, memory of the kiss slid into her mind again and it came to her that, in some subtle, unexpected way, it had meant more to her as well – though she could not formulate exactly in what way, only knew she 'cared for' Matt Locksley, he was in her life and she wanted him to stay there.

But I lied to him! My kiss was a lie and I shall go on living the lie because ... *I have to.* My vow to Marcus stands paramount: *nothing* shall stop me from carrying it out....

CHAPTER 6

A room in Operation Wayfarer's safe house 4, Shaftesbury Avenue, LONDON.

6 May 2008

The room was furnished strictly for its purpose, containing only a plain rectangular table surrounded by six straight-backed chairs. Seated at one end of it Abu Yusuf had Khaled Ras on his right, Faris Mansoor on his left, Rose Daley facing him at the far end of the table and Mahmoud Afsanjani on Mansoor's left. He opened the meeting he had so hurriedly convened, addressing his section commanders in Arabic.

'I summoned you here to disclose to you an important development, but first I would ask each of you to bring us all up to date on progress in his section.'

'Security is being maintained.' Khaled Ras rose to his feet, stood tall and straight, thin hands resting on the table to each side of him. 'With one exception, the training of the martyrs is progressing satisfactorily. I will not name the exception to you since Abu Yusuf has already interviewed and reprimanded him. Rest assured, therefore, that all four will carry their mission to a successful conclusion.'

Looking into the Afghan's lifted, severe face, Rose Daley thought, poor bastards. I've never really understood the young suicide bombers, guess one has to have the compulsion *to be* one to comprehend their motivation.

Faris Mansoor, sitting opposite Ras, stood up as the Afghan resumed his seat, then spoke his piece, very briefly.

'Logistics are all in order, and all information from our sleepers and moles confirms the situation at each of Wayfarer's target trains and stations unchanged both materially and in staffing arrangements.'

'Faris's reports to me,' Rose said as Mansoor sat down, 'are as usual both wide-ranging and fully detailed.' She smiled at the Palestinian, appreciating the strong, well-proportioned body held with self-confidence and the brown eyes invariably bold upon her, suggesting admiration spiked with sexual interest.

As she fell silent, Mahmoud Afsanjani got to his feet. The Irani terrorist kept his eyes fixed on his commander as he said his piece.

'The four bombs required to accomplish Wayfarer will be ready for collection at the appointed time,' he said, 'all component parts required are already in my possession.' A narrow smile thinned his lips. 'Should you order it, Abu Yusuf, I could produce the bombs by tomorrow midday.'

Abu Yusuf favoured him with a brief nod and then, as the bomb-maker sat down, went on to the real reason for his calling them together.

'Yesterday I received from Beirut news that I think you should all be made aware of since although our retaliatory action over there will be swift we have to bear in mind any threat to us—'

'Is there threat to Wayfarer?' Ras's interruption was harsh and imperious.

Yusuf eyed him coldly. 'To Wayfarer, indeed,' he answered carefully polite but inwardly seething at being interrupted: Ras was acknowledged as peerless in the specialized world of training those offering themselves as martyrs; although he was hard with them, his savage fanaticism inspired them, allowing him to mould them into ruthless killing-machines. All of which made it advisable to keep him on side.

'Then get to the point,' Ras said, steely eyed.

Clamping down on his anger Yusuf refrained from remarking

that interruptions frequently led to time-consuming digressions; turning away from Ras, he continued to relay his recently received news.

'Beirut Command has informed me that one of their local agents suspects that a known spy for British Intelligence resident in the city has been activated—'

'To what purpose?' Again Ras thrust his question into the flow of words, but this time it did not annoy Yusuf since it was to the point.

'This traitorous man, it seems, has been attempting to discover more about an incident one of our organisation's Retributive Justice units was involved in back in 2005,' he went on smoothly. 'Apparently British Intelligence has directed this local spy to gather specific information regarding the *identity* of the Hizbollah-affiliated gunman who carried out the actual executions of the Asley brothers at that time.'

Rose had stiffened as he spoke; now sitting bolt upright, she stared at Abu Yusuf. '*Robert.*' She spoke his name with quiet intensity; then licked her lips and, frowning, went on. 'He shot all three—'

'But failed to kill the eldest.' Harshly, Ras eyed her, brooding malevolently on her son's dereliction of duty, his failure to exact proper vengeance, to pursue his mark to the grave as honour demands of those who seek to avenge their own dead.

'The Asley affair will be left to stand as it was when it was first done,' Yusuf said. '*Wayfarer* is our mission here, and Robert Daley is our comrade in prosecuting it to its climax.'

'If Robert is exposed following the activation of this British spy, Wayfarer will fail.' On his feet now, Mansoor turned to Rose. 'Your son properly avenged his father's death!' he said to her with passion. 'One of the Asley brothers betrayed Mohammed Hussain Shalhoub to his death – so all of them paid the blood price. It was just payment, the life of one man such as Mohammed Shalhoub is worth all three taken in exchange for his death. I thank your son, Madame, and count myself honoured now to serve with you, his mother.'

He sat down then. Rose thanked him with a smile and a gracious inclination of the head, but then she thought wryly that the last part of what the Palestinian had said took the gloss off the eulogy: only as 'Robert's mother' was she honoured....

Abu Yusuf too thanked the Palestinian for his tribute, but it was Khaled Ras who got the meeting back on track.

'What is this traitor's name?' he demanded.

'The name is Shasri. Ramadan Shasri.'

Ras's eyes bored into those of his commander. 'Then, presumably, Beirut command will immediately take action against him?'

Yusuf gave him stare for stare. 'The matter is already in hand,' he assured him. 'We can take it that no further information on the identity of the comrade who gunned down the Asley brothers will come to the attention of British Intelligence from him.'

Abu Yusuf left the matter there. Drawing the meeting to a close he himself remained seated, watching the others leave one by one, acknowledging their leave-taking. Rose Daley went out first, Mansoor was close behind her and then, more slowly, Afsanjani.... Khaled Ras stayed sitting, his head bowed as he leafed through one of the files he had brought in with him. Then as the bomb-maker closed the door behind him the Afghan closed his file, replaced it in the slim black briefcase beside him and rose to this feet.

'There is something you wish to discuss with me in private?' Abu Yusuf put his question quietly.

Moving smoothly Ras went to stand beside him and asked his question. 'Why was Robert Daley absent from this meeting?'

'Surely it is obvious?' Abu Yusuf made an open-handed gesture of surprise. 'Were Shasri to identify him to British Intelligence as the Hizbollah activist who gunned down the Asley brothers, M16 would quickly put in place massive surveillance on him. That would seriously endanger Wayfarer. Therefore it is imperative that Daley remains unaware of the fact that domestic Intelligence are attempting to discover the ID of the man who killed the Asleys—'

'You are right.' Ras drew back. 'The boy is rash, quick-tempered, violent by nature and arrogant. Were he to perceive himself threatened it is likely he would take steps on his own initiative and with thought only for his own safety; such action on his part might put Wayfarer at grave risk.'

Yusuf smiled to himself, recalling an English saying he had heard recently which seemed apt: "It takes one to know one."

'Men who are violent by nature are at certain times and in certain circumstances of great use to those like us who are engaged in terrorism,' he observed blandly.

'Only when they have learned *to control* their natural urge to violence.' Ras's dark eyes glinted sardonically. 'We understand each other well, you and I,' he said; then he leaned closer to Yusuf to say what he had remained behind to report to him. 'Rose Daley had a visitor recently who is not one of her regular callers,' he said, his voice making the words an accusation. 'He presented himself to her by the name "Alistair Elliott".'

'What reason have you to believe that was not his real name?'

The Afghan straightened. 'I have no proof but ... she is not to be trusted!'

Abu Yusuf frowned, remembering a certain matter concerning Rose Daley which Ras had spoken to him about earlier. 'This idea you have, that the woman is running a personally motivated operation of her own concurrently with Wayfarer – you still have no factual evidence to support your accusation?'

'Daley's house servant is from the Yemen and is aware that I could have her father killed there within a day of my giving the order for it. The evidence I have received from her is ... suggestive.' Having gone that far Ras stood silent, his eyes fixed on his commander. He was preparing to be met by – not *active hostility* regarding the present subject of their conversation, there could never be that between them, they had shared too much in the past for that – but rather, by a certain *ennui* in relation to it. However, as Ras well knew, what Abu Yusuf said or pretended to feel on anything was not necessarily the whole picture, he was a master in the art of disguising his true attitude or intentions towards situations and individuals.

'Evidence that either Daley or her son are involved in some disloyal activity?'

'So far, none to be classed as definite.' Ras never told a direct lie to his commander during the course of a mission. In fact he had already received, and was continuing to receive, reports from two of the agents he had set to surveillance Robert Daley's private life which had reinforced his suspicions regarding the young man's commitment to Wayfarer. However he still had no irrefutable evidence against either him or his mother. Therefore he now met Yusuf's eyes with a practised neutral expression, his face giving away nothing.

'Answer me this, then, Khaled Ras: considering the lack of proof against Rose Daley and her son, what reason have you to be so convinced that she is being treacherous to our mission and to me as her commander?'

But Ras had closed his mind against him; he would bide his time, he decided, and changed the subject.

'Sir,' he said, 'Robert Daley has many friends at the college he attends and from his sporting prowess, and it is my opinion that certain of them merit further investigation.'

'Surely, this is off the point!' Yusuf interrupted impatiently. 'When – and if – you obtain definite evidence against Rose Daley, you will inform me of it as once. Only then will I have the right to take action against her.'

His tone and manner made it plain that the words were a dismissal; however, Ras knew his commander well, too well to be deceived, making the polite salaams required, he withdrew at once. There was no doubt in his mind that Abu Yusuf was taking seriously the still hypothetical duplicity of Rose Daley. Therefore as he went on his way Ras resolved to cast more widely his surveillance on not only the woman herself but, also, on her son and his particular friends (to the Afghan, the word 'friend' meant 'men who are known well to one or might be useful in furthering one's own interests or ambitions').

12 May

Jacko's café in Ealing.

'*Jacko's*' was popular with the students from Eaton Towers, including Robert Daley and his particular friends. Only five minutes' walk from the main college buildings it was brightly lit, played the latest pop hits and from midday on served drinks and good, reasonably priced snacks. A few of the waiters were also students; but they worked under the eyes of two professionally experienced men who ruled the café floor with an iron fist...

Elianne went in through the double glass doors and looked around her. She spotted Vincent Jenner at once: in designer jeans and dark-red denim shirt, his jacket draped over the back of his chair, he was sitting facing her at a table for two against the wall. As soon as he saw her come in he was on his feet, smiling in welcome.

She had not found it hard to 'get in with' Robert Daley's friend Jenner. Having acquired Daley's address from Locksley she had carried out relentless investigation of him, found out the location of the college he attended, discovered *Jacko's* café to be the place at which he and three of his friends liked to hang out together. By the use of more striking make-up and a couple of new dresses suitable for discos, she had set out to attract and hold the attention of Vincent Jenner. She selected him after careful observation of the four friends as the one most likely to 'fancy' her. Observing him in the café, she had sensed in him a kind of vulnerability; it had seemed to her quite possible that the virile, handsome exterior he presented to the world was a sort of protective façade he had created for himself to mask an inner uncertainty and a kind of loneliness.

'Elianne! I'm so glad you could make it,' he said as she came up to his table giving him a smile and apologies for being late.

Slipping off her light jacket she sat down across the table from him: young and lovely in her sleeveless summer dress of apple-green silk. As he looked across at her Jenner could hardly credit his luck in pulling such an attractive and also intelligent and *serious-*

minded girl five nights ago and then *holding* her interest, keeping her with him, still happy to date him. To Jenner, this seemed a wonder beyond price, and, although this was only their third evening together he was already her slave. Also, because he perceived in her a kind of essential innocence, he wanted and worked for her approbation of him as a man.

'What are your friends doing tonight, Vince? Robert Daley, Damon Ashford and the one you call Blakey?' Elianne asked, for after enquiring what she would like to drink and then ordering from the waiter her requested glass of white wine and a cider for himself, Jenner had sat restless in his chair, fiddling with the cutlery on the table, clearly at a loss for something to say.

'They've all gone to the pub, it's a darts night.' Gratefully, he followed her lead. 'I expect we'll meet up with them later on at the club, after we've eaten here.'

However, Elianne and Vincent did not go to the club that night and meet up with Robert Daley and his mates. Anxious at all costs to avoid meeting Daley face to face – she planned for that to come to pass only once, and at that meeting she would be the one with the gun, he unarmed – and aware of Jenner's interest in films and music, she had other plans for their evening. So after enjoying pizza and salad followed by ice-cream, she suggested they skip the club and, instead, go to a cinema she knew of that specialized in showing classic films and was currently screening *Anna Karenina*. Jenner thought this a great idea and his Porsche convertible took them there in twenty minutes....

Coming out of the cinema around eleven o'clock they went for coffee to a late-night café nearby; it was small and slightly seedy but neither of them paid any attention to that. Each was interested in the other, but their respective interest was completely different in nature. Jenner was falling in love with her, so he was eager to discover more about the persona of 'Elianne Asley'. Whereas she, intent on using him, was building up a closeness between them so that she might exploit it for her own ends: she saw Jenner as her 'enabler' to finding out the living-patterns which shaped Daley's days and weeks so that she might plan her revenge accordingly.

In the moodily-lit, almost empty café, seated at a table for two as far as possible from the self-service counter, enclosed in their own small world, Elianne and Vince talked themselves close to each other. She shaped the conversation to serve her own purpose; entranced, Jenner opened up freely, telling her about his friends and giving of himself gladly in the hope that Elianne would do like-wise – in her own time, of course, he would never pry.

'... My mother is a very worldly-wise, hard person,' he told her when she asked about his parents. 'She was much younger than my father when they married. She was his P.A. and a great help to him as he built up his fortune. He was in construction, he'd made a pile by the time he was forty ... I was always his son more than hers ... I think she was glad when he died. I know that's a horrible thing to say, sorry. She's ... well, she gives me a huge allowance, but nothing else.'

Reaching out, Elianne touched his hand where it lay on the table.

At once he looked up and smiled into her eyes. 'As far as I'm concerned, that is the one good thing about her, that she's never been mean about money,' he said, 'but that's easy when you've got as much as she has, I guess. Still, at least she does *give* to charities as well as me. All she asks in return, from me, is that whenever required I escort her to social events, Ascot, the theatre or what-ever. I loathe all that stuff, but I've been well trained, I can carry it off with loving-son-attentiveness.'

As they lingered over a second coffee, Jenner asked her why she was studying in London – not in Beirut or, possibly, America where, he'd heard, a great many Lebanese went to college. So folding her arms on the table Elianne gave him a brief, heavily edited version of the night of the Hizbollah attack on her family home; realizing Jenner was bound to ask sooner or later, she had prepared a sanitised account, presenting Marcus as alive and well now, an eye-surgeon in the prime of life, and excising Tomas and James from the 'story'.

'You're lucky to have a brother,' Jenner said when she fell silent (and at his words her heart contracted in agony).

But she kept her nerve. Took momentary refuge in sipping her coffee, then forced the image of Robert Daley's face into her mind's eye to blank out the memories. She then found it easy to continue leading Jenner on to hunger for her to be close to him.

She was careful with Jenner that night: careful to show that her interest lay in him, refraining from asking too many questions about his friends. Nevertheless, she gleaned certain facts on which she could start building a picture of Daley's way of life. Among other things, she learned that Daley, Blakey and Jenner were working together on what he called an 'enterprise', which, she suspected, was ... outside the law. To what degree that was so, or of that 'enterprise's' actual nature, she had no idea. The moment she showed real interest in it Jenner laughed the whole thing off saying it was no more than some sort of 'adventure', a 'spree out in the country', he'd said. Not quite believing him and determined to find out more, she immediately accepted his invitation to have dinner with him the following evening.

... Jenner had not been able to contain his delight that she would go out with him again so soon, Elianne recalled, smiling to herself as she slipped into bed an hour after midnight. And for a few minutes then she lay on her back, hands linked behind her head.

'It has begun,' she whispered to the darkness cocooning her. '*I* have begun it: Robert Daley will pay with his blood.'

24 May
BEIRUT

Ramadan Shasri, his wife Nadia and their only child, 5-year-old Naseem, lived in a villa set within its own tree-surrounded walls halfway along a street ten minutes' walk from Hamra, West Beirut's thriving shopping centre. Ramadan taught mathematics at a secondary school which lay half an hour's drive away through the city's anarchic traffic.

Nadia's custom was to leave the house around ten o'clock every morning and, taking Naseem with her, walk along to the nearby group of general stores to buy fresh milk, bread, fruit and vegetables for the day. Naseem always carried home the fruit whatever it might be – though he always hoped it would be oranges because if it was he would be given one as soon as he was inside the house provided he had behaved well throughout the morning's shopping expedition. That day being a Thursday, the day before the Friday holiday, school finished early, at midday, so Nadia was expecting her husband home well before one o'clock.

But there was to be no orange for Naseem that day although he had behaved impeccably at the shops. Letting herself and her son in through the front door, Nadia closed and locked it behind them, slid the heavy bolts top and bottom into place then picked up her shopping bags to take them on into the kitchen.

There came a soft, discreet knocking on her front door and thinking from its quietness that it must be her friend and neighbour Jameela she put the bags down again, unbolted the door and turned the key in the lock.

The door was slammed back against her body as two men rushed inside, the first one seized her by the throat as she reeled back, then swung her round and pinned her against the wall. He held her there half-choking as his comrade kicked the door shut behind them, grabbed Naseem by the shoulder, slapped him hard across the face, then prisoned him against his jeans-clad legs with his left hand while with his right he drew his pistol from the holster at his belt and dug its muzzle into the soft flesh below his captive's right ear.

Shock-rigid, Nadia stared across at her son.

'*You make a sound and we'll blow your son's head off.*' The words came to her one by one, spoken by the man who had her by the throat. What he said was voiced quietly, but she believed with absolute certainty that these men would do what they said, therefore, although she longed to call out to her son – even just to say his name so he would know she was thinking of him and loved him – she closed her mouth.

'I'm going to ring your husband on his mobile now,' the man went on. 'He is not in class at this time so I expect he will be in the staff-room. While I am talking to him you must remember what I have just told you.' Then taking his mobile from the pocket of his dark-blue jacket, he tapped out the number he wanted. When next he spoke his voice sounded quite loud in the utter silence of Ramadan's villa, Nadia could hear every word.

'Mr Shasri,' he said, 'you must listen very carefully to me now because the welfare of your wife and son is in my hands as I speak to you ... Do you understand the implications of the situation between you and me now?'

The pause as he waited for an answer was very brief (Shasri had grown up in the civil strife tearing at Lebanon's vitals – he knew and understood only too well). Pressing her back against the wall, Nadia shut her eyes to prevent Naseem from seeing her fear. Her son stared at her wide-eyed with pain and terror.

'Good. That is well.' The man's tone was conversational, there was no threat in it; he knew overt threat was unnecessary, knew Shasri would be fully aware of the various 'flashpoints' embedded in such situations as the one he was now entrapped in. 'So, I will tell you how you must proceed. If you have any commitments between now and four o'clock this afternoon you will cancel them as soon as I terminate this call. That done, you will go on with your work at the school until it closes, and during that time you will of course make no reference *by any means whatsoever* or to any *person* at all to this call or to what is now happening to you and your family. I don't need to elaborate on that point since undoubtedly you know what would follow were you to inform on us. After school closes you will drive straight home, by yourself. On arriving here you will park your car as usual and walk straight to your front door, carrying nothing at all with you, and let yourself into your villa. We will take over from there.' He paused for a moment to allow Shasri to assess the situation and take on board the orders given him, then, 'You agree to abide by all these instructions?' he demanded.

He received his answer almost immediately, and Nadia heard the man laugh out loud as he did so.

'Then we look forward to seeing you, Shasri,' he said then. 'Take care not to get killed in a traffic accident on the way here, but don't drive slowly, either. If you're not here by 13.45 you won't like what you find when you do make it.'

Ramadan Shasri let himself in through his front door at 13.10; he came in empty-handed, having left his school briefcase in his car. As he entered the hall he saw his wife Nadia sitting on the straight-backed chair alongside the hall table to his right. She looked across at him when he came in and love, longing and despair flashed between them.

'*Over here, Shasri!*' The command came hard and fast from his left and, recognizing the voice as that of the man who had given him his orders, Shasri at once turned and went to him where he stood with his back against the wall with his silenced handgun held loosely in his right hand ready for use.

'Where's my son?' Shasri demanded harshly as he moved, not taking his eyes off this tall, dark-haired man who had trapped him in this nightmare.

'Behind you, over by the door.'

'May I turn and look at him?' Halting a yard short of the man with the gun Shasri held the dark eyes.

'Briefly.'

The ghost of a smile slipped across Shasri's accepting face and was gone. 'Condemned man's last wish granted,' he murmured, then turned his head and looked towards the door: saw Naseem sitting on a wooden-armed chair placed near the door, his guard standing beside him cradling his gun. The little boy was huddled back in the chair and he looked terrified and exhausted. But he and Nadia were alive, and knowing this made a quiet gladness sing inside Shasri's head. He thought, so basically all is not lost. Let's get this over with, best not to stir still waters or evil beasts may rise from them to do dreadful things.

'Shut your eyes for a bit, Naseem,' Shasri called to his son, 'you look as if helping your mother with the shopping has tired you out—'

'*Enough!*' Flashing out his right hand the gunman pistol-whipped Shasri across the face and then, as with effort Nadia's husband straightened up and held himself steady, he aimed his gun at his chest. 'Turn round and get down on your knees,' the man ordered, eyes feral for the kill now, boring into those of his prey.

For a second, Shasri held those eyes; then he did what he had known he would have to do from the moment he heard his wife and son were hostage to the enemy.

Stepping up close behind him the executioner shot him twice at the base of the skull.

Shasri's body crashed down, his head disintegrated, he spasmed once then Naseem screamed thin and high again and again until his guard slapped him hard across the cheekbone and then for a moment there was no sound at all.

The executioner stalked across to Nadia where she sat by the hall table, slave to the will of the two killers from the moment one of them put his gun on Naseem, the son she and Ramadan had made together.

'You will keep your mouth shut about what has happened here. Within five minutes of our leaving men will come to remove the body,' he said to her bent head. 'See to it that neither you nor the boy go out of the house until tomorrow morning.'

She looked up then. Stared at him out of eyes that had no expression whatsoever in them, were bereft even of hatred. 'I understand. I know what your kind expect of those who survive one of their attacks,' she said quietly to his grim face. 'Now you have done what you came here to do, go.'

Her lack of humility sparked in him a sudden, fierce anger: but he had never yet struck a woman and he turned on his heel and strode towards the door. But as he drew close to Naseem he noticed the boy staring fixedly at his face and stood still, holding the boy's eyes.

'Your father's dead,' he said to the child. 'I killed him. What do you see in my eyes that you're looking into them so intently?'

No tears on the tense, scared little face. Naseem thought about what he had been asked for a moment; then his eyes shifted sideways, found refuge in the shopping bag he had been carrying when he and his mother came in and which now lay crumpled on the floor.

'Nothing,' he answered, then looked back at the man who had just shot his father dead. 'Nothing,' he said again, straight to his face.

So the man with the gun raised it for the second time and shot him – just the once, and the bullet ran true to enter Naseem's forehead dead-centre and give him a quick death. Then, holstering his weapon the killer went on to open the door.

'A pre-emptive strike,' he remarked to his comrade as he passed by him. 'The boy's Shasri's only son: give him another twelve years or so and he'd likely come gunning for me to avenge his father's death.'

26 May
Esher

Locksley was clear of Outer London by 09.30. He'd set off from his flat in Thornton Heath to drive to Esher fairly early; he had an appointment with a retired Intelligence officer whose brain he wished to pick about Rose Daley's life before she went to Lebanon and married there. But just as he was settling down to enjoy travelling on the relatively clear minor roads which would take him through countryside to his destination, his mobile demanded his attention. It was the handset connected with the 'urgent call' instrument in his office, so he pulled into a handy lay-by and answered it with a brusque, 'Yes?'

'Todd here, sir. I'm on a secure line.'

'What gives?'

'Bad news from Beirut. They got to Shasri, he's dead, execution style—'

'When?'

'Thursday, early afternoon … Sir, they killed his son, too—'

'Ah, Jesus. Poor Nadia … How did the news reach us?'

'I picked up this envelope addressed to you as I signed in this morning. Parker was on duty, filled me in on how it got there. Seems it was brought in by a young bloke, early twenties, dressed like a student. He spoke heavily accented English, produced this envelope, said it was for Superintendent Locksley and he had to deliver it in person—'

'Cut it short, man.'

'So he got Parker to go off with it to your office, said you'd recognize the handwriting and want to see him—'

'Oldest trick in the book, what the hell was Parker thinking of.'

'Yeah, exactly: when Parky gets back, no student. So Parky puts the letter in the safe, gives it to me as I come in so as per instructions I opened it and read its contents.'

'And?'

'Two more envelopes. One contained a report Shasri had completed the day before he was murdered. The other was handwritten and stated that Shasri—'

'Handwritten by whom?' But Locksley knew, really; and felt for her. Nadia had had IVF treatment in London because in Beirut she had worked for the British Council.

'By Shasri's wife, Nadia.'

Sitting behind the wheel of his Renault, Locksley made a mental note to despatch a 'safe and secret delivery' letter to Nadia that evening—

'Sir, Shasri had made a good start on the Asley case. His report in with the letter confirmed the earlier info that the killings were Hizbollah-initiated, a three-man hit squad in on the action, one man only the killer. Through her work with the Council Nadia knew and was friendly with Katie Asley—'

'Marcus Asley's wife, yes. What did Shasri get from her?'

'It seems that Katie Asley told him that on the night in question she heard the gunman who carried out the killings addressed as "Hussain" by one of his henchmen—'

'And we know that before he changed his name by deed poll soon after entering Britain, Robert Daley was known as Hussain Rashid Shalhoub.'

'Yeah, *but*. Half the male population of Beirut have got "Hussain" somewhere in their full name.'

'More like three quarters ... Why didn't Katie Asley tell this to anyone else earlier on, I wonder?'

After a slight pause, 'Likely at the time she wanted the killing to stop,' Todd said quietly. 'Changed her mind as time went by.'

'Anything else?'

'Yes, sir, nothing big, though. You instructed Shasri to dig into Daley's – Hussain Shalhoub's, as he was then – life in Beirut prior to his move over here with his mother, and see if he could unearth any new info about him that for one reason or another hadn't come to light when they were vetted in connection with their application for domicile here. Well, Shasri got us two such facts: first, that although Shalhoub was never charged – which is why we didn't get it before – he was questioned by *his local police* in 2003 about his involvement in a hit similar to the Asley assault but that killing by knife, not gun. And second, that in Beirut that same year he attended a month-long intensive course in close combat, on the pretext of intending to join the army.'

'Interesting. Be in my office when I get back, I should make it around three, we'll talk things over then.'

'Shall I alert one of the other Beirut sleepers to take over—'

'No. Since Hizbollah were on to Shasri, they'll he looking for us to do just that ... Get the usual local support and protection going for Nadia with all possible speed.'

'Shall we offer her safe haven over here?'

'Offer it, of course. But she may turn it down, like others have. People react to deep grief in different ways. To fight back helps some, she may be one of them.'

'But a lone woman?'

'She's not alone in the wider sense. The Asleys will be there for her, Katie will see to that and it might help her a bit ... Not that anything can help much, I think....'

CHAPTER 7

Jenner had not taken his yacht *Mockingbird* far out from land that afternoon. Nevertheless, anchored on a calm sea with the sun shining from a cloudless sky Elianne and he could see the south coast from Bexhill to Fairlight. The boat rocked gently on blue waters idling their way ashore.

Stretched full length on a sunbed on the starboard deck, Elianne said, 'We used to have a sailboat in Beirut, had a lot of fun on her, I remember.' Then turned her head to follow the flight of a gull heading out to sea.

'Not now, though?' Leaning on the rail alongside her Jenner had been enjoying looking at her for the last few minutes. Her long-limbed, golden-skinned body entranced him. At night he dreamed of it beneath his own, skin-to-skin close and wildly exciting.

'No, not now.' The gull had settled on the water, so carefully shutting away memories she turned her head to him, thinking again as he smiled down at her what a mixed-up but basically good and interesting young guy he was.

Jenner looked away, wishing that like her, he had brothers or sisters but keeping the self-pity bottled up inside him and hating himself for it as he had always done.

'I'm glad I wasn't an only child,' she went on. 'Growing up with siblings gives one a lot of hard knocks, but it gives you such a lot of good things too…. Acts as a sort of bedrock, something you can stand on safely while you find out about life, I guess.' Then she smiled at him again. 'You must have been very lonely sometimes—'

'Alone *and* bloody lonely.' His interruption was bitter, but then abruptly both his body language and his voice changed entirely: straightening up, he smiled at her. 'That's why I went in with Robert and Blakey on this "adventure" thing they're into,' he said, a self-confidence in him she had never seen before. 'Robert asked me to join them and I find it … satisfying, somehow; they say they couldn't get on with it properly without what *I'm* doing for them. We're a team working together to get something done that *ought* to be done, something meaningful. And it's a great feeling, being part of it.' That said, he leaned back against the boat's rail, a little embarrassed by his own outburst.

'So what *is* it, this "thing" you're into with them?' Elianne was wide awake now and, sensing she was about to discover something really important about Jenner she took the risk, and pressed him further. 'Whatever it is, Vince, do please share it with me. I feel close to you and you know you can trust me, trust me with anything …. And something which is as important to you as this obviously is, is important to me, too,' she ended, holding his eyes.

'D'you *mean* that? Really mean anything that matters to me, matters to you too?'

Smiling to him, 'I've always thought that lies between friends are a dreadful waste of time,' she said to him softly, then continued her pursuit of him. 'Is it subversion of some kind you and your mates are engaged in?' she asked, leading him on, sensing him vulnerable to her. 'Like I said, you can trust me, Vince; you know you can, in your heart. And I'm not judgemental about the way people I care for act and think about that sort of thing; if I like someone very much I don't care—'

'Elianne, Elianne! I'd trust you with *my life!*' Pushing himself away from the rail he reached down for her hands and pulled her up to stand close in front of him. 'I want so much for you to know me, to be part of my life. I've been wanting to tell you about all this for days. It's a kind of punitive action we're taking on, and it's good to know you're not judgemental about that sort of thing, it means I can talk freely to you. What we're now planning to do, it's not against Britain; it's against a man who, years ago now, committed a terrible injustice....'

A wonderful sense of having her approval blossomed in him and Jenner drew her to Mockingbird's seaboard side where there was nothing to look at but beautiful blue sea. He gave her Cold Call then. Not all of it, cut and dried, of course, not even the name of its target or where he lived, but enough to – as he saw it – enable her to understand that he, Vincent Jenner, was a man not afraid to take action to right perceived injustices.

When Elianne got back to her flat in Lime Tree Road from the afternoon aboard Mockingbird, it was nearly midnight. Hoping Matt Locksley would be at home, she went straight up to her bedroom, dropped her hold-all on the floor then sat down on the bed and called him.

'Locksley.'

'Matt! Matt, thank God you're there.' His voice immediately eased the nervous tension which had consumed her since Jenner had let down the barriers guarding his secret. 'Can we talk for a bit? You're not busy or … anything?'

'No, I'm not busy or – anything,' he answered mildly, guessing she had added the last word because it had suddenly occurred to her that he might at that time of the night be entertaining a lady friend. 'I'm alone in my sitting-room enjoying a whisky-soda. I'd be delighted to talk.'

'Listen—' But she broke off, engulfed by fear again. 'Is your phone … I mean, can I speak freely? There're things I have to tell you that are to do with terrorism.'

'It's safe for you to tell me anything, my phone's secure. Elianne, you sound … are you all right?'

'It's OK, I just … You see, there are things I've only just learned and it took me back to Beirut, to activities I never thought I'd find

127

here in England.' Then she went on, her voice suddenly self-accusing, 'I realise that's stupid and blind of me, knowing what Britain's suffered.'

'Never mind that. Tell me what you've found out.'

'I went sailing with Jenner, he's got a boat down on the south coast. He and I … well, we get on well, he likes me because he finds me easy to talk to, about himself, I mean. Other girls he knows find him boring, at least he thinks they do; he told me that on our second date so I always make sure he's sure I don't. Don't find him boring, I mean—'

'Relax. Just tell me what you got out of him today.'

Because it was Matt Locksley she was talking to, Elianne became her usual, quietly-spoken self and was able to carry on more coherently.

'Jenner told me that he, Robert Daley, his mother Rose Daley and a young man they call "Blakey" are engaged, and I quote, "In a hit that's Rose Daley's revenge on a man, a retired judge, who—"'

'Why the hell is he telling you these things?' Incredulity was making him angry.

'Because he wants me to understand why he's in it with them! Don't you see, Matt? Jenner's a loner who doesn't want to be one! He longs to be a member of some group that actually *does* things to put right what they see as being wrong—'

'It massages his ego,' he cut in.

'In a way, yes, I suppose so,' she said soberly. 'But there's more to tell you, Matt, dear Matt. And it's worse. Jenner is aiming to move higher than personal stuff like revenge on this judge. His ambition is to belong to a major terrorist organization active in Britain, and he told me Daley and his mother are members of such a terrorist cadre presently engaged in a mission called Wayfarer that's actually in progress here, *now*!'

'So Jenner does the little op with Robert and Co. in the hope that after it's done he'll get recommended by them to the big group as a promising recruit?'

'*Yes*! And apparently this small operation – he said it's code-named Cold Call – has to be kept secret from the people running the big one—'

'It would be, because if the Daleys were found out to be running a secret, personally motivated mission *at the same time* as being involved in a major operation, there'd be hell to pay; it's a cardinal sin in their book. But, Elianne, it's that big op we have to concentrate on now,' he went on, his tone curt as the wider implications of what the girl had told him coalesced into a series of priorities in his mind. 'We have to get to work on it at once, find out its dates, targets, nature of action—'

'Stop it, Matt, *please*!' In her bedroom she was on her feet, the words he was throwing at her were awakening frightful memories.

He intuited it. 'Sorry, Elianne, forgive me,' he entreated with soft urgency. 'I shouldn't have gone for it like that, forgive me. I take your hand in mine and beg you to forgive this miserable, clod-hopping, insignificant specimen of humanity you are kind enough to call your friend.'

As he fell silent a thin, breathy half-laugh came to him along the line and then,

'"You sorry – me sorry – all well now,"' she whispered to him, and the little joke mantra which had come into being between them months ago now re-established ease and trust between them.

'Elianne, listen. What you've discovered is almost certainly terrorist activity here on a scale we've been unaware of. So, I'm asking you, are you willing to go on with this, to find out for us more about it? It's a lot to ask. Bear in mind that as you delve deeper into the plans of these two operations, via the services of Mr Jenner, those who are active in them may become suspicious of you and may—'

'I know what you mean, Matt. I grew up with this sort of stuff, you don't have to spell it out to me. And Jenner ... he would never do, or be part of, anything that might harm me, I'm sure of that.... But Blakey, I don't know about him, of course, I only know him by sight.'

'And Robert Daley?'

'Hussain Rashid Shalhoub.' She gave the name weight, then went on quietly. 'As for him, I have to make sure he doesn't come to suspect me. I shall go on keeping out of his way.'

'Make *sure* he has no reason to suspect you,' he said sharply, trying to hide his fears for her safety. 'Just be careful,' he added quietly after a moment, her silence making him regret his asperity. 'When we go to Hermit's Hill on Sunday we'll have plenty of time to talk this over.... Pick you up around ten?'

'That would be lovely, Matt.' But then, 'That second, big mission. When Jenner told me it was code-named Wayfarer, he was very annoyed with himself that he had. But he couldn't take it back, could he, the thing was done.'

'It's worth knowing that he was aware he ought to have kept it to himself.... About the other one, Cold Call: revenge for Rose Daley, you said it was, and not a big operation. So might they be gunning for this retired judge? Straight murder?'

After a brief pause, 'I don't know. Maybe. But I suspect it may not be as simple as that, so straightforward – that's just a feeling, though. I don't have any facts to base it on.'

'How d'you mean, a "feeling"?'

Again that pause before she answered. Then, 'Don't read too much into this, Matt, but I got the impression that Jenner doesn't like what Cold Call's making him do. It's almost as if ... as if he's *ashamed* to be doing it and—'

'He'll have to grow out of that sort of thing if he's hoping to go into grand scale terrorism!' Locksley observed drily. 'Why should he feel himself shamed by getting into it, I wonder? You must know him pretty well by now, any ideas?'

But he had lost her: his sarcastic remark had made her protective of Jenner. 'No,' she said stiffly. 'Vince and I .... He's a complicated, introverted, somehow very *young* young man, and I don't think it's easy to get to know him, to really know him.'

Soberly, Locksley sought to mend fences. 'I spoke out of turn there,' he said. 'In my experience I've found that the psyche of the majority of terrorists is clear black-and-white, but I have to say that I've interrogated several whose rationale for what they're engaged in is frighteningly ... well, confused. And Elianne, that might prove useful to us: from what you've told me Jenner seems to fall into that second category and, therefore, he's likely to be more *accessible* to you.... You're ready to make use of that accessibility, are you?'

'Through him, I'll bring Robert Daley to justice,' she said sharply – then gave a quick little laugh and added, 'With a little help from my friends over here, that is.'

Elianne ended her call then. Switched off her mobile and sat quiet on her bed, thinking over all that had just passed between herself and Matt Locksley of British Intelligence. After a few minutes she smiled to herself.

'The only thing is, Matt,' she whispered to her quiet, well-ordered bedroom, '*my* idea of what constitutes justice for the man who gunned down my brothers in cold blood is not at all the same as yours.'

2 July

Cold Call's personnel always varied the location of their regular meetings. This day, they met in a sparsely furnished back room in the house of one of Rose Daley's sleepers in Balham. Rose, clad in a trouser suit of taupe linen, sat at the head of the centrally placed square table there, Blake facing her across it, her son Robert to her right and Jenner on her left. She opened proceedings without preamble.

'Cold Call continues on schedule to climax on 14th August,' she began crisply. 'We shall—'

'Isn't our bomb-maker attending today?' The interruption from Blake was quiet but incisive as he leaned back in his chair and looked her in the eye. He had no time for Robert's mother; he called her a "bossy, vain, stuck-up bitch" to the others, excluding Robert.

He was unaware at that time that her son agreed with him and strongly resented his mother's assumption of authority over him.

'No, he is not. He called me this morning giving his apologies. Since his part in the operation is relatively passive, and he assured me that his preparations are complete, I excused him.' She stared Blake down, then turned away and continued with her agenda. 'As you know, I despatched observers to Oakchurch village to monitor and keep me informed on progress in the police investigation into the murder earlier this year on Martindale's property. To date, they report the case has stalled for lack of evidence, with rival criminal gangs still suspected of the crime. But no proof has been forthcoming.'

'Which suits us just fine,' Robert remarked as she paused.

'Nevertheless, it would have been better for us if no murder had occurred on Martindale's land. Police activity there has inconvenienced us from time to time; luckily, no more than that.'

Her son smiled at her and said nothing more. Privately, he congratulated himself again on keeping her and his mates ignorant of the fact that it was he who had carried out that murder.

Rose turned to Jenner: she valued his contribution to Cold Call, but also found him vaguely irritating because he seemed so introverted and too slow to make decisions, always wanting to talk things through exhaustively – and then through again.

'I found your report on the general situation at Martindale's house excellent,' she said to his dark, handsome face, then with a look which included the others, continued. 'From Jenner's take on the situation there I see no reason for any alteration to our plans for Cold Call's climax,' she said to them. 'To summarize those: Jenner will be on watch outside Oakdene that afternoon, Robert and Blake gain entrance to the house around 13.30, by which time Mr and Mrs Martindale and their four grandchildren will be absent from the house—'

'It's definitely decided that they will leave mid-morning,' Jenner put in. 'Charlotte Grover has instructions to remain in the house until they return, which will be around six o'clock....'

'Amazing, what a young, handsome bloke with an equally hand-some bank balance can achieve.' Robert whispered the aside out of the corner of his mouth to Blake, sitting next to him.

Smirking, 'That's jealousy speaking, pure male jealousy,' Blake murmured back.

'… Blake then engages the attention of the housekeeper down-stairs while Robert places the bombs upstairs, setting the timers for 01.00 hours as he does so.' Rose sat back, a small, closed smile on her beautifully made-up face.

Robert turned to look straight at his mother. 'I'll place those four bombs just the way you want them, one directly beneath where each kid's head will lie,' he said to her softly, aware that she would never tire of hearing accounts of her planned revenge on Anthony Martindale. Then because he knew she had searched out photographs of Martindale and his grandchildren at the village fête that year which had been printed in the local newspaper he added, 'There won't be any pictures of his pretty grand-kids in the press after that day.'

Satiated, Rose Daley sat forward again and, somewhat perfunc-torily now, dealt with the remaining agenda then ended the meeting.

As the young men stood up and gathered together their various belongings, Jenner edged round the table to Robert who was still standing by his chair. Keeping his back to Rose.

'Rob,' he said quietly, 'how's it going with the thing about me working with you afterwards? You bringing me to the attention of Abu Yusuf, the commander in charge of Wayfarer?'

'Watch it, Vince,' Robert muttered angrily, 'You know Wayfarer's supposed to be secret even from Cold Call's agents so shut up about it when my mother's around, you fucking well *know* that.' Then looking over Jenner's shoulder he saw that Rose was already at the door; she couldn't possibly have heard what Jenner had said so, turning his back on Jenner he followed Rose out. But he was furious with himself for ever mentioning Wayfarer to Jenner – this was the third time he'd done that. However, Rose would never find out he'd done so: only he and Jenner knew – and with Jenner being Jenner, who the fuck else would he get to talk about such things with? It wouldn't be the sort of thing the lovely Charlotte would be interested in, would it....

5 July

As Elianne had already explained to Jenner, the Lebanese Club was simply a fairly small purpose-built hall with cloakrooms to right and left of the door as one went in and a bar across one of the far corners. Situated in the spacious grounds of the residence of a wealthy Lebanese businessman, it was invisible from the house, and was approached along a single-track road leading in from the side of the property. As Jenner followed her inside he felt pleasingly – and for him unusually – 'at home' there within minutes of looking around him.

'It seems so ... so welcoming,' he said to her. The ambience of the place was already seducing him, he felt at ease there in a way that was new to him and which gladdened his heart: its colours were light and friendly, its chairs richly upholstered in rose red, with walls and curtains in pale greens and cream. There were several small round tables of polished wood in the softly lit bar and, although there were people everywhere, it felt uncrowded and everyone looked happy in each others' company.

'The bar serves coffee and tea at one end,' Elianne said, then smiled as he turned to her. 'But now I'd like us to share a bottle of Lebanese wine, and tonight you're my guest so I'll order my favourite, a white Ksara – if the idea pleases you?'

'Elianne, whatever you choose would be fine with me.'

It was to be "Elianne's evening". 'It'll be a thank-you for all the lovely times you've been giving me, Vince,' she had told him the day before, 'I'd like you to meet some of my friends.' They had met at six-thirty, eaten pizza and salad at Mitzi's, a small restaurant nearby and now she was introducing him to the Lebanese Club as her guest. He had asked her whether these friends of hers would be Muslim, or Christian like she was, and she had laughed and said, 'Some are one, some the other, so it will be interesting to see if, after you've met them and spent a little time with them, you can tell me which is which.'

"Elianne's evening" went well; her friends welcomed him into the gaiety they were making together. He met four of them that night, two young men with their girlfriends; Jenner enjoyed their company very much, but for him the best part of the evening came much later....

It was around ten o'clock when he collected a tray of coffee-for-two at the bar and followed Elianne to a sofa in a secluded corner at the back of the main hall. In the course of their conversation over the next hour she discovered two new facts that she tucked away carefully in her memory, to be relayed to Matt Locksley next day. First, that Cold Call was scheduled to take place some time during the coming August; second, that Damon Ashford, Robert Daley's third friend in the group was, for the duration of his student days, living in a small but very well-appointed bungalow his parents had had built for him at the bottom of their extensive garden....

Leaving the club at eleven-thirty Jenner drove Elianne home, parking his Porsche as he had become accustomed to doing after they had spent an evening together, alongside the secluded spinney at one end of Lime Tree road. The last three times he had done so they had kissed goodnight standing on the grassy verge there; however, that night was different. After the first kiss they leaned apart still holding each other, and he smoothed the palm of his hand over her breast then gently caressed her nipples. Feeling them respond to his touch, he murmured, 'Oh, Elianne.' Then he tore his hand away and crushed her to him fiercely, his face pressed into her black fragrant hair. 'Forgive me,' he whispered to her. 'I shouldn't have but ... Oh Elianne, please forgive, *please*....'

How very refreshing it is to find a young man who isn't convinced he's God's gift to women, she thought, her eyes tracing shapes and shadows amongst the birch trees of the spinney behind them as the breeze danced among the leaves. Then she held him to her a moment longer before pulling away.

'Nothing to forgive,' she said to him quietly, looking into his eyes unsmiling and thinking, Jenner's truly mine now so providing I play him right and carefully I'll be able to use him as I wish. 'By asking for forgiveness you've made what you did a lovely thing.' And turning away then she walked along the road to the flat she shared with Roz Hunt and let herself in, closing the door behind her.

Sitting in the kitchen over a glass of orange juice Elianne thought over all she had learned from Jenner that evening about Robert Daley and his involvement in both Cold Call and the operation called Wayfarer.

I will tell Matt almost everything I have learned about both operations, but I have to begin keeping small facts from him at once. When I call him tomorrow I'll tell him everything Vince told me tonight – except for one thing. I will *not* tell him anything more about this fellow student called Damon Ashford who is a close friend to Daley, but does not know anything at all about his being a terrorist. That knowledge must stay my secret: little things like that may enable me to take Robert Daley's blood before the British counter-terrorist forces arrest him when they strike against Wayfarer.

During the week commencing 7 July, Abu Yusuf made four separate train journeys out from London terminals to check for himself the logistics and general fitness-for-purpose of each of Wayfarer's target trains and rail stations. They were: Rugby, Exeter, Brighton and Southend. To each of them he took a train scheduled to arrive there close to 11.30. At each, he spent an afternoon and evening visiting his agents and sleepers in that area to receive their latest reports and confirmation that, in his or her particular sphere of observation, all preparations were going according to plan. At each, he stayed overnight in some small local hotel, completed his check-up visits during the following morning then returned to London in the afternoon. As a mission commander credited among his peers with being a hands-on operator (except at the sharp end of suicide missions, as one of those peers had cynically commented behind his back) he made a point of familiarizing himself with the layout of each station involved and the various amenities it provided for travellers.

On Sunday 15 July at 17.00 hours, he walked into the café at Exeter station, bought himself a cup of coffee at the service bar then carried it across to a small table on the far side of the room and sat down there. His train back to London was not due to depart until 17.45 so he had no need to hurry. Loosening his jacket he looked around him. The whole place was busy, the bar-counter thronged with people and the tables nearly all full and a constant coming and going of travellers.... He sipped his coffee, grimaced in revulsion and replaced cup in saucer, reflecting that in the matter of making coffee the English had never emerged from the Dark Ages.... His tour of Wayfarer's targets was now complete, and at all four of them he had found everything in good order for the success of the mission: there had been no potential difficulties to overcome or alterations to be made to the operational schedules.

'Would you mind if I sat down here?' The tall, middle-aged man asking the question was standing facing him with one hand on the back of the empty chair across the table. He was smartly suited and his voice and manner were polite and amiable. 'I've just missed my usual train home, so as I've half an hour to kill I'd appreciate a little casual conversation with an intelligent fellow human being.'

Abu Yusuf stared him coldly in the eye. 'Go away,' he said brusquely. 'It is not my habit to converse with total strangers. I doubt your conversation would be of any interest to me.'

The hand was removed from the back of the chair, voice and manner stiffened. 'I apologize, sir,' the stranger said, carefully cour-teous, his eyes hard as ice. 'I'll leave you to enjoy your own company. I wish you a pleasant journey. Good day.' He did not relish the prospect of reporting failure to his paymaster Khaled Ras, but he knew how to deal with rude rebuff.

Abu Yusuf watched him walk away and out of the café. Slightly surprised at his own discourtesy he put it down to bad temper brought on by foul-tasting coffee and returned his mind to operation Wayferer's overall strategy.

'Mrs Daley? Is that you?'

Rose never gave her name immediately on answering the phone. 'Who is calling?' she asked, though she did not really need to, she had recognized his voice.

'Vincent Jenner,' he answered, then rushed on nervously, fearing she might be annoyed at his presumption in phoning her. It was a Cold Call rule that ancillary personnel were barred from initiating contact with their commander except in an emergency. 'I apologize—'

'You have sufficient reason to call me?'

'Yes, ma'm—'

'Then state it, Jenner.'

'Ma'm, I ... I wanted to ask permission to visit you as I have information that ... that it is better to give to you in person and in private. I think you ought to know it, but it's sensitive—'

'Relevant to me in what way?'

There came a brief pause; then, hesitantly, 'It's about that murder at Oakdene, on Martindale's property—'

'Stop there, Jenner. Come to my flat immediately. How long will it take you to get here?'

'I have my car, ma'am, I can be there in fifteen minutes—'

'I shall expect you in that time.' She cut the call, then stood staring out of her sitting-room bay window, frowning.

'Jenner? What the hell did he want?' Sprawled at one end of the sofa off to one side of her, Robert looked up from the newspaper he had been glancing through.

'He says he has information about the murder at Oakdene.' She did not turn round as she answered him; she was recalling

Martindale's house and lovingly cared-for property. She had been there just once, choosing a day when she was sure the retired judge and his wife would be out (their daily routine easily available to her through Jenner, via his girlfriend Charlotte Grover). The desire to go there had been overwhelming: she had to see with her own eyes the house where, at long last, her visceral hatred of Martindale would have its cataclysmic resolution, blasted to pieces like the four children who were the living heart of the judge's life. Driving down there one afternoon back in May, she had told the pretty girl who opened Oakdene's door to her that she had an appointment with 'Mrs Richards' – only to be informed, of course, that no lady of that name resided there.... In her mind's eye she visualized the house dark and still, at peace in the gentle night – then suddenly its upstairs bedroom windows explode in fire and searing heat and shrieking terror.

'D'you know, I believe you'd like to *be there* when those kids of Martindale's get blown to bits, you'd enjoy actually seeing it happen.' Robert was on his feet and walking towards her, half smiling. He had never fully understood why his mother's hatred of Martindale was so all consuming. Drawing level with her he spoke quietly to her averted head. 'You've never told me exactly what it was your mother did that put her up before Martindale,' he said to her, sensing her vulnerable in a way he had never experienced before and seizing on it, intent on exploiting it to his own advantage.

Rose turned to her son. 'Why do you want to know?'

He held her eyes. 'It's *you* I want to know.'

Swinging round to look out of the window again, she told him then. She didn't see the road outside her London flat as she spoke, she was recalling past events which had, later, shaped her life.

'It was 1976 and my father had been dead a year, shot in an attack on a British watch-tower. My mother vowed to take the life of a British soldier in payment for her husband's life, as was her right. She set her cap at one particular young rifleman who had taken part in fighting off the attack my father was killed in.... She was quite beautiful, Caitlin, which helped, of course....

'How did she do it?' Watching her, he saw her hands, hanging loosely at her sides, clench slowly into white-knuckled fists.

'Enticement. She lured him to her.... She'd moved in with a non-political family elsewhere and was pretending hatred of the IRA, pretending she blamed *them* for her husband's death. Using their house as her base she visited certain nearby pubs, got to know this British soldier and then, one night when the family had all gone on holiday, and she and the soldier had eaten out together, she promised him sex in her bedroom. But as soon as he was inside the house she shot him with my father's gun. She shot him in the shoulder....'

Rose fell silent and watching her in profile, Robert saw her tilt her chin up and close her eyes. She was 'living' what had happened in the house that night, between her mother and the British soldier she had lured there; and, as he realized this he felt – briefly – closer to her than he ever had before.

'Go on,' he said. 'There's more to it, isn't there.'

Rose opened her eyes and faced her son. 'Caitlin knew none of her friends would come visiting during the small hours of the night,' she said, her voice as untroubled as a sunlit summer sea. 'She took her time over that killing, and I had it from her own lips that she enjoyed every minute of it.'

'But – they got her for it.' Which in his eyes equated with failure.

'Oh no. It wasn't like that.' With a grimace of triumph, Rose shook her head. 'Caitlin gave herself up to the police next day, and when she was brought to trial she didn't deny any of it.... And Martindale jailed her for life.'

'And she died in prison.' Mother and son were enclosed in a small, tightly defined world of their own peopled by her memories.

After a moment, Rose broke the silence. 'And quite soon, she escaped them,' she said. 'She took her own life.'

'Surely that was difficult?' Startled, he stared at her, frowning. 'She'd have been watched—'

'I helped her....' Rose smiled to herself, remembering. 'Caitlin was very strong in herself. That was the first time in my life she'd allowed me to help her in any way, any meaningful way; so when she asked me – begged me – I was happy to help her do what she wanted to do.'

'How, though? In that situation?'

Rose told him then; told him the secret which, until that moment, she had confided to no other person.

'It took time; a long time. I got the drug in powder form – the IRA helped with that, it could be obtained in powder form and they had contacts for that sort of thing as well as for Semtex. Then I sealed minute quantities of the stuff into thin, flat plastic sachets and stitched those loosely into the clothes I wore to visit her – into the cuffs of blouses, the front of the waistbands of skirts, any place I could slip them out of when I visited her, just one at a time…. So, Caitlin died one night: died at a time of her own choosing and so escaped them….' Then quietly, after a pause, 'Would you do for me what I did for her, Robert?' she asked him, voice whisper-thin, her eyes brilliant, gazing into his. 'If it ever comes to it, will you do that for me?'

Meeting them, he saw that she was certain he would agree to do whatever she asked of him – and on the realization he tore himself free of her remembered world. Stepped back from her. 'No, I will not,' he said deliberately, a kind of triumph in him. 'That's a coward's way out—'

'*Shut your mouth!*' Striking cobra-fast she hit him hard across the face, a swingeing, flat-handed blow that caught him across the cheek as he jerked aside to avoid it. Then she controlled herself; stood stiff, her head up. 'Get out. You'll take that word back and apologize to me for using it before you enter my house again.'

Turning on his heel Robert left without a word. As he opened the front door of the building he found Vincent Jenner on the step.

'She's in a foul mood,' he warned him with a faint grin. 'I just said the wrong thing at the wrong time to her.'

'Personal trouble, or Cold Call?'

'Personal. Nothing I can't handle, though.' Robert was already restored to his usual self-confident self. 'I'll give it a bit of time, then say I'm sorry.... Don't worry, Vince; she'll come round. She needs me more than I need her at the moment, I'm lead man in Cold Call and she knows that if I walk out on her I'll take you and Blakey with me.' Then punching Jenner lightly on the shoulder he walked on past him, out into the street.

Rose recovered her composure as fast as her son had done. When Jenner went in on hearing her call 'Enter' in response to his diffident knock, he found her sitting on the sofa, straight-backed, hard faced.

She did not invite him to sit down. Regarding him coldly as he came towards her, she left him standing when he halted in front of her, remarked that he had taken longer than he had said to get to her, then told him to give her the new information he had regarding the murder at Oakdene.

'I was at Oakchurch village yesterday,' he began, 'and in the evening Charlotte Grover and I—'

'What did you get out of her that we do not already know?'

So Jenner got to the point. 'There's a strong rumour going round the village that the police have matched the DNA of the man who carried out the murder that night,' he said.

'Is that all?' She was frowning.

Unnerved by her hostile regard and seeming lack of interest in his news, he looked down. 'Well, ma'am, we had to call off our surveillance of Oakdene for nearly a month after the killing and we still take extra precautions in case the police return, so I thought ... well, it'll be a lot better for us if the murderer is caught before the climax of Cold Call, and if they've got his DNA—'

'It is a point, yes,' she conceded.

'If it's really true it will open up a whole new field in the investigation, I imagine.'

'Obviously.... Your contact down there, is she as it were level-headed, or is she the sort who would exaggerate what she's heard so as to make a good story of it to keep you interested?'

'I pressed her about the rumour – not too much, of course, in case she starts to wonder why I'm always so interested in what's going on at Oakdene – and I think the police really do have that DNA.... And with respect, ma'am, Charlotte is not stupid,' he added, gearing himself up to give the answer because it was true and because his feeling of guilt at deceiving Charlotte the way he was made him want to defend her against Rose Daley.

'I'm glad for your sake that she isn't.' Faintly smiling, Rose got to her feet. 'See yourself out, Jenner. Thank you for your information, it is indeed worth knowing.'

Actually, however, she dismissed Jenner's news as irrelevant. And, disappointed by her cool reception of his information, Jenner also came to the conclusion that the fact was merely incidental as far as Cold Call was concerned and for this reason he did not bother to pass it on to Robert Daley or Blakey.

11 July

It was early evening as Locksley sprawled at his ease in a cushioned chair at the far end of Charles Gray's lawn. Life doesn't get much better than this, he thought lazily.

'His grass needs cutting.' The words came from the other side of the cedar-wood table between him and Elianne. She gave him a careful smile, her mind on other things as she continued. 'I promised to do it for him so I should get started, I guess.'

'Very bad for grass, I've heard, to cut it before the sun's below the yardarm ... or something like that,' he murmured, eyes half closed against the brilliance of the sky. 'Don't cut grass, stay and talk to me.... Tell me about the flowers of Lebanon,' he invited, thinking to please her, she usually loved to reminisce about her home country.

But intuition had failed him, straightening in her chair she looked around her and after a moment said coldly, 'I think all Lebanon's flowers must be dying out. I had a letter from Katie this morning.'

Keeping his movements very steady, Locksley too sat up; glanced at her. 'What was in the letter?'

'I didn't mean to tell you, but now I find I want to. It's Nadia, Katie's friend Nadia. You've heard me talk about her – Nadia Shasri and her husband Ramadan, and their son Naseem.'

'Yes, I have,' he said, feeling his skin crawl as he remembered.

'I didn't know Nadia well, she was more Katie's friend than mine, but Katie used to talk a lot about her, then as we got older about her husband and son – and now Ramadan and little Naseem, they've both been killed by terrorists, Matt! They held the two of them hostage to get Ramadan home from the school he teaches at, then they told him he was a traitor and shot him dead. Naseem, as well.' Falling silent Elianne looked away at nothing in particular. After a few moments turned again to Locksley, stared him in the eye. 'If you're wondering why they should do that to a boy of five I'll save you the bother of asking: the terrorist who killed him feared that when the boy came of age he would make it his business to find out who had murdered his father, then set out to kill him in revenge.'

'You can't know the gunman would think that way.'

'Katie said she heard the gunman say words which meant just that.' But then quickly her eyelids slid down to hide her anger: blood for blood was the very ethos which, God willing, she herself would put into practice as soon as opportunity came ... Sitting in cool evening sunshine with Matt Locksley close to her yet unaware of what she was thinking, Elianne felt a chill of loneliness she had never known before: she realized that the love she already felt for Matt would never flower into sexual love and that they would never know the marvellous one-ness which comes when spirit and body combine as she had seen happen between Katie and Marcus.

'Elianne, does what happened to Nadia's husband and son make you afraid? Afraid that someone might find out about you and Jenner and come after you on account of this operation Cold Call?' he asked. Then, after a pause, he smiled grimly and phrased it more honestly. 'What I really mean is, do you want to stop helping me find out about Daley and his activities—'

'No!' She cut in hard, leaning across the table towards him, her face suddenly fierce with anger and determination. 'No, Matt, *no*! Never that! I want Daley' – she almost said dead, but managed to bite her tongue in time – 'brought to justice,' she went on carefully 'and I want to be a part of that process. I will get more out of Jenner,' she went on, quite quietly now. 'He is vulnerable to me, I believe he'll tell me more yet.'

'He doesn't suspect? He trusts you?'

She nodded. 'Yes, he does. Because he's falling in love with me. I'm leading him on and....' But her voice trailed away into silence, she looked down.

So after a moment, 'Are you ashamed to be doing that?' he asked.

'Ashamed? Why on earth should I be? Given who he works with and what they're planning, why in God's name should I be ashamed?' Then she laid both hands flat on the table and looked across at him. 'I'd do anything, anything at all, to help you bring Robert Daley to justice,' she said to him. '*Anything at all*,' she repeated; and to herself she added, But then I'll kill him before British justice steals him from me.

'You seem more committed than ever.' There was something about her that – now, quite suddenly – began to disturb him.

Quick thinking provided her with an answer. 'It's because of this terrible thing with Nadia Shasri. I don't know what it was that her husband was doing or had done, but to be executed—'

'Does Nadia know?' He was careful to keep the urgency out of his voice.

'Katie says not. Says, too, that's making it all harder for her.'

'Leave it now, Elianne.' But I'm lying to her, Locksley thought in anguish. It may only be lying by omission, but that doesn't exculpate me since for her the result's the same. Nevertheless, I have to do it: this thing's likely to be far bigger than either of us....

So he put to her the idea he had been considering. 'You know, there *is* a way you can do more for me with Jenner: something which will enable me to get *on record* information which may give the case a higher priority and get more personnel allocated.'

'If I can do it, I will.'

'I need what Jenner's telling you *on tape*, otherwise it's only hearsay and doesn't have the necessary clout. So I'd like you, when you're with him, to wear a "doctored" brooch I can provide you with: it's crafted to contain a high-tech miniature microphone and recording device. At the back of it, close to the pin, there's a tiny switch to give you "on" and "off" control, you can activate it when you've steered the conversation to Daley and these operations he's involved in.'

'When can I have it?' she asked, her face tight with resolve.

You're *obsessed* with this whole thing, my love, aren't you? Locksley thought (accepting the truth behind those two little words of endearment then blanking them out of his mind). Reaching out, he took her hand.

'How soon will you be able to use it?' he asked.

'Tomorrow morning.' Her tone matched his in intensity. 'You understand, with Jenner I only have to suggest we meet and do something together and he agrees, asks me out to dinner, the theatre, whatever I want.' Turning her hand under his she clasped it firmly, as one making a pact. 'I'll call him later tonight, arrange to meet him tomorrow morning.'

'So shall I send the brooch to your place by secure messenger, to arrive between nine-thirty and ten o'clock? Will that be OK?'

She nodded. 'And I'll call you as soon as I get anything of interest from him.'

Bound together by their unity of purpose – the destruction of the terrorist Robert Daley – they sat a moment longer, hand clasped to hand, their eyes locked showing their sharply focussed commitment.

Then withdrawing her hand from his, Elianne Asley sat back and gazed around her as the tension between them died away.

'Grass still needs cutting,' Locksley remarked, carefully light-hearted.

'Are you volunteering?' She was quick to follow his lead in scrambling back to safer topics, away from the dark heart of terrorism and the need – the imperative – to confront it when ever one was given the chance.

'Not me.' Standing up he stretched, then faced her and grinned, ran a hand through his tousled hair. 'It's Charles's grass, Charles cuts it,' he said. 'My idea is, you stay where you are and look beautiful while I fetch wine and glasses, then together we drink and watch the sun go down.'

She laughed, said what a good idea that was, then watched him walk away across lawn, over the terrace and in through the French doors. Both sensed that there had been a sea-change that evening in their relationship, but neither was aware of certain facts that the other had kept secret.

CHAPTER 8

12 July

Abu Yusuf was a well-respected member of the community he lived within as a successful businessman: an executive director with an import/export company based in East London. He gave regularly and generously to three charitable institutions, attended prayers as laid down for all 'true believers'. He was a member of two local organizations, one dedicated to aiding the poor among them, the other political, its stated aim to promote nationwide 'harmonious understanding between different religions and cultures'. He lived a blameless private life, maintaining in suitable comfort a household composed of a devout and strictly home-based wife, three male and two female children now all in their teens, together with a large number of retainers and domestic staff who ministered to the family's respective needs. By its nature his business necessitated frequent, sometimes week-long absences from home. During these he based himself in a privately owned service flat in Tottenham Court Road, but spent most of his time in one or other of the safe houses maintained in the capital by his parent terrorist organization.

On this Saturday afternoon, for his meeting with Khaled Ras he drove out to a safe house south of the city, a pleasant detached dwelling owned and lived in for many years by Said Hassan, a Jordanian and one of the longest serving sleepers in his organization. Hassan had placed his study at the disposal of the commander of Operation Wayfarer, a project of which he himself knew nothing. Overlooking the drive the room was sumptuously furnished, its rugs and carpets were especially beautiful.

Arriving around midday Abu Yusuf had lunch with Hassan and his wife – his second wife, a sophisticated lady twenty years younger than him who was au courant with his undercover subversive activities. At two o'clock, the time at which Ras had been ordered to present himself, he repaired to the study, sat down at the antique oak table alongside the window overlooking the drive and set out on its polished surface the three files he would need for the meeting.

A little after two, Khaled Ras was shown into the study. This safe house was already known to him from previous visits so, greeting Abu Yusuf as he went, he strode over to the chair facing his commander across the table, sat down in it and extracted a sheaf of papers from his black briefcase. Setting them down in front of him he looked up expectantly.

'What shall I report on first, sir?' he enquired. His Arabic was tainted to Abu Yusuf's ears by his time in tribal areas of Afghanistan when he was in his mid-twenties. It was at this period in Ras's life that terrorist act as gratuitously brutal as it was courageous had brought him to the attention of certain movers-and-shakers in the world of international terrorism; they saw promise in his fervent savagery and, enlisting him in their forces, gave him the opportunity to practise his undoubted talents in a wider field of conflict wherein they could be developed to their full potential.

'I'll take the sleepers' reports on the situation at each of our martyrs' target stations first,' Yusuf answered.

Ras had no need to refer to his paperwork, Wayfarer's action and its progress were all clear and ordered inside his head, he lived them through each evening in the silence of his mind.

'With the exception of Southend the situation at all stations of importance to us remains unchanged apart from minor, quickly resolved local staffing problems that have no bearing on our plans,' he said, his guttural voice a kind of challenge to the expensive elegance of Said Hassan's study.

'So – Southend?'

'Last Saturday there was some sort of "war" between two local gangs, it originated at the station and the platform amenities were trashed. All is now back to normal and local informants say there will be several weekends of peace before tensions reach breaking point again. That gives us a time-scale which leaves Wayfarer unaffected.'

'So all is well.' Yusuf nodded, thinly smiling. He then opened a file in front of him. Unlike the others it had a hard cover: white in colour, this had a surah from the Holy Quran printed on it in black, the Arabic script was elegant, yet clear and bold, as suited the surah's content.

'The martyrs, Ras,' he said. 'I trust all are now well in body and steadfast in spirit?'

The Afghan's face had taken on a closed expression, however. Stiffening, he sat upright, dark and still, eyeing Yusuf.

'Mouchtar is troubled,' he reported harshly. 'The other three look only forward to Friday the 15th of August, as to a bright star in the firmament of their lives; their one desire is to bring about the deaths of the greatest possible number of infidels, the non-believers. Those three already have the glow of the martyr about them.'

'But Mouchter does not?' The question was put coldly for, although he used such men without mercy, Abu Yusuf had always considered fanatics too time-wasting to be indulged unless doing so served a specific purpose: he made use of Ras's fervour, but when it flowered into words it bored him.

'Mouchtar has been destabilised by news from home.' Ras's austere face was forbidding. He wanted to point out that it had been on Yusuf's own order that Wayfarer's suicide bombers had been allowed to receive one letter a fortnight from their families during their final training period – he himself had asked for a total ban on such an arrangement. It took Ras some effort to restrain himself, he was aware that Yusuf's post-Wayfarer reports on his captains would influence their future progress within the organization.

'His favourite brother has been killed in a so-called road accident,' he went on, 'and this has ... distracted his mind from the duty he has committed himself to.'

Yusuf frowned. 'I will converse with him personally in private and bring him back to the realities of his situation,' he said curtly. 'Arrange it for tomorrow morning, safe house Nine.'

'Sir, I can correct him myself, save you the time.'

'And how would you do that? I remember the boy; he needs careful handling.'

Leaning towards him across the table, 'I would speak to him thus,' Ras answered, his eyes narrowed, afire with grim intolerance. '"What would you say to your father and your four remaining brothers, Mouchtar, should you return to your family and tell them you ... you *what*? What words would you use, Mouchtar, to explain away the shame you will have brought upon them? The soul-searing, undying shame that will make every member of your family despised and loathed for generations to come?".'

'His father would of course kill him—'

'His father would have to fight his own sons for the honour of doing that. Which is a fact I would point out to him.'

For a moment Yusuf held Ras's eyes; then he sat back, already decided to move on to affairs closer to his own interests. 'Correct Mouchtar along those lines, then,' he ordered curtly. 'Now, turn your mind to the matter of the Daley woman. Have you succeeded in discovering evidence of her disloyalty to me?'

'Regrettably, none sufficient to warrant action against her on your part, sir. Information received from our Irish sources confirms that her mother died in prison while serving a sentence for—'

Yusuf gestured his impatience. 'Leave the woman's past life, Ras. Concentrate on her present and widen the net of investigation,' he ordered, then turned his attention to discussion of the general security of Wayfarer.

Returning to London, Khaled Ras wasted no time in 'widening the net' of his secret surveillance on Rose Daley.

12 July
18.00 hours.

There were no more than half a dozen other cars in the parking space at the Lebanese Club as Elianne slipped her apple-green KA in close to the club entrance. Grabbing her purse from the passenger seat she scrambled out – she was already fifteen minutes late, he might have left! She locked the car and ran for the front doors, sunshine everywhere as she ran across the tarmac, her black hair flying free on the summer breeze. She had chosen a sky-blue cotton blouse and a broad leather belt which cinched in her narrow waist....

To Vincent Jenner sitting waiting for her at a small table on the far side of the room she came in like a goddess, sunlight behind her and she hurrying towards him, her smile only for him. Plainly she was pleased to see him and, as he realized it, his heart sang. Last night beneath those trees near her house I caressed her breasts again, he thought – and he went to meet her, took her hand.

'I was afraid you weren't coming,' he said.

'Good,' she answered, laughing. 'It shows you care.'

'You know that already,' he said, wishing she had said 'love me' not just 'care'; having seen her seated in the chair facing his across the table, he asked her – since she had arranged honorary membership of the club for him – what she would like to drink.

'A glass of Ksara, please, Vince,' she said – as he had known she would. He'd learned on the first night they'd come to the club that it was her favourite wine and at that point it had become his, as well.

She watched him as he walked across to the bar, received his order then carried the two glasses of wine back to their table. She felt no guilt, now, for deceiving him, for setting out to enslave him in order to make use of him. It had been easy, so surprisingly easy: he was the perfect 'soft' catch, the 'dude' open to manipulation; through him, God willing, she would give her three brothers due vengeance on Robert Daley.

'Thanks,' she said as he placed her glass in front of her then sat down with his own. As she spoke her right hand moved up to fiddle with the square, quite large enamelled brooch pinned near the collar of her blouse, seeming to make sure it was securely fastened there.

Its colours were black, green and gold. 'That's an attractive brooch you're wearing,' he said, 'I haven't seen it before.'

'It was a present from my grandmother, years ago,' she lied coolly, 'and it's one of my favourite things. I thought I'd lost it, but last night it turned up again, I'd put it in the wrong drawer. I shall wear it often now, to make up for its months in the dark.'

Jenner raised his glass to her, and they drank a silent toast to each other. He was hoping she would go on telling him about her family; he longed to know everything there was to know about her. And he was filled with wonder and gratitude towards her for staying with him, for being interested in the life and thoughts of 'Vincent Jenner'. Never before had he spent time with a girl so ready, so eager to discuss 'life' and 'human values' as Elianne Asley was – and she understood his aspirations and his longing to be recruited into an organization that took action, that actually *did* something about what they believed in. In Elianne, it seemed to him he had – at last! – found a girl truly and deeply interested in such things. She always listened enthralled to his ideas and then discussed them with him. Earlier that day he had determined to confide in her that evening more detail of the 'operation' he, Robert Daley and Blakey were engaged in – because by doing so he'd really show her how sincere he was about it all, he wasn't one of those who 'talk the talk', he was the real thing, he 'walked the walk' as well....

That evening Elianne told Jenner a little more about her family in Lebanon. However, quite soon she turned their conversation to Jenner himself, to his ideas about 'life' ... then on to those of his friends who were of like mind to him and what action they were taking....

11.45 that same evening

'Matt, oh Matt, *listen*! That operation Jenner and his friends are taking part in, Cold Call – no, don't interrupt, just listen – it's against a man named *Martindale*. Jenner told me—'

'Elianne, hold it! Calm down.... Where are you now?'

'At the flat, sitting on my bed. I've just got back from being with Jenner, I pleaded a headache, left him early after an evening out together.'

'He *named* their target to you? Straight out?'

'No, of course not.... Sorry, I've cooled down now, you see being with him I've had to keep my feelings bottled up.... He and I were talking about how sometimes people can't let go of some terrible events in their lives, they hold on to them, it stays with them and they sort of shape their lives round it, wanting to make whoever caused the terrible event to ... *suffer* for it....' Her voice had gone quiet and sad as she spoke, and now she fell silent.

Sensing her thoughts returning to her own tragedies, Locksley felt for her; nevertheless he brought the conversation back on course at once because he felt sure she had vital information to give him.

'Please, Elianne, think back now,' he said to her gently. 'How did this name Martindale come into what you were talking about with Jenner—'

'Sorry, Matt. I didn't mean to go all soft like that. I'm "cool, calm and collected" again now, the way I should be.' Her voice gave Locksley the truth of what she said (and he offered up silent thanks for her resilience and bravery). 'I remember how it came up. Jenner said, "She'll have her revenge. Martindale will pay a heavy price for what he did years ago." But that's all there was, Matt: he clammed up immediately after he'd said it. I asked him who Martindale was, but Jenner has these mood swings sometimes, they're very sudden, and they seem to come when he realizes he's done or said something he regrets, wishes he could take back.'

'Did you ask him to go on? To tell you more?'

'No. I didn't get the chance because at that moment a guy he's got to know at the club came up and greeted him so we got talking to him.'

'And you left it there?'

'Yes, I did. I had what he'd said on tape so it seemed wiser not to bring it up again straightaway.'

'You were absolutely right. And leave it alone now, Elianne. Don't mention the name again with him – and if he does, play not interested.'

'But it's interesting to you, the name? Useful, I mean?'

'Enormously. It's almost certainly a good lead, it should open Cold Call up to us—'

'And then Hussain Shalhoub, aka Robert Daley ... will get what he deserves.' She spoke that last phrase quietly. So quietly that the short pause she left between it and Daley's name passed by Locksley without his noticing it and – perhaps – wondering exactly what she meant by it.

'I'll send a special messenger to your place tomorrow morning to take out the tape and insert a fresh one,' he said. 'And thanks, Elianne. We should be able to get moving on Cold Call now.'

No nightmares came out of the past to violate Elianne's peace of mind that night; she slept well. So did Locksley, but not until after he had called Nicholas Anson, a fellow Intelligence officer who was no less than a wizard in the practice of IT investigations. He asked Anson to trawl all IT sources available to him – which he knew to be legion, since in addition to having access to all Intelligence Services' IT network, Anson maintained a private network of (sometimes criminally active) informers. These contacts would on his behalf clandestinely probe an underworld ring-fenced against official penetration – in this case for information on a man by the name of Martindale.

'No, sorry, I don't know anything about him other than his surname,' he said to Anson's expletive-laden response to being expected to come up with a "whole man", as he put it, out of no more than a name, and only a surname at that. 'Sorry, Nick, but then that's what The Almighty put wonder-workers such as yourself on Planet Earth for, surely?' he added, half joking but aware that Anson's ego was never averse to a little flattery regarding his special talents.

'Can you give me some idea of time-frame?' Anson asked. 'For instance, what age is this man Martindale?'

'I hadn't thought of that—'

'Then do now, for Christ's sake! It's 1.30 in the morning, Locksley, I was asleep, your call woke me up and I bloody well want to get to sleep again.'

'I guess he'd have to be somewhere between 45 and 65. Could be older, though. Sorry. There's a long period to cover.'

'IT was born to let mankind roam time itself at will, was it not—'

'You're talking nonsense.'

'That's because you haven't given me any facts to work on—'

'Because I haven't got any.'

'In which case I'll say goodnight,' Anson snapped, and switched off his mobile.

But, knowing Anson liked nothing better than a serious challenge to his expertise, Locksley slept easier after that call: once hooked by a case, Anson never gave up on it, he would play his 'fish' until he'd landed him.

Sitting side by side at one end of the table in Rose Daley's front room bay window, she and her son had just finished checking through the travel documents – visas, plane tickets, hotel reservations and so on – that would be required by Khaled Ras when, three days after Wayfarer's climax, he left England and travelled to Pakistan. Slipping the papers into their own plastic envelope, Rose sat back and relaxed.

'Mansoor's good to work with,' Robert remarked. 'He admits it when he's got something wrong—'

'And unlike Ras he's honest with others about what's going on in his mind, what he's really thinking.' As she interrupted, Rose stood up and stepped closer to the window, staring moodily out into the street.

Surprised and intrigued – never before had his mother been judgemental, to him, regarding any other member of Abu Yusuf's cadre – Robert sat up and took notice.

'This is the first time I've worked with Ras on a mission, and I hope it will be the last, I find him very difficult to get on with,' he observed, hoping to encourage her to elaborate on her opinion of the Afghan. For, although often at odds with his mother on a variety of matters, he had great respect for her opinions on the strengths, failings and aspirations – those last best kept secret! – of their fellow cadre members. She had after all known or known of all of them for many years.

Unseen by her son, Rose grimaced wryly. 'I've worked on a mission with him twice before,' she said, 'and I've found doing so full of tensions. For one thing, he's a dyed-in-the-wool misogynist: he loathes women, he thinks we're … not fit for purpose, as they say, simply because we're not of the male sex…. And there's another thing, too,' she went on, swinging round to face her son. 'You never know where you are with Ras. On a mission, you are quite likely to find he's busy behind the scenes on some private agenda of his own.'

Robert grinned. 'Hey, hold on there!' he said. 'Isn't that exactly what you and I are doing here? We're beavering away on Cold Call while the main op is Wayfarer—'

'Shut your mouth!' It came out fast and in gutter-slang Arabic.

He held her eyes, stood very still. 'And you watch *your* mouth,' he warned grimly, in English. 'Remember, you depend on me and my friends for Cold Call: if I pull out of it I'll take Jenner and Blakey with me and you'll be sunk – you'll have lost out, won't you? Martindale will continue to enjoy life with his lovely and beloved grandchildren…. And you wouldn't like that, would you?' he added quietly, with malice.

Quickly, Rose controlled herself. She dropped her eyes and

made herself relax, one hand resting on the back of her chair, the other smoothing over her immaculately styled hair.

'Talking of Cold Call,' she said after a few moments, 'is Jenner keeping properly in touch with the girl Charlotte? We need to be absolutely sure there's no change in the arrangements for—'

'Stop it! Of course he's doing the job, why do you keep asking?' Robert had not moved, but his voice and manner had hardened. 'You've never liked Vince, right from the start. He's a good guy; stop downing him.'

'He's … immature. I should never have allowed him to assist in Cold Call.'

'He's perfect for the job he's doing for us; he's very good-looking, he's well-off and free with his cash – a good date for the maidens of the village of Oakdene.'

'But there's a weakness in him. The way he's always looking for approbation from others, especially women.'

Her son smiled, a wide, open grin that (to her eyes) made him look too young to be the front-line terrorist he was (and had been brought up to be, by her).

'Well, Vince doesn't get much in the way of "approbation" from me and Blakey, I can tell you.' But then he gestured an apology. 'Jenner's got for us what we have needed right from the start of Cold Call and will go on needing until it has climaxed,' he said, 'Up-to-date info on Martindale's plans for his grandchildren's visit to Oakdene during their summer holidays. *We need him,* mother—'

'Don't call me that!' Resentment flaring at his truly reasoned disagreement with her about Jenner, she reproved him for a minor, but to her infuriating habit. 'I must have told you a thousand times since we arrived in England that you are to address me always as *Rose.* That must become natural with you because within our organization family relationships have no place and must be seen to have no place.'

'And you live for that organization, don't you!' Angrily, he challenged her. 'Always have, always will. In your heart, you bitch, you never truly mourned the deaths of my brothers, you saw only your-self as nobly "giving them" to The Cause – and I know you would happily do the same with me, if the cards fell that way!'

Staring him furiously in the eye, 'Do you *not* live for our organization then?' she demanded. 'Because if you don't you would do well to get out of it before they discover your lack of total commitment and have you executed!'

But her son refused her the answer she wanted; smiling tightly, he drove a wedge between them.

'They would never dispose of me. I'm too skilled in the various arts of killing, thanks to my father's brilliant instruction and your ferocious encouragement,' he said. Then added, softly but with menace, 'Maybe, Rose, considering that Cold Call is without question in direct contradiction of the organization's code of conduct – maybe you should watch your own back.'

14 July

Locksley sat longer than usual over his breakfast coffee that morning. At 18.00 the previous evening his boss had called him in for an emergency session, with other officers attending, on an unexpected but possibly threatening development in an under-cover operation in progress in the Midlands. Discussion and argument regarding the nature and timing of the action – if any – to be taken in the light of fresh intelligence had gone on very late. Getting up next morning had called for the exercise of willpower. Nor was he in the best of moods, so when his mobile sang out he switched it on wearily and muttered 'Hello'.

'Anson here,' his caller announced, 'and you sound as grumpy as I felt the other night when you rang me at some ungodly hour—'

'Sorry, on both counts.' Tiredness forgotten on the instant. 'What've you got for me?'

'A Martindale who I think ticks all the boxes you wanted ticked, though whether he's actually the right one only you can determine.'

'Give.'

'First name, Anthony. Married, two children, four grandchildren. He was a judge.'

'Sounds as if we might be on to something, then. Judges can have serious enemies, the nature of the job makes that inevitable—'

'The scale of the antagonism varies enormously, though.'

'Point taken, but the scale has been known to go extremely high.... You didn't come up with any other "Martindale"?'

'None that didn't drop out as I continued probing along the lines you gave me.'

'You must've worked hard.'

'It's a fairly uncommon name, which helps in such searches.'

'So dig deeper into this one now, will you? Trawl through his cases for ones where the sentences he handed down might generate in the recipients thereof such a strong craving for revenge that only a killing would satisfy it. Take in the close relatives of the guy who was sentenced and get me the dates of any such cases together with details of the background of each individual convicted and sentenced by Martindale. I want—'

'Hey, hey! Stop there, friend! Maybe MI6 can get by for a couple of days without any help from me but I doubt they'd take kindly to the idea—'

'Then set a couple of those sleek and shiny young blokes who litter your office on to it – no, wait! *Wait a minute*!' Breaking off Locksley pushed himself to his feet and for a few moments stood stock still, assessing in turn the possibility, probability and sheer feasibility of the hunch that had just flashed into his mind. Then, decision made, 'Cancel that first idea, Nick, for the moment anyway,' he instructed, 'I've thought of a name for you to have a go at first. It could turn out to be a dead duck but it might pay off. Dig as deep as you can go into any case that came up before Martindale in the name Daley.'

'First names?'

'It's only a hunch, Nick, forgive me if it turns out I'm wasting your time but – try Roisin, or Rose, it might get us somewhere.'

'Right. Leave it with me. And as they say, Matt, "Don't call me, I'll call you". OK?'

'More than OK. Thanks, as always.' But Locksley could not hold back his sense that time was running short on the Martindale affair. 'Make it as fast as you can, Nick,' he said, low and hard, 'it could matter.'

'Trust me.'

'Fast as you can, indeed,' Locksley murmured to himself as he switched off his mobile. What the hell more can I do? he agonized, what the hell more...?

But nothing came to mind.

CHAPTER 9

28 July
The Hungry Hunter Inn, 30 miles south of London 19.00 hours.

'Do you often come here?' Elianne asked; gazing across the lawn stretching from the back of the inn down to a brook marking its western boundary she put the question idly, glass of white wine in hand. Locksley had driven her out of London for dinner, and the last part of the journey had taken them through restful countryside, she was feeling relaxed. It being a sultry evening they had decided on a drink in the open air before going inside to eat.

'Fairly often. The food's excellent, and as long as I don't come at weekends I find it a good place to, metaphorically speaking, put on my slippers, sit back and be thankful for any small mercies that might come my way.' Locksley was watching her; he liked looking at her and she was, he thought (as he quite frequently did) a delight to the eye. That evening she was wearing a summer dress of some silky material: full skirted and pearly white, it left her arms bare and emphasized her young, lissom body.

'You say "I". Does that mean you usually come alone?'

'This is the first time I have brought anyone here to dine with me.'

'Then I feel honoured.'

They had talked very little on the way there, but he had sensed in her an anxiety, a kind of heart-ache which was troubling her;

so he was pleased now, to see her smile. He thought to remark that he was the honoured one that evening, but he left the words unsaid.

'You know, Matt, Vince Jenner puzzles me,' she said after a little silence. 'I don't know exactly what it is that's different about him, but he seems to have become sort of *divided* about himself and what he's doing.'

'Doing in this op Cold Call, d'you mean?'

'I don't know. Maybe. Or perhaps about the bigger operation, Wayfarer, though he hasn't said anything more about that to me since that evening when he referred to it then changed the subject.... Have you found out anything about it?'

'No. There was nothing there to work on, he only gave you the name,' he said, frowning. But then his mood changed and, raising his half-pint of lager to her, 'I salute you, Elianne, for all you're doing to help us get to the heart of this op Jenner named to you as Cold Call,' he went on, smiling across at her, 'so I'd like us to drink to you soon getting from him some facts that will enable our security forces to frustrate it.'

They drank to that, touching glasses and hands. Then, 'I'd like to add a sort of private bit to what we've just drunk to,' Elianne said. 'It's about Jenner.'

'And important to you?'

She frowned at the question, suddenly uncertain of herself, but after a moment went on, slowly. 'I'm not sure *why*, but yes, it is important to me. Maybe because ... well, I'm *using him*, aren't I, and ... I'm beginning to dislike myself for doing that.'

'What he's into in Cold Call is criminal.' He said it harshly, meaning to hurt.

'Nevertheless, I hope that, when everything comes out about Cold Call, some sort of *mercy* might be shown towards Jenner because those others have used him too, they've perceived his vulnerability and used it.... They've *bent* him, Matt.'

She loves him Locksley thought: not sexually, and maybe only a little, but – she cares about him.

'I'll do what I can, when and if the time comes,' he promised her, quietly.

'I'm not in love with him, you know.' Defensively, but her eyes telling him there was more to it than that.

'But he's in love with you?'

'Yes. That's what makes what I'm doing sort of ... disgusting.'

Locksley nodded, his face impassive, but then after a silence he forced that side of the situation out of his mind, asking,

'So, Elianne, is there anything that's likely to give me any sort of lead on this latest tape you've got for me?'

'I believe so,' she leaned back, smoothing her long black hair away from her face, seemingly glad to distance herself from the personal complexities attendant on the relationship between herself and Vincent Jenner. And she sensed herself and Locksley were 'together' on a different level now; they had returned to their usual level of close friendship broadened and deepened by the instinctive trust that lives between comrades-in-arms.

'Go on,' he said.

'It's about that terrorist group Vince said Robert Daley is a member of, and which Jenner hopes to be recruited by, the one presently involved in Wayfarer. In a high position within it there's one man who Daley, according to Jenner, is afraid of. I don't know *why*, but Daley fears him.'

'Did Jenner mention his name?'

'Just in passing. It's "Khaled Ras".'

'That might get us somewhere. I'll follow it up. Anything else?'

'Maybe. It sounded as if it might be important, but I'm not sure it is.'

'Why not?'

'Well, Jenner wasn't sure so how could I be? I was about to tell you when you interrupted.'

Instantly contrite, 'Sorry, sorry,' Locksley said. 'Please go on, in your own time.'

Giving him a fleeting, preoccupied smile, she told him then. She was unaware that the information she was giving him would allow certain disparate but vital facts regarding Cold Call and Wayfarer (both of them to-date lacking definition to MI5 and MI6) to cohere into a scenario that would enable further investigative action by the Intelligence and Security services.

'Jenner thinks – as I said, he doesn't know it as a fact – that Robert Daley's mother is, like him, involved in both those operations he's named to me.'

'Christ!' Stunned, Locksley leaned towards her, his eyes fixed on hers. 'We've long suspected that Rose Daley has past form,' he went on, 'but we've never had anything against her that would stand up in a court of law; there's only unproven stuff linking her with family connections in Ireland in the '80s, then later in Lebanon with the terrorist activities of her husband and sons when she was domiciled there. But we've never discovered anything directly incriminating her. However, what you've just told me, together with what I hope to get from having this man Khaled Ras named to us, should open up the whole Cold Call and Wayfarer situation to penetrative investigation.' Locksley was looking past her, no longer at her as he worked out his way ahead. 'I'll take the whole thing higher up now I've got something to base it on: get some real clout behind me. Surveillance the Daleys' movements closely, discover their contacts—'

'Matt.'

His eyes refocused on her. 'Elianne, you are without doubt the best thing that has ever happened in my life,' he said, half smiling at her.

But he got no answering smile. 'I'm turning out to be quite an accomplished....' Voice trailing off into silence she searched for the right word – then suddenly broke eye contact with him, looked away towards the brook; when she went on there was a deadness in her voice. 'What am I, Matt, by doing what I'm doing to Jenner?' she asked, words spaced evenly across the cool evening air. 'I know two cruel and viciously degrading phrases in Arabic for a woman who uses pretended loving to steal secrets from a man; but until now I've never found the need to express that in English—'

'The words you should use are simply "honey-trap",' he said coolly, then waited in silence.

After a few moments Elianne got to her feet, turned to him. 'I remember reading somewhere that "simply" can mean "no more and no less". Doesn't help much, though, does it?' she said quietly, putting it to him without challenge, holding his eyes, allowing him to see the angst gnawing at her. But then without waiting for his answer, she went round the table in a swirl of pearly silk, stood close to him and smiled.

'Let's leave all that now, Matt, dear Matt,' she said, her voice warm and a little throaty. 'This evening is for you and me, I won't allow Hussain Shalhoub to steal it from me.'

But for him the change was too fast. 'It's not so easy, Elianne. I'm a counter-terrorist officer and as such—'

'And I'm a student in criminal law – and as such I'm very hungry,' she interrupted, slipping him her gamine grin, not giving an inch in her determination to break free, for a little while, of the world of terrorism. 'Each of us, "we are what we are", isn't that what they say? So please, feed this starving student now.... Please?'

He stood up and made a somewhat over-elaborate gesture towards the open doors of The Hungry Hunter inn. 'Dangerous thing, to stand between a ravening student and her dinner,' he said, taking her hand and leading her that way. 'Let's eat.'

5 August
Locksley at his service flat

20.00 hours.

Arriving home the following evening, Locksley cast aside jacket and tie in the hall, provided himself with a glass and a can of Foster's from the fridge and sat down in his favourite armchair in the sitting-room; stretching out his legs, he filled his glass and drank gratefully.

Two minutes later he set his drink down on the floor beside him and pulled from his shirt pocket the folded, typed report he had found waiting for him on his return to his office at four o'clock; after studying it he had issued certain urgent orders relating to its contents. Nevertheless his mind could not leave it alone because – surely? – in the light of what Elianne had so recently told him, the info the report gave him had to refer to the operation Jenner had named to her as 'Wayfarer'.

The report had come from Tug Graham, the MI6 officer whom, late the previous night and after dropping Elianne off at Charles Gray's place around midnight, he had called and ordered to carry out an immediate, top-level search on a man named Khaled Ras. Graham had worked hard and fast. His report read thus.

KHALED RAS

Age 56

Arr UK 2000. At that date status resident only.

Under MI6 observation since arrival. Standard of observation on arrival: low level.

Commencing Jan 2007, began regular but infrequent visits to Flat 1 – Arnold House – KINGSWAY LONDON.

Duration of visits usually 3 to 4 hours.

Surveillance of this flat imm instigated.

This established:
   a) flat rented and occupied by SALIM ANWAR (no known suspicion attached)
   b) flat visited by four young men at times coinciding with those of Ras. These young men arrived and left separately therefore assumption is that each in turn met with RAS or ANWAR or both.

These four young men resided at separate rented accommodation until June 2008, but at the end of that month all moved into the same hostel in Tottenham Court Road. Their visits to Anwar/Ras have continued therefore surveillance has been increased on MI6 orders.

Relevant info gained during July surveillance as follows:

1 Ras travels at varying intervals to Southend – Rugby – Exeter – Brighton always by train and always between 09.00 and 16.00.

2 Ras stays one night at each place. Different acc. at each, but always uses small hotels usually commercials.

3 Each of the 4 young men ref. above has accompanied Ras twice so far on his visits to the above cities – same young man to same city each time.

During these visits they spend their time 'sightseeing'.

Graham's report ended there. However he and Locksley had worked together frequently, and at the end of the report Graham had written in his barely legible hand, 'suicide bombings in the planning here, d'you reckon, Matt? I could meet you for a beer, talk it through? If you'd like to give me a bell pronto. Tug.'

Dropping the report in his lap, Locksley took out his mobile and called Tug Graham.

However, much later that night he received a phone call which blew the Martindale case wide open to immediate action by the security services. It came at 01.23 according to his bedside clock as he lay sleepless in bed, hands clasped behind his head, his mind worrying at Cold Call and Wayfarer like a masterless sheepdog harrying an untended flock because 'that's his nature, that's what it's in him to do'.

'Matt,' Elianne said to him without preamble, 'Jenner's told me what Cold Call's going to do to the Martindales and it's appalling and he says it's going to happen soon so I had to ring you the moment he'd gone.'

'Gone where?' Funny, how the mind can hook on to trivia.

'Back to his flat. Does it matter?'

'No, not the slightest—'

'Then can I tell you straightaway while it's clear in my mind? Without your interrupting? Please?'

'Of course. I'll keep my questions till after you've finished.'

So she explained as much as she knew of the plan for Rose Daley's revenge on the man who to her way of thinking had 'murdered' her mother....

When Elianne came to the end of it Locksley took her right through it again, noting down her answers to his tightly constructed questioning so that when he was done he had Cold Call's plan of action as clearly imprinted on paper as it was in his mind.

'I'll get to work on this immediately,' he said then.

'But it's the middle of the night.'

'I couldn't sleep on this.'

'I think I can. Now I've told you, I can sleep.'

'Why did Jenner tell you all this, Elianne? Surely you—'

'No, we didn't make love, Matt. He told me because he's finding it very hard to live with being involved in such a dreadful thing.... And sexually, he is a very respectful young man. It wasn't after making love that he told me. He told me because he's in love with me so he trusts me, thinks I'm ... what I'm not, and craves my understanding.... Good night, Matt. Call me tomorrow and tell me what you're doing.'

CHAPTER 10

10 August
Martindale's house.

'A n-thony!' Leaning out of the casement window of the first-floor bedroom overlooking the front lawn, Olivia Martindale called down to her husband who was playing rounders there with his four grandchildren. However, on the far side of the row of tall firs marking the boundary between Oakdene and its neighbouring property someone was cutting grass with a motor-mower, and the retired judge did not hear her. Instantly entranced by the summer's-day charm of the scene below her, Olivia leaned her forearms along the windowsill and, squinting a little against after-noon sunshine, smiled proprietorally.

Out there on the grass she could see her husband and the grand-children giving the ball game their all. Anthony had his shirtsleeves rolled to the elbow, the kids were tearing about shouting to each other – but wait a second! Only three of the four were to be seen! Four small heaps of tee-shirts or floppy sunhats marked the four 'bases' required by the game. The two boys were bare-chested, she noticed, Jack was fielding not far from her, off to her right below the bedroom window, Melissa was doing likewise over by the broad path which led from the house to its front gate; Nicholas was batting and Anthony was bowling (sensible fellow, no running about after the ball called for). So where was Elise, Olivia wondered, but at that moment Nicholas put rounders bat to ball and the ball flew towards her offering Jack a splendid catch – but he muffed it, got a finger-tip touch to it but fell sprawling as it bounced on past him and came to rest beneath the window.

Scrambling to his feet Jack went after it, picked it up then stared ruefully up at her, his sweating thirteen-year-old face mortified.

'I should've got that,' he called up to her, scowling, then swung round and threw the ball low and hard straight into his grandfather's waiting hands.

'Good throw-in, Jack!' Loud and clear the words sailed across the warm summer air as Martindale praised his eldest grandson.

'Come on down and join us, Nan.' Turning back to Olivia, Jack grinned up at her, his pride restored. 'We need more fielders.'

'I will if I can be back-stop,' she offered (not much running about in that position either!).

'Good-o, sure you can. See you out here in a min, then,' and he was off, speeding back to rejoin the game, a skinny, tall-for-his-age, agile boy moving swiftly over the grass.

I just can't find it in myself to say 'no' to any of them, can I? Olivia chided herself as, without haste, she made her way downstairs, went out of the front door – and to her surprise saw Elise way over to her left: sitting cross-legged with her back against a full-grown horse chestnut tree the little girl was stroking Tiger's ears, the golden-haired retriever lying stretched out on the grass beside her.

Near-silent over the soft earth Olivia went to her. 'Hello, Elise,' she said.

The dark-haired head came up fast, the hand rested still on the soft-to-the-touch head of the dog.

'Hello.' Blue eyes solemn, a little sleepy. 'Are you going to play rounders with the others?'

'I am. Want to come?'

'No, thank you. I'm thinking.'

'What about?'

'About being nine years old on Saturday the 15th of August.'

I'll be here for ever if I get caught up in this, Olivia thought. 'I expect Tiger helps a lot. With you thinking about your birthday, I mean,' she said, beginning to turn away. Then she checked and looked back. 'Change your mind about playing?' she asked. 'It's fun out there, with your sister and the boys.'

'OK.' Elise was on her feet in a flash, slipped her hand into Olivia's. 'Let's go … I'll be almost the same age as Tiger on the 15th of August,' she went on seriously as she hurried her grand-mother on towards the game of rounders. 'But did you know, Nan, that it doesn't work out equal between us and dogs because one year in their lives is like seven in ours, so really Tiger will be around sixty on my birthday but I'll still be only nine….'

10 August

Damon Ashford's bungalow at the far end of the long lawn at the rear of his parents' house in Richmond. 18.30

After a warm day the rambling, landscaped garden at the rear of the big house was pleasantly cool, as was the paved veranda of the bungalow on which Robert Daley, John Blake and Vincent Jenner were taking life easy. That afternoon they had watched their friend Damon Ashford play for his club in a locally important football match. After the game a triumphant Ashford, bruised, pouring sweat and wildly happy, had spared a moment to tell them, 'Go on back to the bungalow, you guys, key's in the usual place, make yourselves at home and I'll join you later' before being swept on towards the changing rooms by his jubilant team-mates.

On arriving at Ashford's place, Blake had fetched bottled beer from the fridge, and the three of them had settled down on the veranda, relaxed and pleased with life.

'Good match Dash played back there,' Blake observed to no one in particular. Then hitching one hip up on the flat wooden capping of the balustrade edging the veranda, he glanced across at Jenner who was sat at the small, white-painted table at the far end of the paving. 'You should try the game, Vince. It's good for learning to be a team player,' he said with a sly grin, hoping Jenner would rise to the bait.

'It's a game I enjoy watching.' Jenner answered him quietly, not looking at him, aware that the suggestion was bait, but refusing it.

This exchange had passed by Daley unheeded. Stretched out on a cushioned lounger, bottle in hand, he had been dreaming of what to him was the only truly interesting activity – terrorism. Cold Call he considered to be of little account, barely worthy of his time; Wayfarer, however, was a useful stepping-stone to international operations which would allow him hands-on action with grenade, knife or gun, but preferably knife. Nevertheless, he was doing his best for both ops since both would figure on his terrorist CV – with Cold Call carefully excised from certain presentations thereof, of course! – and, consequently, would influence his future career.

Now his mind turned to his immediate commitments. 'Hey Blakey!' he called, turning his head to his mate, 'd'you reckon there'll be any chance of us getting to use our knives down at Martindale's place?'

'Can't see much hope of it.' Blake's tone light-hearted, amiable. 'There'll be no one in the house bar Vince's girlfriend, and from what he says we can count on her being easy to deal with when she opens the door to find a couple of young handsome blokes standing there with ID in hand and a brilliant line in sweet talk from me to make her think it'd be much more fun if *with her help* I do the ground floor – and leave you, poor sucker, to do upstairs.' But then his voice hardened. 'And you watch your step, Rob. Keep that knife of yours stuck in its sheath there at your waistband,' he said grimly. 'You go upstairs with your clipboard and your hold-all, and fix those bombs under the beds of those kids. Then you stick around up there till I call up to you and ask if you've done. You then say you are, and we get out. Out and away, fast.' Then he drank the last of his beer, pushed himself down off the balustrade. 'I'm off to that pub along the road,' he announced, voice and body-language that of everyone's friend 'Blakey' once more. 'Those we've just had were the last in the fridge.'

'Good idea, then.' Daley eyed him, smiling, taking the 'advice' in good part because Blake was a professional – and his good friend, he was sure of that. 'And you bring back plenty cold ones, Dash'll be thirsty when he gets here.'

'You think he and his mates'll have been drinking lemonade back there? Ha, ha! … see you. Ten minutes should do it.'

A brief silence followed Blake's departure. Jenner sneaked a glance at Daley's supine form, wondering whether this might be a suitable time to ask him how things stood with regard to him and Abu Yusuf, the man he hoped to impress with his work in Cold Call … Rob looked to be in a friendly mood, he decided, so he ventured into that territory since it was a fine opportunity, he didn't often have time alone with him.

'That Operation Wayfarer, how's it going, Rob?' he asked.

By chance, Daley too had been thinking about that, 'No problem.' Sitting up, he looked across at Jenner. 'It's a good op, Vince. It's uncomplicated in its basic format – and believe me, that can be a big plus.'

Getting to his feet Jenner strolled across to the edge of the veranda, leaned his arms along the balustrade and gazed out over the garden: the evening was turning sunless, sky clouding over.

'Tell me about Wayfarer, Rob,' he said. 'I'd like to have some idea of how a big mission works – to get that from someone like you who has actually *done* terrorist stuff at the cutting edge—'

'"Cutting edge"; I like that.' Briefly, Daley smiled to himself. But then his face hardened. 'Wayfarer is from a different world to Cold Call, Vince,' he said. 'It's leaner and meaner. Also it's snake-in-the-grass stuff; designed to eat into the heart and soul of the people it targets and cause them to lose faith in their own political institutions – and in themselves, too, because they realize then that all the time their enemy was living in their world with them, was close to them and yet they failed to see through him to what he really was and save themselves.'

'How exactly d'you mean, "close to them"?' A kind of excitement stirring inside him, Jenner kept his voice low. Never before had Rob talked with him so openly, telling it as it was, one-to-one, man-to-man, the way true comrades should; and he hungered to keep things on that level between them.

Daley stood up and padded across to lean his arms on the railing beside Jenner. Inside his head he was running over the action sequences of Wayfarer.

'It's a suicide bombing,' he said softly, his eyes on the flowers and green grass in front of him. 'Four men with bombs in their backpacks board their allocated trains out of London; they have their tickets with them, the bookings made a day in advance. Each makes himself comfortable among his fellow travellers, chats a bit with them, maybe about the English weather—'

'Where are they going?' Jenner asked.

But deciding to preserve his 'superiority', Daley checked himself. 'That's not for you to know, Vince,' he said. 'The real point is that all four martyrs detonate their bombs at precisely 11.30, at which time two of the trains will just have arrived at stations near their final destinations, while the other two will be approaching theirs.... So we have four simultaneous "terrorist outrages", as they say,' he ended, smiling to himself.

Detonate their bombs. The words pierced Jenner to the heart and through a split second of intense agony of spirit he 'saw and comprehended' the wildfire, cataclysmic horror of the instant when a terrorist bomb explodes amongst a crowd of people. Then he screwed his eyes tight shut, put his head down and fought his way back to sanity.

'Like I said, Vince, "leaner and meaner", see? All it takes is planning, careful brilliant logistics to achieve the desired correlation regarding train-times and an experienced bomb-maker. Also, of course, four men ready and willing to forfeit their own lives in order to take plenty of the enemy with them when they go.... Not my scene, that.' He turned to Jenner, his face suddenly malicious, mocking him now. 'How about you, Vince? You got it in you to "make the ultimate sacrifice"?'

However luck was with Jenner that day for as he stood lost for words to answer with, caught rabbit-in-headlights shocked, staring into Daley's eyes, he heard Blake's voice.

'Bottoms up, you guys! Supply lines are restored – and guess who I met as I came back?' Blakey called to him as he rounded the corner of the bungalow with an obviously weighty sportsbag in one hand and Damon Ashford by his side.

'Don't worry, Vince, such self-sacrifice won't be required of you.' In a quiet-voiced aside Daley let Jenner off the hook – then turned to Blake and Ashford. 'You took your time, Blakey! Hi, Dash. Come on over, let's celebrate....'

21.15 approx

Locksley was late arriving back at his service flat that evening. Satisfied that preparations for the thwarting of Cold Call were well under way he settled down in an armchair in his sitting-room, mobile and a glass of whisky-soda to hand on a low table beside him. Switching on the TV, he began searching for a news programme. Two minutes later, his mobile sang out so he switched off the TV and answered it.

'Hello, Matt,' Elianne's voice.

'Hello and how are you? I guess you're at Charles's place—'

'Matt, listen. I don't have much time.' Her voice told him she was uptight, even frightened. 'No, I'm not at Charles's, I'm in the ladies' rest-room at the Lebanese Club and I have stuff to tell you that you should know – and act on, I imagine, and act fast. I'm here with Jenner and I mustn't be long talking to you because he'll think it odd. And I'll have to talk quietly because although there's no one else in here now someone might come in any moment.'

'I get the point. Go on.'

'What I'm about to tell you, Jenner had straight from Robert Daley so you can be sure it's authentic.' Her voice had gone lower and was tightly controlled. 'That operation Jenner gave me the name of earlier, Wayfarer – it's big, Matt,' she said. 'There will be four suicide bombers on separate trains going out of London—'

'*My God. When?*'

'I don't know when or where, or any other details. He said it would be "soon", and that the martyrs would detonate their bombs at an agreed time and simultaneously—'

'Elianne.' Realizing he was confronting civic terror and destruction – four trains loaded with summer holiday passengers, it would be carnage, no other word for it – Locksley interrupted again. 'Stop now. It's imperative I hear the tape myself.'

'I had it switched on, of course. I'll be home around midnight, come to the house at half past. Park away out of sight and walk round to the back, I'll be waiting there by the gate, you know it. I'll give it to you then.... Wait, though! Shall I go on with the subject, with Jenner now? Try to find out more?'

'No – no! Could make him suspicious.'

'Then I'll go back to him and we'll go on as planned. Though God knows how I'll get through the rest of the evening—'

'Think on the miracle you've performed here tonight, Elianne. That should help you through the next few hours.'

'Yes. Yes, it will, won't it.... Until soon after midnight then, Matt. See you.'

The inane valediction came to him quiet and a little shaky; and as she spoke it he felt so close to her that he 'saw' her in his mind's eye. For the first time, too, knew himself to be seriously afraid for her. For should Robert Daley find out somehow that Jenner was bragging to his latest girlfriend about his 'direct action' activities, and was letting slip to her vital info about them – what then? What would Daley do?

Cutting off that line of thought Locksley sat down at his bureau and, taking into account everything known to him about the current situation, decided what steps he should take before he heard for himself, on Elianne's tape, exactly what information Jenner had given her that night. Then using an emergency number he put a call through to a certain high-ranking officer at M16 and requested a meeting as soon as possible. The reasons he gave were briefly put, but they were enough to win him a one-to-one meeting at the home of that officer in one hour's time.

CHAPTER 11

Wednesday 13 August
The day before the climax of Operation Cold Call.

That morning Rose Daley made two phone calls before going about her customary Wednesday routine. The first was to her son Robert. Having checked with him to be sure that John Blake and Vincent Jenner were properly prepared for the action of Cold Call the following day, she instructed Robert that *on no account whatsoever* was he, or either Blake or Jenner, to telephone, e-mail or fax her after she ended her current call to him: all three young men must, repeat *must*, wait for her to communicate with them – which she would do, she assured him, late on Friday evening, well after the climax of Wayfarer. When he protested, saying he would prefer to contact her on her mobile soon after he and Blake had completed the placing of the bombs at Martindale's house, she slapped him down hard, reminding him that all day Thursday and Friday she would be working with Abu Yusuf on Wayfarer's business – and that since even the slightest thing connecting her with Cold Call would immediately arouse his suspicion she *must* not risk that happening, she must keep herself clear of anything which Yusuf might interpret as disloyalty on her part....

'So, Robert, see to it that the three of you understand that there is to be no attempt by any of you to contact me in any way from now on,' she said, reiterating her orders to make them absolutely clear to her son. 'All of you will wait for me to call you, which I shall do after Wayfarer has run its course. *Is that understood?*'

Smiling tightly to herself as he at once assured her that 'Her commands would of course be obeyed by all her Cold Call agents', Rose proceeded to make her second call. This was to the secretary of her bridge club to inform her that she, Rose Daley, would not be able to make it to their usual session that evening due to an unspecified but unexpected event in the family.

Then, phone calls done, she made the ten-minutes-either-way walk to the local newsagent to collect her copy of The Times; from 10.00 to 11.00 she was at *Andre's Salon* for her weekly wash-and-blow-dry, then it was home for lunch before her afternoon stint at the RNIB charity shop in the High Street. The rest of the help there all thought her 'a lovely lady', unaware that to her they were simply background 'characters' in her carefully cultivated cover story and that, privately, she despised them for their kindliness towards the world in general and herself in particular.

Later that evening, dressed with quiet, stylish elegance, she summoned a taxi to take her to *Pierre's*, a French-cuisine, upmarket restaurant a mile's drive away, where she enjoyed a leisurely, excellently cooked and presented dinner in softly lit, deep-carpeted surroundings.

She drank a little wine at dinner. But on arriving home around 22.00 she changed into a beige trouser suit of raw silk then opened a bottle of champagne, drew closely shut the rose-red velvet curtains in her sitting-room and sat down in one of its deeply cushioned armchairs with the champagne in its ice-bucket and one exquisite Lalique flute on the table at her side.

With her first glass of champagne she drank a toast to Caitlin Daley her mother, recalling her suicide in a prison cell. As she poured the second, her mobile rang....

Olivia and Anthony Martindale spent that Wednesday at Oakdene with their grandchildren. It was a cloudy summer day, but warm. The children – Jack, Melissa, Nicholas and impatient-to-be-nine-years-old Elise – were out in the garden all morning, playing together. At first Tiger joined in the fun, but as soon as things became too boisterous for a dog of mature years the golden retriever padded off to lie down in one of his favourite 'resting' places, the grass beneath the copper beech at the edge of the lawn, up by the house. The retired judge kept an eye on the kids from his study to the left of the porch while sitting at his desk attending to his correspondence – 'nothing but bills these days,' he would grumble to Olivia when she brought in the tray of mid-morning coffee and sat down with him for a chat over their elevenses of good coffee and two chocolate digestives each....

'I'll take smoked salmon sandwiches for you and me tomorrow,' Olivia remarked, gazing out of the study window to where, at the edge of the shrubbery alongside the path leading from the front door to the gate on to the pavement and side road beyond, Nicholas and Jack had constructed a rough 'home-base' from fallen branches for the game of hide-and-seek now in progress. Only Jack was to be seen there at the moment, he was the present 'seeker' so the others had all rushed off into the shrubbery to hide. 'But for the children I think we'll take peanut butter ones, and of course some with plum jam in for Elise—'

'There'll be one hell of a scene if you don't put some of those in,' Martindale said, a grandfatherly grin softening his strong-featured face. 'Thank God we can buy ice-cream down there on the coast and won't have to transport it.'

After a moment's silence, 'I'm glad they're all going next door to Penelope's this afternoon,' Olivia said.

'Thanks be that she and Tom have got a pool.'

Olivia wasted no time in seizing this opportunity. 'I still think it'd be a good idea for us to have one,' she observed, 'there's lots of space for one out at the back—' She broke off, starting to her feet as, through the open study windows, a child's voice howled in sudden pain. 'Oh God, what's happened now?' she cried, heading for the door.

'Don't panic, Olivia. It'll be Melissa with a minuscule cut on her little finger, she always makes a hell of a fuss at the slightest thing as you well know.' Nevertheless he too was on his feet – but he contented himself with leaning out of the nearest window to see what the trouble was (ready, of course, to go out and take charge if a man's help was needed).

But there was no blood, no serious hurt. Nicholas, smashing his way through the shrubbery to reach home-base with Melissa close behind him, had let a hazel branch swing back hard behind him and it had hit her in the face—

'If I hadn't been quick to get my arm up it would've hit me right in the eye!' she protested as her grandmother stroked better the barely visible mark on the tanned little forearm. 'Nicky should be more *careful*. He's always like that, he's, he's a *tearaway*, he's a thoughtless *bugger* and I'll never speak to him again!'

I hope Anthony didn't hear that horrible word, Olivia thought, where does she pick them up I wonder. 'Let's go across and say hello to Tiger,' she suggested, 'he's looking lonely over there....'

Peace was restored. Melissa agreed to speak to her brother again. An al fresco lunch was enjoyed out on the lawn, and at two o'clock the four children, carrying towel-wrapped swimming gear and a large box of chocolates for Penelope (fierce argument as to who should present it to her successfully defused).... And when they returned to Oakdene it was nearly seven o'clock and they were all absolutely dead-beat.... Heaven, thought Olivia as they trooped in: supper, shower, then bed. No trouble at all, perfect heaven.

Ten o'clock, and Anthony and Olivia Martindale were sitting outside on the terrace, relaxed in their cushioned reclining chairs. They hadn't talked much since putting the children to bed: used up by the various problems and wonders of the day they were happy to be alone together now it was safely ended.

Linking her hands behind her head Olivia gazed out across the lawn, watching the afterglow fade from trees and sky.... Such a lovely day it had been, Anthony and herself and the grandchildren. And the next day, Thursday, should be great: the drive down to the coast, sun, sand and sea.... Then come Saturday, because it's Elise's birthday Penelope and Tom come over to us with *their* grandchildren and we have a barbecue....

Life was pretty good, Olivia Martindale thought, watching the sun go down that Wednesday evening.

The day before Cold Call was scheduled to climax was a difficult one for Robert Daley, it refused to pass quickly enough for him. Impatient for the time for action to arrive, he filled in the time as best he could, watching football on TV, hanging out with some of his mates.... A glowering young man with predatory eyes, he prowled through the day restlessly, hungering for the coming strike with a growing anger at what he considered to be the tedium, the sheer boredom of life in England. Even the imminence of Cold Call and Wayfarer, since he had no 'aggressive action' part to play in the actual killings both would inflict, could not quell his lust for hands-on physical violence.

And while Rose Daley was watching the sun go down in its special glory, a few miles away from her across London her son sat down in a catchpenny bar he had never been in before with a bottle of beer and planned his escape from her to a life of his own choosing. As soon as his present two ops were done, he would make the break: head back to Lebanon. He'd get in touch again with the captain of the Retributive Justice unit who, because Robert was the only surviving son of a celebrated terrorist killed in action, had awarded him the execution of the Asley brothers.... Robert recalled that he had wanted to kill the Asleys with his knife, but the captain had overruled him, saying that with Beirut in the febrile state it was at that time it would be preferable to use the gun and make a quick exit....

At least with the captain I'll sometimes get the chance to kill with my knife, Hussain Rashid Shalhoub told himself, drinking alone in a seedy London pub. Then finding his bottle empty he bought himself another beer, sat down again and drank at leisure, dreaming on his past killings in Lebanon – and on those to come, those surely written into his future back in his native country....

★

Locksley's one-to-one late-night meeting with Assistant Commissioner Margaret Morris was brief but testing. After a rigorous question-and-answer session by which she'd brought herself up to speed on the present situation regarding Wayfarer, she explained to Locksley that, following his call, she had summoned an immediate 'war council'. She'd brought together the movers-and-shakers required to put in place such wide-ranging measures as might have some hope of frustrating the intended hit.

'They're all waiting for us in conference room D along the corridor,' she went on, getting to her feet. 'We'll join them now and get to work on this.'

As he followed her out into the corridor, 'Won't be easy, will it,' Locksley said. 'Flexible planning required.'

'That's a bit of an understatement, I think. With us not knowing from which London stations the bombers will board their respective trains, the logistics are, well, overwhelming,' she answered. They trod parquet flooring, he towering over her slight, trim figure, the straight blonde hair capping her poised, beautifully shaped head. 'Is there any chance, d'you think, of our getting definite info on that – and, of course, on date and timing?'

'To get all that we'd need little short of a miracle as far as I can see.'

'I'm told they do occur from time to time.' Half turning to him at a door standing ajar Morris flicked him a wry grin then pushed the door fully open and went in.

Then I'll pray for one to happen between now and … whenever, Locksley thought. As he followed her into the conference room, he saw the faces of the men-of-power seated around the long mahogany table turn towards Assistant Commissioner Morris and himself. They clearly hoped the two of them would know more about Operation Wayfarer than they had as yet divulged.

When it swiftly became apparent that this was not the case the movers-and-shakers accepted the fact without argument. Over the course of the next few hours they worked out a skeleton plan framed to frustrate the four-pronged terrorist attack and awaiting only, but of course crucially, the provision of the timing and place-names needed before it could metamorphose into a specific response.

'Thanks to you, Matt, at least we've had a modicum of warning and this thing won't come at us out of the blue.' Morris smiled up at him as he passed by her on his way out.

'I'll keep my source focussed; hopefully we'll get more detail....'

Wednesday 13 August
23.00 hours
Abu Yusuf's Flat in Chelsea

Abu Yusuf put his mobile down by the clock and the hardback book on his bedside table, took off his black silk dressing-gown, laid it across the bed, then turned back the sheet and the summer-weight coverlet and got into bed. His manservant had prepared everything for him as usual; the commander of Wayfarer liked to read for a while before sleep so the two pillows were plumped up against the headboard, the glass of bottled spring water stood alongside the clock. Settling himself to comfort Yusuf reached for his book – a George Smiley novel, he found Le Carré's plots inter-esting and enjoyed trying to pick holes in them – but even as he did so his mobile chimed.... Having earlier switched it to urgent-only mode, he answered it immediately.

'Yes?'

'It's Khaled Ras. Salaam, sir. I have a matter for your ears only which, clearly, requires immediate action on our part.' The Arabic was harsh in the Afghan's voice and, it seemed to Yusuf, it was cut with a kind of triumphant malice.

'Proceed.' Snapping out the word, he replaced his book and sat upright: Ras was not the man to chase after moonbeams, informa-tion he had come by deserved proper concentration.

Even so, and in spite of his own previous suspicions regarding the person concerned, the stark facts stated in Ras's next words shocked Wayfarer's commander.

'Sir. Rose Daley has indeed, since the start of this year, been setting in place here an operation of her own which serves solely her own ends. It is scheduled to come to fruition within the next two days.'

In Abu Yusuf, shock was smashed aside, white-hot fury ruled: what Ras had reported was disloyalty of the basest, most despicable nature. Nevertheless, Yusuf knew he must first guard *himself* in the resolving of the situation.

'You have *irrefutable* proof of this?' he demanded.

'I have. From two independent sources, both impeccable.'

From Ras, that was sufficient: Abu Yusuf believed him. 'Then it is imperative we act against her without delay,' he said.

Realising the intention behind the very deliberate emphasis his commander had placed on his last two words, Ras asked, 'Shall I act without reporting the matter to headquarters and requesting their permission?' he asked.

Abu Yusuf refused him the answer direct. 'There will of course be an official enquiry after the event,' he said, 'but with Wayfarer so close to climax *immediate* action is called for and permissible in the face of such flagrant disloyalty. Nevertheless, we must proceed with care: it is essential that at that enquiry we are able to ... satisfy the executive's criteria.'

After a brief pause, Ras asked, quietly but with infinite satisfaction, 'Then we kill her?'

'The code of honour our organization lives by decrees that the act of setting in place and running a separate, *personal* operation concurrently with an official mission in progress and initiated by the organization's executive carries the death penalty.—'

'And,' Ras interrupted, 'it exonerates from personal blame all or any of its members who, in line with proven circumstances as above noted, enforce that penalty on any such traitors.'

Yusuf smiled to himself. 'As commander of Wayfarer, the mission affected, I award to you summary execution of the traitor, Khaled Ras,' he announced in formal tones, well aware – and in this case glad of – his 2i/c's appetite for hands-on violence. He himself preferred more subtle and long-lasting forms of punishment.

'Shall it be tonight?' Ras's voice lubricious as anticipation coursed in his blood.

'Tonight, indeed. No time must be wasted. Contact her on your mobile and instruct her that on my orders you will call upon her without delay to pass on to her certain vital new orders concerning movement of personnel after Wayfarer's conclusion. Given that reason for such a sudden, late-night visit, she cannot refuse to receive you.'

Ras nodded. 'Good. That is very good.... I shall use the knife; cut her throat—'

'Ras! Come to your senses! You will use a silenced gun. This is an execution for dereliction of duty, and must be dealt with in the manner laid down.'

23.50 hours

Comfortably dressed in beige silk trousers and blouse, Rose Daley opened the door of her flat to Khaled Ras.

'Come in,' she said to him curtly, her long-standing, instinctive dislike of the Afghan surfacing immediately she saw him standing at her door in his dark suit. Everything about him annoyed her, from the stance of his wiry body to the fierce narrowed eyes. 'These new instructions you have for me from Abu Yusuf,' she went on, turning to face him as soon as he had entered and she had closed the door behind him, 'Are they written, or will you deliver them verbally?'

But Ras gave her no answer. For a second he stood silent, bird-of-prey eyes brilliant with triumph and hatred – then in one swift movement he whipped a handgun from his belt and aimed it straight into her face—

'Down on your knees, woman.' The concentrated savagery driving him was palpable, it fouled the air enclosing him and Rose Daley.

To her, knowledge of what was to come was instantaneous – and the shock of the perceived imminence of her own death paralysed all self-command: without a word, her eyes never leaving his, she knelt before him.

'Now, sit back on your heels.'

She sat back on her heels.

For a moment, Ras stared down at her, exultant, savouring her humiliation. Then,

'You are a proven traitor to our organization,' he said to her, softly and with infinite malice – and stepping closer he leaned forward and pistol-whipped her across the face, two swingeing blows powered by the arid, ancient loathing running in his blood.

The force of it sent her sprawling. She lay on one side, her body turned towards him, blood flowing from her wide open, silent-screaming mouth – but then looking up into his eyes she knew what was coming next and tried to curl herself into a self-protecting ball. Lacking the strength to make it happen her hands and feet only scrabbled feebly at the floor, achieving nothing.

Ras kicked her in the stomach – twice, polished leather toecap driving into her soft undefended flesh. He stood back a little then, staring down at her, a man about to express the hatred consuming him by killing in its name.

'Turn over,' he ordered. 'Lie on your front, pillow your forehead on your hands.'

His words came faintly to Rose as she lay in the small, tightly constricted world of pain that he had trapped her in. He is master, he rules her world now. Slowly and with agony she does exactly as Khaled Ras has ordered.

And he executes her then. Two bullets to the back of the head.

CHAPTER 12

Thursday, 14 August
Outside Oakdene House in Pilgrims' Way

A hot, lazy summer afternoon. Oakchurch village lay quiet and still. The few villagers who worked locally had had their lunch at home and then walked, driven or cycled back to their work-places; holidaying children were off to hang out with their friends at the local swimming pool or the council-run sports area south of the village. While in several gardens men and women had rolled up their sleeves and were removing garden detritus to enhance the beauty of flowering shrubs and annuals.

However, in tree-lined Pilgrims' Way running past the front boundary fence of Oakdene House all was quiet. Each of the residences lying to either side of it stood centred within its own extensive land, and all guarded their privacy with hedges and trees, especially on the roadward side....

Approaching Oakdene on foot Vince Jenner turned into Pilgrims' Way at 2.15, his dark-green designer jacket worn loose over an open-necked white shirt, regulation jeans and trainers. Walking along to the red pillar box ten yards or so beyond the gate into Oakdene's drive, he loitered around it for a few minutes then looked back along the road he had come in by.... Rob Daley and Blakey would drive in the same way, he thought to himself, tense with excitement and nervousness. They would park the dark blue KA outside Oakdene and – dressed in their suits, of course, polished black shoes, slick hair – they would walk down to the house, each carrying a holdall for their files and lunch boxes – and in Rob's bag he'd have the four explosive devices. He'd fix them individually beneath the bedheads of the kids when he went upstairs to do the council check.

'Lovely afternoon, isn't it?' A girl's voice came from behind him, bright and friendly and – to him at that moment – utterly terrifying.

Swinging round to face her, he saw she was about fourteen and wearing a pink sleeveless top, matching shorts, and had her blonde hair pulled back into a pony-tail tied with a pink ribbon.

'Hello,' he said, getting it out somehow and thinking – please go back to wherever you came from, go fast, go *now*! 'Yes, it's nice today.'

'I got sent out to post my father's mail,' she confided wryly, and turned away to slip a handful of letters into the postbox; then facing him again she favoured him with a flashing grin – and, whirling round, was off back the way she had come, pony-tail bouncing and catching the sunlight. ''Bye!' she called over her shoulder. 'Have fun!'

''Bye!' he called back, a cold sweat of relief breaking out on him, he could feel it beneath his shirt as he watched her disappearing through the entrance into a house a cricket pitch's distance away along the road.

Pulling himself together Jenner glanced at his watch, saw it was 2.28 p.m. so reached into his jacket pocket for his mobile. As he took it out his hand brushed against the waistband of his jeans and he felt the hard metallic butt of the narrow little automatic thrust securely into it there. As he touched it, his head lifted in pride at being a member of a cadre of 'terrorists' and entrusted with a gun by them, a loaded gun.... Since he was the look-out posted at the gate of Martindale's property, the fate of Rob and Blakey was in his hands, they were depending on *him* for their safety! In fact the whole operation Cold Call now depended on *his* vigilance. As soon as he had seen Rob and Blakey arrive safely, park, get out of the KA, go in through Oakdene's gate and start off along the drive to the front door, he himself had to move closer to that gate and take up a position from which he could see both Oakdene's front door *and* for a good long distance along Pilgrims' Way, in both directions. From there he had to keep a sharp eye on the road and the pavement and, should he spot either pedestrian or vehicle approaching the house he must use his mobile immediately. Any movement in the street meant he must call Rob and report what was happening in Pilgrims' Way, and from that moment on must keep Rob informed on any developments in the road, thereby giving him and Blakey time either to carry on with the hit as planned, or make a quick exit without arousing suspicion in Charlotte's mind.

At the far end of Pilgrims' Way he saw a dark blue KA turn in and come towards him. At once, but with apparent nonchalance, Jenner turned his back on it, took a step or two towards the postbox ... then, on hearing two car doors slam shut, he retraced his steps to Oakdene's front gate. Loitering outside it he stuck his hands in his pockets and, pretending to be unconcerned, watched Rob Daley and John Blake walk in through Martindale's gate and then along the drive leading up to his front door. Each had his hold-all in hand, Robert the blue one containing the four bombs, Blakey the grey one innocent of menace. They looked their part, he thought, both neat and correct in their dress and with an air of 'I'm-on-government-business' as they walked along in step....

Jenner saw his Cold Call fellow-agents come to a halt at the door and either knock or ring for attention. He saw the door opened to them, there was a pause while doubtless they showed their ID and explained their business then the door was opened wider, they both went inside and the door was closed behind them.

For a moment Jenner stood rooted to the spot by a powerful sense of utter loneliness and fear as the silence of Pilgrims' Way closed around him. For an instant the implications of what he had become swamped him. He realized that as a result of what he was doing four children would be blown to bits. Oh Christ, what have I done? How am I going to live with *what I have done* this day?

With a tremendous effort of will he got his guilt under control, counteracting its effects with the exhilarating hubristic arrogance implicit in the knowledge that he was an action-comrade to Robert Daley – a member of a full-blown terrorist cadre.... Squaring his shoulders he strolled back towards the scarlet pillar-box, mobile in hand, eyes ever busy, watchful for threat to his comrades.

He saw a woman emerge from the house the teenage girl had gone back into. Elegantly clad in dark trousers and a tailored buttercup yellow overblouse she began to walk towards him. She was obviously taking the dog for a walk, the beautifully groomed Borzoi she had on a lead looked even more self-assured and well-tended than she did, Jenner thought. The dog reminded him of one of the same breed owned by a relative of his mother's and for a moment he looked at it with pleasure and admiration – but then quickly turned away to check up and down Pilgrims' Way, make sure the coast was still clear for Rob and Blakey. Found everything OK there, no cars or people anywhere to be seen in either direction.

'Looks as if you're having to wait a long time for your friend,' she said from behind him, a touch of amusement in the cultured, friendly voice. 'Anyway, at least it's not raining, that's a plus, isn't it?' she added as he swung round to face her.

'That's a lovely dog, Borzois are superb, aren't they?' he said and, anxious not to seem anxious and thus perhaps arouse suspicion in the woman, he bent forward and offered the back of his right hand towards the Borzoi's muzzle for it to smell—

'Vincent Jenner I'm arresting you for complicity in a terrorist strike!' Fast-moving and highly trained in such manoeuvres, WPC Ann Harker seized his stretched-out right arm in a grip of iron just above the wrist as she spoke. She slipped round behind him and jerked him upright, grabbing and securing his left arm as she did so; then holding both arms against his spine, she handcuffed him while she completed the obligatory warning that anything he said might be used in evidence against him. That done, she searched him for weapons, discovered the automatic and relieved him of it.

She glanced at her watch, saw it was 2.34 p.m., then slipped him a mocking grin.

'Dead on time,' she said, and at that moment saw an unmarked police Volvo turn into the far end of Pilgrims' Way and drive towards them.

It pulled up alongside her, and a young, strongly built male officer got out from beside the driver and came over to her, smiling.

'Got your man, I see,' he said. 'Was he armed, like they thought?'

She handed him Jenner's handgun. 'He was easy,' she said sombrely. 'I only hope the others are as lucky with his mates inside.' But then she shook her head and got on with her part in the exercise. 'You take Jenner in the back with you, will you? I must return this handsome beast to Mrs Henderson.... Wouldn't half mind keeping him myself, he's beautiful *and* well behaved, I could love him....'

CHAPTER 13

Pilgrims' Way 14.30
Oakdene House

Getting out of the passenger seat of the KA Blake hauled the two hold-alls out of the back and carried them round the car to where Daley was locking up. Handing him the blue one, the heavier since it contained the bombs, Blake turned and walked across the pavement to the gate into Martindale's property, as he did so glancing towards the pillar-box and checking that Jenner was in position there. Daley joined him a few seconds later, and going in through the gate they walked along the drive to the front door and halted before it, standing side by side.

'Got your ID ready?' Daley murmured, reaching into his jacket pocket for his own.

Blake had his in his hand.

Three thumps of brass on wood brought no immediate response, but then as Daley lifted a hand to repeat the summons they heard footsteps within the house and a couple of seconds later Oakdene's door was opened to them.

'Good afternoon,' the pretty young woman facing them said quite sharply, one hand on the door frame, the other holding the edge of the door, effectively blocking the way in. Then, 'Can I help you?' she went on, softening her tone because ... well, two nice-looking, neat-and-tidy young blokes facing a girl when the 'top lot' are away for the day – it can fill in the time pleasantly, can't it? Better than polishing the fucking silver, anyway.

'Good afternoon to you, Miss.' Holding his ID towards her for inspection, Blake stepped forward a little to establish in her eyes his position as the senior of the two. 'We're from the Council, Housing and Planning Department. Would you like to verify our bona fides?'

'Yes, I would.' Charlotte checked both ID cards, compared photographs with faces; then handed the cards back. 'What is it you want, then?' she asked, smiling at Blake. He looked a real man, she was thinking. OK, for sure he wouldn't have so much cash to throw around as young Vince did but he looked as if he might be more interesting. 'Mr and Mrs Martindale aren't at home and they won't be back till six at the earliest—'

'Their presence is not required, miss.' Blake was at his most charming, making flirtatious eye contact all the while: he was finding no problem with that, the girl had a luscious figure – also blue eyes that were telling him she thought he looked pretty good himself. 'All we have come to do is check the number and approximate size of all the rooms in the residence.'

'Why? What for?' Charlotte asked. Mustn't let him think I'm stupid she thought.

Blake had prepared for the obvious questions. 'Council tax update,' he said – then gave her a grin and added, 'Hell, Martindale might've built a whole new flat out the back since our last check, mightn't he?'

Charlotte giggled, her pretty face flushing attractively.

'They're not like that,' she protested. 'Still, I have to admit there's one or two over in the village who might be, so I can see you need to keep an eye on things.'

'We won't take long.' Unzipping his (innocent) hold-all Blake brought out a clipboard with several pages of a typed questionnaire fixed to it. 'We have these forms, they just need us to put ticks in the right places and we're done. Me and Jake here' – he nodded towards Daley – 'we usually work together and Jake usually does the upstairs while I do the ground floor.' He smiled again, "chatting her up" with his eyes. 'The ground floor of these big old houses is usually pretty complicated,' he went on, 'so if you can spare the time I'd be glad if you'd come round with me, it'd be a great help.'

Charlotte took her hand away from the doorpost – but then thought to make one more check. 'So what's in the bags?' she asked. 'They look at bit heavy for note-taking and forms.'

Nodding, Daley picked up his hold-all. 'In here I've got a camera and folding tripod in case we think there's "added value" to the property,' he said. 'Outside stuff, lovely views from the upstairs windows, maybe, that can up the price of a place. Also there's our lunch boxes, so that we can claim lunch-out cash – don't let on to the council about that, though, will you?'

Charlotte giggled conspiratorially and opened the door wider. Daley went into the house first. Moving past Blake he stepped into the medium-sized hall and stood still, checking its layout. Blake followed him inside and Charlotte shut the door and began to walk on across the hall, past them both. Daley found everything in the hall exactly as shown on the sketch-map of the ground floor plan Blake had made after his investigative break-in-and-entering job at Oakdene. He noted the closed doors to left and right giving access to study and sitting-room respectively and, open straight ahead of him across the hall, the door into the corridor leading on through the house to the back door and the garden at the rear—

'*Armed police! Armed police! Don't move! Stay where you are!*' Shouting their warning, guns levelled at Daley and Blake, four counter-terrorist marksmen erupted simultaneously from the study and the sitting-room, two of them targeting Blake, two Daley.

They got Blake, one of them felled him with a single swingeing blow as he reached for the gun in his jacket pocket, then stood over him with aimed weapon while the other hauled him back on to his feet, jerked his arms behind him and cuffed them.

But Daley was too quick for his two marksmen. Luckily for him Charlotte had unwittingly stopped in their way as they were closing in on him so, for two vital seconds, they lost the drive of their attack, giving Daley time to hurl his hold-all at one of them, dart through the door into the corridor and run for his life. Pelting along he dashed out through the back door and hared across the lawn. Hearing gunshots behind him as he plunged into the bordering shrubbery, he charged through it to the back fence, scrambled over that and was away....

CHAPTER 14

M16 Operations Room
Portland Place, London

'Locksley here,' he said, seated at one of the tables in the Ops room.

'Sir. WPC Harker, reporting from Pilgrims' Way.'

'Go ahead.'

'Suspect Vincent Jenner arrested here outside Oakdene House. Suspect was armed, one handgun, loaded.'

'More fool he. Did Edwards pick you up OK?'

'On the dot, sir.'

'Bring Jenner in, then, and—'

'*Sir*!' An urgent male voice called to him as Tom Cox, working at the radio and computer equipment, swung round to raise the alarm. 'Daley's escaped! He's off the Oakdene property and on the run—'

'Hold it, Tom.' Speaking to Harker, he ordered her to report to him in person as soon as Jenner was safely in custody, then went across to Cox and took over radio control of the incoming report from the arresting unit at Oakdene House.

'... over the boundary fence at the back of the house. Vehicle A has been alerted to pursue. Sergeant White also chasing, self holding Blake pending back-up.'

'Right. Keep him there and await further orders. Locksley out.' Handing radio contact back to Cox he swung aside and, shoulders hunched and with his head down, concentrated on forming in his

mind a complete 'picture' of the situation in regard to both operation Cold Call and Wayfarer. One of his top priorities was to try to
gain information regarding Wayfarer from Robert Daley.

Shortly, Locksley had decided on his course of action. One: well
hidden plain-clothes attack-and-arrest units to be positioned at all
Daley's places of entertainment or refuge known to the
Intelligence services with orders to effect his immediate detention
should he turn up at any of them. Two: intensive searches to be
carried out at Daley's place of residence in the hope that details of
Wayfarer might be discovered there. Three: an arresting unit to be
positioned at Rose Daley's residence to lie low, maintain surveillance – and detain her should she attempt to leave home. Such
detention to be effected only when she was well away from her
residence lest her son was himself watching the place with a view
to hiding out there.

All relevant orders issued, Locksley went back to the radio
connection to Oakdene and had Cox send out the following
instruction:

'Squad car 3 Rapid Response unit to proceed immediately to
Robert Daley's place of residence at 12 Nelson Road, Ealing,
London and await my arrival there. Should any person enter the
building before I get there allow him/her to do so and hold back;
should any person *leave* it, he/she to be held pending my arrival.'

15.30 on the same day

'I see Rapid Response have got their look-out well hidden,'
Sergeant Eastwood observed as he turned the black Escort into
Nelson Road in Ealing, a street of greystone terraced houses, and
drove on along it.

'Didn't see him myself. Where's he placed?' Beside him,
Locksley's attention was on the house at the far end of the road,
the one lived in by Robert Daley.

'He's lurking by that telephone kiosk we just passed.' Six foot tall and built with it Eastwood was young and supremely self-confident. 'We'll have Daley to rights if he shows up here, no sweat.'

Locksley said nothing. Minutes earlier he had been in radio contact with the senior officer of the RR unit on watch at Daley's house and received a 'No action here' report. This whole situation wasn't going to be wrapped up easily, he was sure of that. The arrest of Daley wouldn't be the end of it: looming somewhere ahead, at some unknown further date, lay the shadowy operation known as Wayfarer.

'Park well short of Daley's, shall I, sir?' Eastwood was slowing down.

'Do that.'

The Escort slid into an empty slot alongside the kerb. There was no one to be seen in the street. Unhurriedly Locksley and the sergeant walked along to the end of Nelson Road. They went in through the open gate of Number 12, covered the short paved path to its front door in a few strides then turned on to the narrow lawn on their right and went round to the back of the building. The gardens were untended and again everywhere was very quiet, no people to be seen or even heard – except for the monotonous beat of a pop hit with heavy base coming from a house three doors away.

Halting at Robert Daley's back door, Eastwood squinted up at the rain clouds, cast a quick glance across the neighbouring gardens and, finally, ran an experienced exploratory eye over the door into the house.

'Nice and peaceful all about, sir, and a door that wouldn't trouble a child of ten,' he murmured, then looked at his boss standing beside him. 'OK to go in?'

Locksley nodded and said quietly, 'Go ahead, but limit the damage as much as possible.' Eastwood took a couple of steps back, eyed the door for the best pressure point, lined himself up for striking it – then with carefully judged force lunged at it with hip and shoulder.... The sound of surrendering wood was no more than meaningless counterpoint to the rhythmic pounding beat from three doors away. As Eastwood stepped back he saw that the door was now hanging at an angle, in place but loose, detached from the doorframe at the locking side. Quickly he eased it a couple of feet open, making the way into Daley's place clear. As far as Locksley could tell the house Daley lived in was his one hope; it was the only point of contact he had to Wayfarer.

Following Eastwood in, he found himself in the kitchen.

'Get straight to work,' he said, turning to the sergeant. 'You're here as the IT expert so while I get the house searched for all Daley's documents you go to work on his computers. God knows how much there'll be and a lot of it will be his college stuff, but like I was telling you on the way here, Operation Wayfarer is what we're after. You'll probably have to dig deep—'

'If there's anything for us here, I'll find it, sir. You'll sing out to me, won't you, if anything that's up my street turns up where you're looking?'

'You can count on that—' He broke off to respond to his mobile, motioning to Eastwood to go off and get started. 'Locksley,' he said.

'Commissioner Woods. Has Davies reported to you yet?'

'No, sir. Eastwood and I are in Daley's house now, just beginning a search.'

'Good. There's been an interesting development here. An officer working on Robert Daley extended his computer search to DNA found on recent murder sites – and he struck gold: Daley's DNA is a match for bloodstains found at the scene of that killing months ago at Oakdene House, the would-be housebreaker—'

'Good God.' Locksley was gobsmacked at the sudden random kindnesses of Fate. 'So whatever happens we'll have him for plain murder.'

From daybreak that Thursday Elianne stayed at home waiting for Matt Locksley to call her: he had promised to do so when he had time and give her some idea of what progress was being made in the combined Intelligence-services and police exercise being mounted against Cold Call. She found it difficult to fill in the hours. He would call her when he could spare the time, she reminded herself as the hours crept by: given that promise she would, somehow, manage to wait all day if necessary.... She cleaned the house, used the washing machine twice and then, unusually for her, prepared complicated and time-consuming Lebanese food for her lunch – only to leave it barely touched.... She made herself a mug of black coffee, then took it through to the big mahogany desk in the living-room and sat down there, mobile and books on criminal law to hand, and tried to concentrate on the half-completed essay required of her by the end of the vacation....

He called a few minutes after five o'clock. Told her in short sharp sentences that the 'exercise' at Oakdene House had resulted in the arrest on scene of Vincent Jenner and John Blake and the confiscation of the four bombs intended to kill Martindale's grandchildren—

'But Robert Daley?' she broke in harshly. 'What about *him*?'

'He evaded capture. He's on the run, Elianne, which is why I've made time to call you—'

'*I don't believe it!*' she said, anguish and a wild tide of anger and protest welling up inside her.

'You have to! That's the way it is, there's no arguing with it. So listen to me now because perhaps you can help us find and arrest him. Are you listening?' May God give her strength, he thought.

'Yes, yes, Matt, I'm listening.'

'Here's how things stand at the moment. Daley escaped arrest at Oakdene and is known to have got clear of that area. I'm now in his house in Nelson Road, we're searching it for info regarding Wayfarer. But – we want Daley. We have men watching his mother's house, but we've no clues as to any other place he might run to in the hope of lying low there. So, Elianne – can you help us in that? Can you think of anywhere else he might go in the hope of sanctuary? A bolt-hole, some place he hopes, even expects, the authorities don't know about? Do you know of anywhere like that? Somewhere Jenner might have mentioned, perhaps? ... Think, Elianne!' Desperately he prompted her, hungry for anything that would enable him to take positive action against Daley, who must have info about Wayfarer – and might be willing to make a deal.

But Elianne could not call to mind anything to give Locksley; nothing he didn't already know.

However when the call was over she put her elbows on the desk and her head in her hands and thought over the times she'd spent with Jenner: recalled things he had told her about Robert Daley and his mates, searching for something – anything – he had said to her that might give some clue to a hide-out available to his cadre-comrade.

Locksley's search of Daley's house had brought to light nothing of interest: there had been only a stack of material connected with his college work and, naturally, personal trivia about him such as that he had a liking for avocadoes (six in his fridge) and a large collection of designer tee-shirts. Finishing just before 18.00 he went into the kitchen, sat down at the big square table and, having received no progress report for over an hour from the 3-strong squad surveillancing Rose Daley's flat, called through to Donelly, its lead officer.

'No action here, sir.' Donelly's Irish lilt seemed more pronounced over the phone. 'And to tell you the honest truth this surveillance we're on here is boring, this street's so bloody quiet it's like we're in a city of the dead. Neither man nor woman has gone into nor come out of Number 10 since we took up position here.'

Surely she would have realized by now that Cold Call had been busted and done something about it? Even if, Locksley thought, it was just to flee to personal safety? A worm of apprehension stirred in his brain. Surely she wouldn't simply stay home waiting for the cops to come and arrest her? No way would Rose Daley react like that, it wasn't her style at all.

'Go in at once, Donelly!' he ordered, misgivings suddenly crystallizing into a sixth-sense certainty that something was wrong and action was needed. 'Use only such force as is necessary, but get to her fast, don't give her time to destroy documents or send out warnings. You're with me?'

'Sure. One of my boys here is a locksmith, the lady won't know we're in the house till we bust in and take her.'

'Call me as soon as it's done— Locksley out!' He cut Donelly off abruptly as Eastwood shot into view in the doorway calling 'Quick, sir! Come quick!'

'What gives?' Locksley asked, already on his way to the door, Rose Daley instantly dismissed from his mind.

'*I'm on to something, sir*!' Eastwood said exultantly, grabbing Locksley by the arm and hurrying him along towards Daley's room. 'This Op Wayfarer, sir, there's what looks like the outline of its action on one of his computers. I've only just got started on it so hopefully there's more to come, but I thought you'd want to be in on it straightaway. Daley's got four or maybe more computers here, see: this one was a little way off to the side like maybe he's forgotten about it. It doesn't name the op, sir – well, not so far as I've got – but, hell, surely it has to be Wayfarer, doesn't it? They wouldn't be running *two* with suicide bombers on trains, like you were saying—'

Breaking off as he led the way into Daley's room Eastwood strode across to a cluttered table on his left, slid into the chair in front of it, then pulled the small computer closer to him and busied his hands on its keyboard, Locksley at his shoulder.

'Look at this, sir!' he went on as typed information appeared on the screen – and then as his fingers continued flowing across the keys there appeared on the screen the unfolding pattern of a fully planned terrorist strike.

Leaning forward over Eastwood's shoulder, Locksley watched the strategies of Abu Yusuf's mission take written shape before his eyes. On that seldom-used out-of-date computer, Robert Daley had mapped out for himself the proposed action-sequences of Wayfarer. The named London stations from which the four suicide bombers, each carrying his lethal payload, would start their respective journeys and their ultimate destinations: Rugby, Southend, Exeter, Brighton. The departure time of each train was given, followed by its position with respect to its target station at 11.30 on

Friday 15th August. Finally, after Eastwood had been confronted by a blank screen and fought his way past it, were listed names and telephone numbers of the major players in the mission.

'*Jesus!*' Eastwood breathed, leaning back in his chair and rubbing a hand over his eyes and forehead. 'That's it then, isn't it, sir. End of story.'

Locksley laid a hand on his shoulder. 'Not so,' he said quietly. 'It's the beginning of the end for those who dreamed up this nightmare.'

CHAPTER 15

Thursday, 14 August
Robert Daley's house in Nelson Road

'It has to be Wayfarer, sir.' Locksley said to the Commissioner on his mobile. 'Yes, three of its named personnel are already on file, the Daleys, mother and son, and the bomb-maker.... Four bombs, yes, primed for detonation, each one concealed in the haversack of one of the bombers, to be collected from the bomb-maker's house. Until Wayfarer got going the bomb-maker had been inactive here since entering the country years ago, he'd established himself as a law-abiding citizen here—'

'And the Daleys?'

'Robert Daley's still on the run. We've had his mother under tight surveillance at her place of residence for some time, but now I've ordered the watch-squad to force entry and arrest her, I'm expecting a report on that any minute. Documentary evidence from this house is being assembled and should be with you shortly. Transcript of the computer-info on Wayfarer is almost completed, but it's clear that Wayfarer is scheduled to climax at 11.30 tomorrow—'

'So get yourself and that transcript here as quickly as possible, there's some fast action needed,' the Commissioner said. 'By the time you arrive I'll have the senior officers of all relevant forces called to conference, join us as soon as you get here.'

Even as Locksley put his mobile down on a nearby chair, it summoned him again.

'Donelly, sir. I—'

'Why the devil has it taken you so long?'

'Sir, I've been trying to contact you for the last five minutes.'

'Sorry. You've got Rose Daley?'

'In a manner of speaking, sir, yes. She's dead. We found her dead inside the flat.'

Locksley controlled his sense of shock instantly. 'She committed suicide? Damn it, I should've guessed, should've sent you in earlier—'

'It's murder, sir.' Donelly's voice cut in, curt and certain. 'Neither living man nor woman would do that to themselves.... Couldn't,' he corrected himself tightly, 'it's not physically possible.'

'Weapon used?'

'She must've been pistol-whipped across the face, kicked hard in the guts by a shod foot, then shot twice in the back of the head.'

'Well ... poor Rose?' No, he thought, I'll never feel sad for Rose Daley; in Lebanon she and her husband caused far far worse to be done to many others, in their time.... 'You know the drill, Donelly. Main thing is to secure the scene, to leave it exactly as you found it. I'll despatch a counter-terrorist team and forensics to you as quickly as possible. Meantime you and your men maintain a very low profile, detail any caller and inform me immediately. And bear in mind that Daley's son is still at large....'

Friday, 15 August
06.30

Abu Yusuf slept well for the latter half of the night preceding Wayfarer's climax, the night of Rose Daley's murder. Khaled Ras's late-night telephone call reporting the killing had been tailored to include the sentence, 'I found her at home so I was able to give the present into her hands.' After hearing this sleep had come easily to him. He felt his honour as the operation's commander restored with the execution of the Daley woman on his order, his personal order.... And even more satisfactorily, Wayfarer was on the brink of successful climax: by the end of the coming day his name would be ringing throughout the Muslim world in triumph, himself hailed as The Sword of Allah in Glory....

Waking early he ate breakfast and then, taking with him a cup of coffee, went into his study at the front of the house. It was a pleasant comfortably furnished room with large windows over-looking the drive. Settling down at the desk in the back corner of the room, which was equipped with IT equipment enabling him to contact not only each of his senior agents in Europe but also certain high-ranking officials of his organization presently residing in Iran, Syria and Lebanon – he turned his attention to Wayfarer's preparedness. He contacted each of his senior captains to ensure that every feature of his operation's complex structure was fully ready for action at its appointed time. Wayfarer's bomb-maker reported all was in order, the four explosives packages were at his house, primed for detonation and concealed in the hold-alls to be carried by the martyrs. Faris Mansoor, the Palestinian, confirmed that at each of the martyrs' departure stations the relevant Wayfarer agent had reported no crisis or inopportune development.

Lastly he contacted Khaled Ras, seeking assurance that each of the martyrs was not only physically but also mentally and emotion-ally prepared for his sacrifice, that each was afire and eager to '*go to God*' that day. Ras swore all of The Chosen were fully committed and steady of purpose, then as Abu Yusuf began to make celebra-tory farewells, the Afghan asked him if he had been in touch with Robert Daley that morning.

'Of course not,' Yusuf answered impatiently. 'I have no reason to, the boy has no active part in the operation's climax, his usefulness to the mission is already at an end.'

'As is his mother's.' Ras could not resist making the comment. He then returned to the point he wished to make. 'I asked about the bitch's son because early yesterday morning I called him and ordered him to remain at his place of residence from then on until at least midday today since I might need to call upon him for assistance in Wayfarer should one of our other agents fail in some way.'

'Why did you call him this morning, then? *Has* one of our agents failed?'

'No, thanks be to Allah, but I do not trust Daley and I wished to make sure he had obeyed my orders – and now, I find he has not,' he ended, steely voiced. 'So have I your permission to send an arresting agent to his place of residence immediately?'

'You will do no such thing,' Abu Yusuf said angrily. 'It would be a waste of manpower on this day of high consequence, and I do not want you distracted by such sideline affairs.'

Locksley had woken up a little earlier than Abu Yusuf that day. Now, showered, shaved, and wearing a grey shirt and navy blue chinos, he cooked himself bacon and eggs and ate at the kitchen table. His mind was busy with the plans which, during the top-level 'war council' conference held at counter-terrorism HQ the previous evening had been aired, discussed and furiously argued about. Agreement had finally been reached on a schedule of action to frustrate operation Wayfarer and to arrest that mission's front-line personnel.

First, the four suicide bombers. Each in turn is scheduled to call at the house of the bomb-maker, collect his haversack and set off for the station from which his target train will depart. The departure times are different for each of the four, but all, according to Robert Daley's notes, take place between 07.00 and 09.00. The times at which each 'martyr' is scheduled to leave the bomb-maker's house are staggered and, like the route each will take on leaving it, are known to us in full detail. Each of the four will be arrested at a point in his journey when he will be caught *in flagrante delicto* while at the same time the risk to passing citizens is minimal i.e. in a quiet street fairly close to the bomb-maker's house. By 09.15 the last of the bombers will have collected his device – three minutes later our armed officers will arrest this explosives expert and escort him to the unmarked police car parked nearby. He will then be driven to the interrogation centre established for Wayfarer's personnel.

The images of the counter-attack against Wayfarer continued their parade through Locksley's mind until all were played out. He now had a clear sense of how the ground beneath the mission would be cut away from beneath the terrorists' feet piece by piece, its suicide bombers taken out one by one as they set out for their targets and its mission commanders and logistics officers captured in a synchronized series of Rapid Response units' raids.

All this to take place before they realize we've got Wayfarer in our sights and are blowing her out of the water, Locksley said to himself as he drained the last of the coffee in his tall brown mug. Then by the time I arrive at the interrogation centre this Abu Yusuf and his cadre members will be on their way there as well. They will be safely wedged in the back seats of unmarked police cars, one securely hand-cuffed terrorist to each vehicle with an armed anti-terrorist officer to either side of him....

However, that morning events did not work out exactly as planned.

Abu Yusuf's residence
A few minutes before 09.00

Neatly dressed in black trousers, white shirt and black jacket, Khaled Ras arrived later than he had said at his commander's house. No-one let him in: knowing the front door would have been unlocked earlier and left that way for him, he simply opened it and went inside. The house was very quiet about him; Yusuf's wife and children, together with all his domestic staff had been away on holiday near Bournemouth since the beginning of August, spending the summer break as usual in a large rented house there with a big garden and heated swimming pool. In their absence Abu Yusuf was served and watched over by Ahmed Mohsen, his middle-aged, obsessively devoted body servant, who that day had departed at 07.15 to pass the weekend in Oxford with his aged father, a filial duty expected of him twice a month.

As the front door of the house closed behind Ras, surreptitious action commenced at the back of it. Emerging from tree-and-bush cover there, having concealed themselves either side of the narrow lawn, four armed assault officers clad in dark green combat gear advanced at a crouched run – their weapons at the ready – to the twelve-paned casement window of the scullery. They stopped alongside the back door near the window and paused in a tensed-for-action, grim-faced group.

Standing nearest the window Pete Brooks glanced at his sergeant, received his immediate thumbs-up so got stuck into the job. An ex-house-breaker by upbringing and practice who had changed careers at the age of twenty, he worked with fast, economical ease. Taking from his backpack a prepared window-pane-sized, well-greased sheet of folded, tough brown paper, he slapped ie greased-side down against the bottom right-hand window pane then smoothed it firmly into place there from its centre outwards to the sides and the four corners. He turned to his sergeant, mouthed 'Ready' to him and received his nod to proceed. Shattering the pane's entire surface with a series of systematically placed hard sharp blows with the heel of his hand, he then spread his palm and fingers across it, pressed inwards hard and felt the glass give under his pressure. As the whole pane gave way, he folded the broken glass in on itself within the brown paper, put the package down on the ground, reached carefully in through the hole he had so quietly made and manoeuvred the window's metal catch free.

A couple of minutes later the four-strong squad of marksmen were advancing through Abu Yusuf's house....

Ras went straight into the study overlooking the drive, where he found Abu Yusuf standing looking out over his garden through the big picture window. Yusuf turned to him as he came in, greeted him curtly then went to sit down at his desk on the other side of the room. Ras followed him.

'Our martyrs will by now be on their way to their departure stations,' he observed, glancing up at his 2i/c, dark eyes aglow with anticipation of imminent triumph. 'Wayfarer is launched, Ras.'

'Has our bomb-maker reported to you yet?' Ras asked. He too was hyped up – also restless with the frustration of not, on this mission, being at the sharp end of the action.

'He is not scheduled to call in until 10.15.' Yusuf watched the Afghan swing impatiently away, stride across to the big window and stand staring out. 'You did a good job last night,' he said. 'Thanks to you the Daley woman will trouble us no longer.' Aware of Ras's continuing craving for hands-on violence, he nevertheless recognized that it was a mindset which needed a touch of commendation at times to help him keep properly focussed on the overall situation, not on his own personal hang-ups. 'I shall make official report of your pivotal role in her punishment for disloyalty in the course of an operation—'

'*Armed police! Armed police! Stay where you are! Stay where you are!*' As the door was kicked open four armed men surged into the study filling it with shouted orders as they came, weapons aimed, fingers on triggers. Two of them headed straight for Abu Yusuf and halted a yard away from him, one with gun-muzzle directed at his chest as he sat at his desk, his mate a little to one side watching Yusuf's hands. The other two had Ras boxed in before he had time to turn round from the window, one of them standing back a bit to cover the Afghan from the side, the other moving fast to get up close, the muzzle of his gun was pressed hard against Ras's spine.

'Get your hands above your head and face me!' he ordered, jabbing his weapon harder into Ras's back to make the wisdom of obedience absolutely clear.

Abu Yusuf had made no attempt at resistance, the lightning-fast suddenness of the attack had been a shock paralyzing all thought and action on the instant.

'On your feet, keep your hands in the air!' ordered the man with the muzzle of his gun barely a yard from the sitting man's chest. And with dazed, clumsy docility Wayfarer's commander pushed himself to his feet; a few seconds later, his hands cuffed behind his back, he was on his way to the door, prisoner to the marksmen close behind him.

Ras, however, was active in his mind although apparently obedient to the orders he received. Even as he began to turn round to face his enemy, he slid his right hand smoothly downwards to get at the pistol in his jacket pocket – only to have his wrist grabbed by the marksman on that side him who then yanked him round one-handed to face him and held him thus while his mate frisked him, relieved him of the pistol but found him to be carrying no other weapon, not even the concealed dagger they had half expected. They handled him hard and, when satisfied, handcuffed him like his commander.

As the two prisoners and their escorting marksmen were approaching the door the telephone on Abu Yusuf's desk began to ring and all the men stopped. Then the sergeant went back and picked up the receiver.

'Faris Mansoor to report,' said a man's voice in his ear, quietly jubilant and using fluent English. 'All goes well at the four stations. Our martyrs are ready to honour their commitment. May God be with them. Out.'

Quietly, the sergeant replaced the receiver. 'Faris Mansoor,' he said to his men as he rejoined them and their prisoners. The group started on towards the door again—

'*Allah Akbar! Allah Akbar!*' screamed Khaled Ras defiantly, hearing Mansoor's name on the lips of his enemy and realizing the completeness of his defeat. And twisting round he hurled himself bodily at the sergeant, trying to head-butt him; his guard fired at him as he charged, but at the same moment the sergeant felled the Afghan with a round-house blow to the jaw so he was already falling sideways and the bullet meant for his shoulder took him in the head. He hit the ground shoulder-first and lay still, his gaunt body already dying. Then, as the sergeant bent over him, the black, hooded eyes glared up at him – and gathering together his last remaining strength Khaled Ras hissed one brief sentence at him in Arabic, then died.

The sergeant checked for signs of life, found none and straight-ened up. Grim faced, he turned to Abu Yusuf who, he had been told, spoke English.

'What did those last words of his mean?' he demanded, thinking they might reveal information of some kind.

Regaining something of his younger, truer self through the manner of the Afghan's death, Abu Yusuf looked the sergeant in the eye, considering how best to answer him. Finally he said, 'You would probably translate it simply as "Thank you for killing me,"' he said. 'But the Arabic words he used convey more than that. He died giving thanks to God for allowing him to die by the bullet of an infidel – which is to die with honour.'

CHAPTER 16

Late afternoon

Sitting tensely on the edge of her bed with her arms braced and hands clamped white-knuckled to its wooden frame, Elianne Asley was hag-ridden. Staring down at the floor she thought with great bitterness of Marcus lying prisoned in his hospital, and in an instant of clarity and determination came to a decision.

Getting to her feet, she went across to her dressing-table and took out her jewel box. It was made of rosewood inlaid with a pattern of delicate ivory roses; she kept it locked and wore its small key on a thin gold chain around her neck. It had been given to her by Nadia who had been presented with it by her husband Philippe in 1976 on the day Beirut descended into the hell of full, open civil war. The gun had been in it then; and it was in it now. Small and lethal, the silver automatic fitted smugly into its white satin bed beneath the top tray of the jewel box: fully loaded – Elianne knew of no source of further ammunition – it had been crafted by experts. 'Use it to safeguard yourself and the people whose values you believe in,' Nadia had said to Elianne as she had given it into her grand-daughter's hands. As she recalled those words now a sudden urgency surged through Elianne: she had to get there fast lest somehow British Intelligence reached Daley first. In the final analysis there was only one truly proper way to avenge her brothers – and that way did not lie through an English court of law.

Lifting out the silver pistol she slid it into the waistband of her jeans, went out to her car and set off for the place that might –

hopefully – be giving sanctuary to the man born Hussain Shalhoub. She drove fast and well, memories hounding her as she thought of what had to be done before Locksley got there and stole him from her.

Robert Daley was congratulating himself on having achieved what he saw as a clever move – or, rather, a whole series of smart, quickly executed moves – that had brought him safely to his present and, he hoped, secure hideout. First he had made a rapid getaway from Martindale's house – hard luck on Blakey, he'd lost out there – then by his cunning use of the knowledge of its environs he had acquired earlier he had worked his way clear of the area. Then he had had this fucking, gobsmackingly brilliant idea. He was weaponless, bereft of back-up of any sort and with police marksmen in hot pursuit. Cash and credit cards he had with him, that side of things was okay, but obviously Cold Call was blown sky-high so he'd be dead stupid to go to Rose's flat for help. His mind had been searching for a viable place where he might have a chance to lie low for a while, have time to make contact with sleepers among Abu Yusuf's network of moles and, with their help, get out of Britain, and take refuge in Lebanon. Then: *Damon Ashford*! His brain had suddenly flashed up the name as, head-in-hands and breathing hard, he'd been sitting on a park bench to get his breath back. 'Seeing' Ashford's name in his mind's eyes he had sat back in relief, lifted his head and grinned up at the sun shining down on him from the beautiful friendly blue sky....

Reaching Ashford's parents' place around five o'clock he had paid off his taxi, sneaked in through the side-gate to the two-car garage then on through the shrubbery to the bungalow way off at the rear of the house. He'd found the key secreted in its usual place.... Good on you, Dash, he'd thought, generous, trusting Dash who'd told his three best mates they were welcome to use his place any time whether he was with them or not – "Just remember to restock with beer and other necessities when you take off again, amigos, and leave everything more or less as you found it, OK?"

Now, soon after letting himself in, Daley strolled out through the door of Ashford's sitting-room on to the paved patio running the length of the bungalow, facing away from the house. He had an unopened can of lager from the fridge cold in his hand. Showered and changed, he was wearing one of Dash's shirts loose over jeans, his own, filthy and sweaty, consigned to the laundry basket in the spare room.

The bed in the spare room was already made up, he'd sleep well that night, Daley thought as he sat down in a cushioned leisure chair at one end of the patio and relaxed, stretching his legs out in front of him. He ripped open the can and took a long drink of the lager (within a couple of minutes of entering the bungalow he had knocked back a glass and a half of water from the tap in the kitchen to take the edge off the thirst burning his throat). While changing he had listened to a News programme on the portable radio, but it had carried no reports of any police raid that afternoon which, he imagined, would probably be presented to the nation's media as a failed burglary.

Cold Call, though, was low level stuff, Wayfarer was the one that really mattered, Daley reflected and, putting the can of lager down on the paving beside him, he leaned back into the comfort of his padded chair. A sense of comparative well-being grew in him as he considered his present situation; he let his mind roam ahead to the future, to plan how he should shape his life from now on. So far, he'd made it! Not only had he escaped a very dangerous set-up at Martindale's but also he was now a free man bunked down in a place where, surely, no one on the law-and-order side would ever think to look for him. He reasoned with growing self satisfaction that he would surely do well to stay put in the bungalow. Dash's fridge was well stocked and anyway he had cash and cards with him and there was a small supermarket ten minutes' walk away.

Yes, he'd keep a low profile for a few days and then, with Wayfarer played out successfully, he could soft-talk Abu Yusuf out of punishing him for going in with Rose for Cold Call and persuade him to safe-route him back to Lebanon under a new name. Once there, the captain of Unit 10 would surely sponsor him. True, the captain had disciplined him for not at once obeying the 'Out now' order that night, but he'd praised him for the efficiency of the actual killings so likely he'd ensure him a speedy return to the kind of life he wanted, sharp-end action stuff....

As Locksley approached Richmond on his way to the Interrogation Centre, he was granted his 'miracle' (that was to be the way he thought of it thereafter in spite of Assistant Commissioner Morris referring to it as his 'brilliant lucky coincidence').

Driving towards the Interrogation Centre in Richmond for his evening session he found himself slowed down on the outskirts of the area by traffic build-up, the vehicles ahead of him crawling along in line. When the car in front of him suddenly stopped dead, he did likewise, and then as he sat tapping impatient fingers on the steering wheel – the miracle happened. His restless eyes fell on the road sign planted low down on the verge on his nearside: RICH-MOND, it announced in big black-on-white letters – and as the name flicked on a switch in his mind, he recalled he had heard Elianne say it to him once early on when they had been talking about Robert Daley's best mates.

Thinking back fast Locksley picked up the name she had associated with Richmond: *Ashford*, Damon Ashford, *yes*! So, as Daley's other two co-criminals – Jenner and Blake – were both in custody, that left Ashford as Daley's last hope, surely? He might run to Ashford's place to hide? ... Elianne had said that young man lived in a bungalow behind his parents' house, hadn't she. But exactly where in Richmond was that? ... Locksley's mind was hot on the trail now so when he came to the next lay-by he pulled in and used his mobile. Calling his office at HQ he told the duty sergeant to check through the recently-compiled records of Robert Daley's friends and get him the address of Damon Ashford, *fast*, then ring him back.

Four minutes later the sergeant was on the line.

'Waverley, Furzedown Avenue, Richmond,' he said. 'Good hunting, sir.'

His Interrogation session postponed with a quick phone call, Locksley used his Satnav then drove to Furzedown Avenue. Cruising along it, to his horror saw Elianne's apple-green KA parked outside a house with a long frontage on to the road and a two-car garage. There were no other vehicles in sight.

'*Christ!*' he said aloud. Then he slid the car to a stop alongside the kerb, scrambled out and ran through the open gate he'd spotted leading in to the garages. Racing on past the big house and onto the lawn behind it, he saw the bungalow way off on the far side of the grass. For a moment he stood still, studying it – and realized that the door must be on the other side of the building.

So keeping to the shadowed darkness beneath the trees alongside the lawn, Locksley sped along towards the bungalow until he was level with it then darted across the grass to take cover behind the back of it. Drawing his gun from its holster he crouched down and crept along close to the side wall, listening for sounds of people inside the place.

The dream of that new life awaiting him in Lebanon enthralling him, Robert Daley reached down for his lager—

'*Both hands above your head, Daley – now!*'

A woman's voice was shouting at him – his head jerked round and he saw her standing at the far end of the patio with the small pistol in her hand aimed straight at him.

'*Do it or I'll shoot! Kill you, like you shot my brothers, the Asleys!*'

Daley's hands shot skywards, the name had said it all. 'I'm unarmed,' he shouted back.

'*So were they!* On your feet, Shalhoub!'

His mind homing in on the knife at his belt, eyes and brain judging the distance between them, Daley stood up, shuffling backwards a little as he did so then standing still as he felt the corner of the bungalow nudge his left shoulder – perhaps he could escape round there?

'Elianne Asley.' He said her name quietly but the fear of death was on him. 'Yes, I remember you. But think now, Elianne. These things play differently here in England: if you shoot dead an unarmed man they'll have you for murder—'

'I'll wipe the gun clean and leave it clasped in your hand, Shalhoub. The only other person who knows I have it is my grandmother Nadia and she's dead – did you know that, Shalhoub? *Did you?*'

'She was very brave that night, your grandmother.' Keep her talking, there're only seven/eight metres between us and I'll bet she's none too fast with a gun so if I drop to a crouch, whip out the knife and go for her in a side-swipe rush I can bring her down – then cut her throat. 'You were brave yourself, Elianne. I'd be proud to have a sister like you—'

Daley choked on the words as a man's arm swung out round the corner of the bungalow behind him to crook vice-hard around his throat. At the same moment a gun muzzle pressed against the side of his chest.

'*Don't shoot*, Elianne!' a man's voice yelled, 'it's Matt Locksley, *don't shoot this way!*'

She held her fire. Lowering her gun a little she watched and waited until—

'*Matt, look out, he's got a knife!*' she cried. '*His right hand, a knife!*'

High pitched and shrill from the far end of the patio, her voice sliced the warning through the air to Locksley.

For although half strangled Daley had reacted lightning fast. Twisting in against his assailant's body he forced back the suffocating agony of the throat-lock, grabbed blindly for the man's gun-arm with his right hand and slid his left down towards his belt, fingers reaching for his knife—

Hearing Elianne's warning Locksley glanced down, saw Daley's right arm, knife in hand, being stealthily drawn back to make the final arching strike up between the ribs – so with ferocious effort pulled his arm away from Daley's throat, swiped him savagely across the face with it then as the blood-suffused face jerked backwards under the force of the blow, shot him twice, high in the right shoulder. The knife dropped from Daley's nerveless hand as, punched backwards by the impact of the bullets, he flung out his arms and collapsed to lie sprawled on the patio, one side of his head thudding hard down on the paving.

And for a moment then there was no movement at all on the patio: Locksley, Elianne Asley and Daley were locked together in a silent tableau. Each in his own way was, momentarily, somehow at peace: Locksley, on account of a man's life having been 'saved'; Elianne, for reasons she had not yet formulated and Daley, obviously, for the simple reason that he was unconscious.... Then,

'What right did you have to ... steal him from me?' Elianne's voice came flat and hard, accusatory. Standing stiff and still, she regarded Locksley as though he were a total stranger.

Bending down he picked up the knife, laid it and his gun down on the windowsill of the room overlooking the patio. And staying where he was he spoke to her quietly, but he did not answer her question. He put to her one of his own.

'Elianne,' he said, 'do you think your brother Marcus would want you to be found guilty of murder? Would he want that, even though the man you murdered was the one who has, in a way, killed him? And would Tomas or James have wanted their deaths to make you a murderer? Judging by the way I've heard you talk about those three men, and I've heard quite a lot, mostly from you but from Charles too, they haven't seemed to me to be the sort of people who would themselves commit murder in cold blood. I think all three would consider doing so – whatever the reason given – a despicable act. Also one that degrades the person doing it,' he added, a sudden harshness in his voice, 'which is why I'm dead certain not one of them would have you kill Daley even though you did it for love of them.'

Sleek silver pistol held loosely at her side, she gave not an inch. 'They are not *your* brothers, are they,' she said to him. Then without another word she left him; turned her back on him and walked away past the bungalow, heading for the road.

A few minutes later he heard a car start up beyond the house. As it drove off he slid his gun back into its holster then got on with his job. Called an ambulance, made a brief report on his mobile to the Commissioner and was called in for immediate debriefing.

Elianne rang him in the small hours of the morning. Letting himself into his service flat only five minutes earlier, he had just sat down in his favourite armchair, with a whisky-soda to hand and his mobile on the floor beside him because he had orders to be available throughout what remained of the night....

Robert Daley was in hospital, under armed guard. That assured, Locksley and certain other officers active in the case had attended an *ad hoc* and off-the-record meeting convened by the Commissioner to decide on a course of action for the following day: assessment had to be made of the entire Wayfarer situation in the aftermath of that operation's frustration. Three hours' sleep I'll get tonight if I'm lucky, Locksley thought. Then his mobile rang.

'Shit,' he murmured without venom, only tiredness in him; then he answered the call, wondering what the hell they needed him for now.

'Matt,' she said, her voice light and easy, a kind of excitement in it. 'There are two things I want to say to you, I *need* to get them said so please forgive me for calling you at this ungodly time of the night. The first is simply, *Thank you*. You'll understand what for – and Matt, dear Matt, it comes from the heart.... The second thing is—'

'Elianne.' Sharply, he interrupted her. 'Before you go on to that, I'd like you to tell me what it is you're thanking me for. I need the words from you.'

After a pause, 'To begin with, thank you for what you said to me there on the patio. You put a lot of truths into words. Things I hadn't thought of, though I realize now I ought to have done....'

'Go on. That's "to begin with", you said.'

'If I'd killed him there and then, you'd have arrested me – you'd have had to, wouldn't you, you'd just seen me kill him,' she went on, the words rushing out now, she was desperate to get her motivation across to him, for him to *understand*. 'And if that had happened I would in time have been convicted of murder. So I would have been sent to prison for a long time and – well, what use would I be to Marcus then? There's only one answer to that, isn't there: *none. None at all.* And Matt, Marcus *is* going to come out of that private hell he's in. I'm sure of it, absolutely sure – and when he does *I want to be there with him,* not stuck in some English jail! … I didn't see all this, before. But I've thought about it, and about other things too since then, so – may I tell you my second thing now?'

'Of course.'

'Matt…. Maybe this sounds a stupid thing to you, but it doesn't to me so don't laugh at me but – I'd like you to be as it were my other brother. I'd like it very much if you would – and when he gets better Marcus will too, I know he will, he's lost two brothers same as I have….' Then to his silence, 'And – please – will you take me out to Hermit's Hill tomorrow, for the whole day? You could call for me as usual and we'll drive out there, have lunch at The Foresters' Arms then walk in the country. Can we do that?'

Tiredly, Locksley rubbed a hand over his eyes and accepted that the age-gap between them was too great.

'Sorry, I can't make it tomorrow,' he said. 'I have to be back on the job by 07.30. I'll call you tomorrow evening, we can talk then.'

'Hopefully we can go out there next weekend, then, I'll look forward to that…. You must be so tired, Matt. I'll go now. And please know, I feel close to you.'

She did not say goodbye and, on thinking about it Locksley was glad she had not because – had she said it at that moment – the word would have had a ring of absolute finality about it, its source the old farewell 'God be with ye'. And thinking about the old saying of how it is 'Better to have loved and lost than never to have loved at all', he decided that whoever wrote that one didn't know what he was talking about.